Blood City

DOUGLAS SKELTON

Luath Press Limited
EDINBURGH
www.luath.co.uk

First published 2013

ISBN: 978-1-908373-71-7

The publisher acknowledges subsidy from

towards the publication of this book

The paper used in this book is recyclable. It is made from
low chlorine pulps produced in a low energy, low emissions manner
from renewable forests.

Printed and bound by
Bell & Bain Ltd., Glasgow

Typeset in 10.5 point Sabon
by 3btype.com

DOUGLAS [illegible] West of Scotland. He has written eleven books including *Glasgow's Black Heart*, *Frightener* and *Dark Heart*. He has appeared on a variety of documentaries and news programmes as an expert on Glasgow crime, most recently on STV's *In Search of Bible John*. His 2005 book *Indian Peter* was later [illegible]pted for a BBC Scotland radio documentary which he presented. [illegible]*od City* is his first foray into fiction.

Acknowledgements

Thanks go to John Abernethy, who first suggested I go back to how these guys began. Also to my reading committee, Karin, Elizabeth and Gary. Kate and Joe Jackson provided some information, as did Big Stephen Wilkie. Anything I've got wrong was either intentional or my fault.

Thanks to Helena for the white suit and the Vauxhall Chevette. To my wife Margaret, who is still providing the cups of tea as I pound the keyboard.

Finally, huge thanks to Louise Hutcheson at Luath for spotting the manuscript as well as Gavin, Kirsten and the team for their help, support and confidence.

Prologue

OCTOBER 1977

...voices, floating...
...rising, falling...
...ebbing, flowing...

When Davie McCall bobbed to the surface of consciousness, he was aware of the voices drifting around him. Hushed voices, and he did not recognise any of them. His vision swam as he opened his eyes and he didn't know at first where he was. There was a blue curtain around him, darker lines waving as if he was seeing them through water. And there were other sounds; the squeak of shoes on polished surfaces, sometimes the clink of cutlery on a plate and even, faintly, the harsh sound of laughter on a television. But then he would be dragged back down into the depths, unconsciousness washing over him and sweeping the sounds away once more.

And each time he was back in that dingy room where the firelight guttered and the stench of blood hung in the air. Back in that room with his father standing over him, the heavy poker wet and glistening in his hand, his face frozen in rage, his eyes cold, distant points of blue ice.

And Davie again felt the pain in his arm and the ache in his head, and tasted the blood from his scalp as it trickled down his face to his lips.

And he felt the fear as his father turned those dead blue eyes on him.

Then, mercifully, the deep claimed him again and he was carried away from that place with its pain, and its terror, and its blood. Not his blood, of course. It was not his blood that clung to the memory of that dark room. Not his blood. Not his.

I

WHEN AT LAST Davie fully burst through the silky surface of consciousness, he knew immediately that he was in a hospital. His previous surges back to the world had been brief affairs, when he had registered the sounds but not the smells. Now he knew he was in a hospital ward, for not only did he recognise the squeak of nurses' shoes on the floor and the muted conversation of the other patients on the ward, but also the smell of disinfectant and, for some reason, boiled cabbage. As he lay on his back he opened his eyes and saw the cracked plaster in the cream ceiling high above his bed. Pale, watery daylight leaked through a window to his left. Surrounding him he saw the light blue curtain with its ragged darker lines and finally the unmistakeable figure of Joe the Tailor beside his bed. Immaculate as always; the trademark deep navy coat, unbuttoned to reveal his blue suit, white shirt and dark red tie. Davie couldn't see it but he knew the Tailor's grey Homburg would not be far away. The old man sat straight-backed in the fold-away wooden chair, one knee crooked over the other, his perfectly manicured hands clasped on top. He might have been praying, but Davie knew he had given that up a long time ago. He also knew, without asking, that the man had been sitting there for a long time.

Joe Klein smiled gently when he saw the boy's eyes snap open.

'Glad to see you are returned,' he said, his voice carrying the faint echoes of a Polish childhood. 'You are in the Royal Infirmary. Do you know why?' Davie tried to pull himself up, but found his body unwilling to obey. The Tailor reached out and placed a hand gently on his shoulder. 'It is best that you remain as you are,' he said. Davie looked at the hand, at the ring that sparkled on the pinkie, and beyond that his own right arm, encased in plaster. He raised his left hand to his forehead and felt the bandages encasing the top of his head.

'We almost lost you,' said Joe, settling back again. 'Do you remember what happened?'

'Yes.' Davie's voice rasped and for the first time he realised how dry his lips were. He tried to lick them but his tongue was cracked and barren of moisture. The Tailor nodded and leaned forward with a glass of amber fluid with a straw. He placed the straw between Davie's lips and said, 'You must drink. They have left water but this is better.' The delicate scent of the old man's cologne was comforting as Davie sucked on the straw and felt the fizzy liquid bite at his tongue and throat. 'The Irn-Bru,' said Joe, smiling again. 'The bringer of life.' Davie drained a strawfull. Joe replaced the glass on the cabinet and sat down again. He shook the folds of his coat until they hung correctly then draped his leg over his knee once more before letting his hands resume their clasped position.

'Where is he?' Joe didn't need to ask who Davie meant, for he had expected the question.

'They do not know,' he replied. 'He has vanished.' Davie nodded, knowing instinctively that his father would not have allowed himself to be caught. 'He came to me, after,' said Joe. 'I phoned the police myself. That kind of behaviour must not be tolerated. They will catch him, or we will, sooner or later.' Davie knew the old man meant what he said, but doubted that his father would ever allow himself to be caught. He knew Danny McCall too well. A madman he may have been – Davie still recalled something not of this world glinting in his father's eye that night – but Danny McCall would have been aware that he had crossed a line. It wasn't just the Law that sought him now, but Joe 'The Tailor' Klein as well, for he had broken one of his cardinal rules. *Thou Shalt Not Harm a Woman.* There was enough of the father in the son to make him certain that Danny McCall would move heaven and hell to ensure he was not found. Joe Klein was a bad man to cross.

'The police will wish to talk,' said the Tailor. 'You must assist them.' This, Davie knew, was an order and there was no possibility of him not obeying. He nodded his agreement as the curtain behind the old man flipped back and the hulking form of Rab McClymont loomed over the bed, two small white cups of tea gripped in his big hands. He was only 21 – just six years older than Davie – but he looked far more mature, thanks to his size and the heavy beard darkening his cheeks. His wide jaw and shock of black hair made him look like a live action version of Desperate Dan.

'This is the best I could do, boss,' Rab offered before realising that Davie's eyes were open. 'Fuck – Sleeping Beauty has woken up!'

Joe frowned as he eased the cup from Rab's hand. 'You must moderate your language, Robert. You are not on the street now.'

'Sorry, Joe,' Rab sounded chastened but when he winked at Davie he seemed anything but. All Joe's boys knew that the boss loathed foul language, but it never stopped Rab and Davie sometimes suspected he did it on purpose to goad the old man. 'You've been out of it for days, Davie son. You want a cuppa tea?'

Davie shook his head. 'Give us that glass down, though,' he said.

'Sure thing,' said Rab and wrapped his fist around the glass. 'What's in it? Medicine?'

'It is the amber nectar of the gods,' said the Tailor with a smile.

'That right?' Rab raised the glass to his face and sucked on the straw. 'Fuck me – it's fuckin Irn-Bru!'

The old man winced. 'Robert, you are incorrigible. Give the glass to David before he dies of thirst.'

'Sorry, mate – here.' Rab handed over the glass and Davie took it with his good hand. He struggled to sit up and Rab put his own cup on the cabinet top in order to give him surprisingly gentle assistance. Davie nodded his thanks before he drained some more of the liquid and looked at the Tailor.

'Where do I go from here?'

'You will remain here until the doctors say you are fit to leave,' Joe answered. 'Your arm is broken, your skull fractured.'

'Aye, you're well fucked up, Davie,' said Rab, then turned to the old man who was glaring at him from the chair. 'Sorry, Joe.'

'And then...?' Davie asked.

'Your auntie – your mother's sister. With her you will stay. But you are my responsibility now.'

Davie nodded, drank a little more and said, 'When?'

'A little while only. You must get better.'

Davie lay back on the pillows Rab had helped prop up and looked out of the window, its surface speckled with rain. The dark grey city stretched out beneath an iron sky. Cars moved down Castle Street towards High Street and further on he could see the top of the Tollbooth Steeple at Glasgow Cross. He stared at the serrated edge of the city skyline etched against the dark clouds. The Tailor had said he must get better, but Davie seriously doubted he ever would. At only 15 years old, Davie McCall knew there was darkness within him with which he would have to come to terms. And that prospect scared the hell out of him.

2

JANUARY 1978

Frank Donovan felt the cold seeping first through his black coat, then his thick uniform and finally his flesh to settle in his bones.

They had only been here 15 minutes but already the Glasgow winter night was beginning to bite. Jack Frost wasn't just nipping at his nose, he was bloody well gnawing. Donovan's ears were burning, a phenomenon that had always struck him as rather strange. How could you be cold, but feel as if someone was holding a match to your ear? He would have pondered this conundrum further, but he was too damn frozen to bother. Behind him he could hear the dark waters of the canal lapping against the stone walls, but he knew the sub-zero air would soon choke the life from the sound and still the surface to ice. From where they stood beside the Forth and Clyde Canal they could look across the dark sprawl of Firhill and Maryhill. A thick frost floated over the city streets, making a white carpet of the tenement roofs and sparkling diamonds of the street lights. The grass at their feet was just beginning to whiten. But the girl lying on it was already white.

His eyes flicked involuntarily to the broken corpse lying just off the towpath. She lay on her back, her arms outstretched, one leg bent under the other. Her skirt was tucked up around her waist, the remnants of her ripped underwear lying beneath her. Her blouse had been torn open and her bra wrenched away to reveal her breasts. Donovan wanted to reach down and cover her, to preserve at least some of her dignity, but knew that would be a cardinal sin. Instead he looked away.

'Fuck me, it's freezing,' said Jimmy Knight, stamping his feet on the cold-hardened pathway beside him. 'When they gonnae get this show on the road?'

'No be long,' said Donovan.

'Better fuckin no be, 'cos soon they'll have another two stiffs to work wi if they don't get their arses in gear.'

PC Jimmy Knight stepped closer to the girl's body, rubbing his gloved hands together to create some semblance of heat.

'D'you know what the tragedy of this is?' Donovan remained silent, knowing his neighbour's question was rhetorical. 'D'you know what the cold, hard, heart-fuckin-wrenching tragedy of this is? It's that she wasnae a bad bit of stuff, the lassie. I mean, if she was a pig it would be sad, but she's no pig. That's the tragedy of it.' He bent lower over the corpse, studying her face. 'How old, do you think? 17, 18?'

Donovan didn't answer. What he wanted to say was that she was too young to die, but he knew it was best to keep his mouth shut. Jimmy Knight disdained sentiment; it was a feeble show of weakness. Jimmy Knight didn't do sentiment and he didn't do weakness.

'Aye, she's no a bad bit of stuff,' Knight went on, his gaze crawling down the girl's body. 'Nice set of tits on her, so she has. Good pair o pins. Wouldnae've minded a wee go at her myself.'

'You've got time now, Jimmy, if that's what you want,' Donovan said, a hint of irritation in his voice. 'They'll no be here for another ten minutes or so. I'll turn away if you want some privacy.'

Knight straightened up and for a second Donovan actually believed he was considering it. Then he shook his head. 'Nah,' he said, 'I'll pass, thanks.' He turned back to Donovan and sniffed. 'Don't want to be guddlin about in another guy's pond, know what I mean?'

Donovan looked away, the other man missing the disgust that flashed across his face. He hated being neighboured with Knight. God knows Donovan was no prude, but Knight was little more than an animal. Everyone knew there was a bit of sexual action on offer to uniforms, but Knight abused the privilege. He didn't care if the offer came from a working lass, a suspect or a victim – if it was up for grabs, he was game. Donovan also had some concerns over the other man's honesty, suspecting for some time that Knight was involved in darker stuff. He was a good cop, though; a cop's cop – a cop who brought in the bodies, who notched up the arrests.

Then, as if to underline Donovan's thoughts, Knight spoke. 'Boy that did her's got some marks on him, by the looks of it.'

He glanced back at Donovan and explained, 'Blood on her fingers, round the nails. She's been strangled, no visible wounds. She scratched the bastard during the struggle.'

Well done, hen, Donovan thought.

A movement on the towpath, just a slight shifting in the darkness, caught Donovan's eye.

'Jimmy,' he said, and the other officer looked back towards him. Donovan nodded up the path and Knight followed his gaze, his eyes squinting against the gloom.

He murmured, 'Someone up there?'

'Looks like it,' said Donovan, keeping his voice low.

'Is it the murder team?'

'No, just one person, he's stopped dead still. Doesn't want to be seen.'

'Fuck that for a game of soldiers,' said Knight and took a couple of steps along the path, his torch in his hand now. He clicked it on and swung the beam along the towpath, the light picking out the frost hanging in the air like mist. 'Come on, pal, don't be messin about. Let's see ye.'

There was a slight pause before the figure stepped into the beam. A young man, still a teenager, his hair long and straggly, his body encased in a blue anorak and blue jeans. There was a white scarf at his throat to ward off the cold. He moved hesitantly towards them.

Knight asked, 'What you doing here, pal?'

'Just walking,' said the youth, still moving towards them. 'Then I saw you standing there and I thought there was something wrong.'

He was well-spoken and Donovan immediately pegged him as coming from the smarter part of the West End and not the immediate Maryhill vicinity – Kelvinside, Hyndland, maybe even Bearsden up the road. The question was, what the hell was he doing walking along the banks of the Forth and Clyde past midnight? The 200 year old waterway was not the place for a moonlight stroll.

'Well, you thought right,' said Knight. 'What's your name?'

The young man came to a halt about three feet away from them. He suddenly looked nervous. He glanced from one officer to the other, his eyes widening behind a pair of round, John Lennon glasses. There was a slight catch in his voice as he asked, 'Why do you want to know my name?'

Knight shrugged. 'Just routine, pal, nothing to worry about. You can see we've got a situation here...' he gestured at the corpse of the girl, but the youth barely looked at her. Knight went on, 'Now you come strolling along here like you're out for a Sunday walk in the park. So what's your name?'

'William. William Lowry. Like the painter.'

'Well, William Lowry like the painter, what you doing here at this time of night?'

'I'm...' he began, but paused, and Donovan knew there was a lie coming. 'I'm going home after a party.'

'Aye? And where's home?'

'Woodside.'

'And where was the party?'

'A flat on Maryhill Road. It's a pal's place but I'd really not like to get him involved in this.'

Donovan thought, *involved in what*? But he let Knight control the interview. He knew to let the other cop follow his own line of questioning.

Knight asked, 'You a student, then?'

The boy nodded and pushed his spectacles up the bridge of his nose. 'Yes. The College of Art.'

'So he's really going to be like Lowry the painter,' Knight smiled and turned to Donovan, his back momentarily to the boy so he could tap two fingers to his throat without being seen. Donovan nodded, looked back at the youth and saw what Knight had already noticed, a smear of blood just at the fold of the white scarf where it touched his neck.

'You got some identification on you, son?' Knight asked.

The boy shook his head.

'Ok, that's Ok, not everyone carries ID, do they? We need to check up on you, though, you know that, right?'

'Why? I haven't done anything wrong.'

'I know that, son, it's just routine. I mean, after all, we've got a dead lassie here.'

Again, Knight nodded to the body and again Lowry refused to look at her. He kept his eyes between Knight and Donovan and barely seemed to notice the dead girl just a few feet away.

Knight asked, 'D'you know her maybe?'

The boy shook his head, his hands thrust deep into his pockets.

Knight said, 'You've no even looked at her, so how do you know you don't?'

'I don't know her.'

'Never seen her before?'

'No.'

'She wasn't at the party?'

'There were a lot of people at the party. I couldn't possibly remember everyone.'

'Why don't you look at her, maybe you'll recognise her.'

'I'd rather not.'

'How no?'

'I'm... well, I'd rather not.'

'You squeamish?'

'Something like that.'

'It might help us, though. Might help us catch the guy who killed her. You'd want that, wouldn't you?'

Lowry didn't answer. He stared straight at Knight, his eyes still wide, his hands moving inside his pockets, the blood on his white scarf now reaching out to the police officers like a bad smell.

'What about it, William Lowry like the painter?' Knight said, moving slightly closer to the boy. 'You want to assist the polis with their inquiries, or what? You want to take a quick peek at this lassie here, tell us if you've ever seen her before? Just a quick look, that's all. It'll be like looking at a picture. Then you can be on your way.'

The boy's head was shaking from side to side and Donovan thought he could see the livid red marks of a recent wound on his neck, scratch marks that had left blood on his scarf. 'No,' said Lowry, 'I don't want to look!'

'Come on, pal,' coaxed Knight, now close enough to touch the youth. 'Just a wee peek...'

Knight lunged, but the boy was quick, jumping back and whirling on his heels before breaking into a sprint back down the pathway.

'Fuck it!' Knight took off after him, yelling over his shoulder. 'Blow it in, Frank – he's the fucker we want.'

Donovan watched his partner vanish into the dark and leaned into the microphone clipped to his uniform collar. 'C 1-3-2, C 1-3-2. C 1-0-8 in pursuit of male suspect on towpath of Forth and Clyde Canal, heading towards Firhill Basin. Request immediate assistance. Repeat, request immediate assistance. Suspect is white male, around 20 years of age, name of William Lowry.'

A voice crackled back, 'Lowry? Like the painter?'

'Affirmative.'

Donovan took his finger off the button and looked back along the pathway. The sound of Jimmy Knight's size tens had long since vanished and he was left once again with the lapping water behind him and the occasional engine on Maryhill Road. There was just him and the girl left now, waiting for the circus to arrive.

* * *

Knight could hear footfalls ahead of him, but he couldn't see their source. He pounded after the sound, a smile on his lips. This was the part of the job he enjoyed, chasing a scroat, bringing him down.

Lowry-like-the-painter was as guilty as Judas and Police Constable James Knight was going to be the man who brought him in. And that would not do his future any harm at all. No harm at all.

He imagined the boy running blindly through the darkness ahead, perhaps occasionally darting a look over his shoulder to see if the tall, dark-haired policeman was still on his tail. *Don't worry, son, I'm here. I'm right here – and I'm not giving up. You're my ticket out of uniform and into plainclothes, where the real action is.*

Lowry-like-the-painter had killed a lassie and made the mistake of returning to the scene of the crime. God knows what had been going on in his sick wee head, but he'd come back and walked more or less right into Knight's arms. And Knight wasn't about to let him slip away. He followed the sound of the boy's feet, his mouth set in a tight, determined line.

Everything went quiet at Firhill Basin and Knight came to a halt to catch his breath. Once this had been a thriving sawmill but now it was silent, a derelict memorial to the canal's bustling heyday where darkness hung heavily around the crumbling buildings and discarded lumber. The canal had fallen into disuse years before and its waters were so choked with weeds and rubbish that he'd heard it called the 'filth and slime canal'.

Sometimes joy riders brought their stolen cars here and set fire to them, but not this night. Sometimes teenagers gathered here to drink and experiment with sex, but not this night. On this night there was only the darkness and somewhere in that darkness there was a frightened little killer. Knight strained his ears for any sound, but all he could hear was the faint gurgle of water to his right.

'End of the road, son,' he shouted. 'Nowhere to go now.'

He paused and listened again, stepping carefully through the darkness, his feet crunching on the crisp ground. He slowly drew a wooden baton from his pocket, his hand slipping easily into the strap.

'Come on, pal – this is a waste of time. We got a good look at you, me and my neighbour, a right good look. We've got your name and I think it's your real name. It's only a matter of time before we get you.'

Knight stopped and held his breath. He thought he'd heard something, just a faint sound, like a sob, coming from a burned-out shed ahead of him. He moved closer, the solid baton hidden in the folds of his coat.

'I'll bet she was asking for it, eh? The lassie. Prick teaser, was she? Leading you on? That what she was?'

He heard it again, another sob, and he smiled. *There you are, you wee bastard. There you are.*

'I loved her!'

Knight stopped when he heard the distraught voice pierce the air to his right, where a skip filled with rotting timber stood.

'So what happened?'

The boy didn't answer. Knight took a couple of steps towards the hulking skip, placing his feet carefully to lessen the rasp of his sturdy boots on the frost. 'Come on, son, we can't help you if we don't know what happened. She two-timing you, or what?'

'She laughed at me,' said the boy, his voice floating through the darkness, 'when I told her how I felt, she laughed at me. I've loved her for months. She goes... she went to the Art College with me and I would see her every day. She's beautiful. And tonight when I saw her at the party I had to tell her. It was now or never, you know? But all she did was laugh at me. So when she left with that guy, I followed her. He's another student at the college. And when they came up here and they... well, they... she let him... I watched. I watched them rutting up against that wall over there.'

Bit cold for a kneetrembler, Knight thought, *but hey – when the sap is rising there's no holding it back.*

Lowry said, 'They didn't see me or hear me, they were so bloody intent on what they were doing. They didn't hear me or see me when I came up behind him and hit him with a rock.'

Oho, thought Knight as he crept forward, *another body maybe. A double killer, this lad. All the better for me.*

'She was really surprised when he went down. "I loved you," I told her. "I loved you and all you could do was laugh." And then I hit her. Not with the rock, just my hand. I would've hit her again, only that bastard moved and I looked away.'

Not dead then. Knight was disappointed.

'She ran off down the path, and I gave the bastard another dose of the rock and went after her. I didn't want to hurt her but she'd laughed at me, you see? I caught her where you found her and we struggled and then I …I …'

'Then you killed her,' said Knight softly and the boy, lost in the memory of recent events, looked up in surprise from his hiding place to see the big policeman standing over him. Knight gazed down at the youth crouched down behind the skip, his knees pulled up under his chin, his arms wrapped around them, eyes big and round behind his glasses, pale face creased with grief and fear and self-disgust. For a brief moment, Knight felt some sympathy for the young lad. There'd been many women he'd wanted to give a wee skelp. This lad had just taken it to the next level.

Lowry nodded and laid his face on his knees. 'I didn't mean to, it just happened. We were rolling around on the ground and my hands were round her throat and I think I just pressed too hard, that's all.'

'Aye,' said Knight, and brought his baton crashing down on the back of the boy's head. Regulations banned blows to the head, but Knight believed an unconscious prisoner was a perfect prisoner, and he knew just how hard to hit without causing permanent damage. If anyone raised an eyebrow he'd say Lowry-like-the-painter had come at him and he defended himself.

He jerked his handcuffs from his waist and chained the boy's wrist to a rusting piece of pipe in the wall behind him. Then he looked back across to the deserted buildings where he was sure he had heard sobs earlier. Somewhere out there was a lad with his head bashed in – and if Knight couldn't have his double murder, then he'd have to settle for saving the boy's life – being the hero.

'Talk about win-fucking-win situations,' he muttered and, with a quick glance at Lowry to make sure he was out cold, he set off into the darkness again, his torch stabbing the frosty air.

3

MAY 1980

IF DAVIE MCCALL EVER felt overwhelmed by Rab McClymont's size, he never showed it. He was just average height himself, big enough for Glasgow, which had more than its share of 'wee men'. But Rab was a giant. Davie was acutely aware of the height difference – when you constantly find yourself eye-level with a guy's shoulder, you can't *not* be aware – but unlike others, he never felt threatened by the big fellow. If anything, it was the other way around.

David McCall had carved himself a reputation far beyond his 18 years. If Danny McCall had left him one thing worth knowing, it was how to take care of himself. Davie seemed to have no fear, constantly inserting himself into situations that would make bigger men pause for thought. And once inserted, he displayed a propensity for violence that bordered on savagery. As soon as he was committed to a course of action, Davie McCall followed it with a cold-blooded efficiency that was rare even in the tough East End streets of a tough city. It was this skill, and a single-minded determination to be the last man standing, on which Joe the Tailor capitalised in his less-than-legitimate enterprises.

Davie, Rab and Bobby Newman stood together outside Luca's

Café on Duke Street, while Joe sat inside for a meeting. Small stores and family traders catering for mostly local customers lined both sides of the street, topped by red sandstone tenement flats. Here there were barbers, butchers, bakers and, this being Glasgow, bars. The exteriors of some of the pubs on Duke Street may have lacked allure, but it was not their intention to attract passing custom. They had their regulars. These were no wine bars or licensed restaurants. They weren't even watering holes. They were pubs, pure and simple, and the men who spent their time in them came to smoke and to drink and to let the world outside spin on its merry way without them.

No big department stores or nationwide chains here, they kept themselves to the city centre, but the street was nonetheless busy for a weekday. Old women with hats pulled over tight perms, wearing shapeless coats even on a warm May morning, trudged past carrying ancient leather bags or wheeling tartan shopping trolleys behind them like old and faithful dogs. Younger women moved faster, but those who pushed prams or dragged unwilling children at their heels could be a danger to other pedestrians. Young girls flitted singly or in pairs, their arms crossed over their breasts as they walked. Sallow-skinned and narrow-faced young men with watchful eyes scurried by, shoulders hunched as if to fend off the cold. They cupped lit cigarettes in their hand against the wind as they hurried to the pub or the bookies or wherever they went on a weekday while out of work. Occasionally one dodged the cars in order to cross the wide road, it being somehow unmanly to use the pedestrian crossing nearby. Sometimes, eyes darted to the café door and the pace would quicken as they recognised the trio standing there, guessing that whatever was going on inside was not something they wanted to be anything near, thank you very much, pal.

The man Joe was meeting was known to Davie and his pals, by reputation if not by acquaintance. Johnny Jones was a former safeblower and founding member of a crew the press liked to call The Backroom Boys, a tag they earned because one of their MOs was to hide in premises until they closed and then loot it six ways from Sunday. They were also known as Robbery Inc, a loose confederation of like-minded felons who came together only when there was a big blag on – hospital and factory payrolls, bank cash transfers, anywhere there was a big score. That Jones and the Tailor were together in the same room was something of a coup, even if it was just a wee café with no other customers. It was named after Luca Vizzini, a tousle-headed little Sicilian, but Joe owned the place, and any hungry or thirsty locals who Davie and his pals might have to turn away would be no real loss to turnover. Anyway, they'd be back.

The Tailor hadn't revealed why he was meeting Johnny Jones, and Davie was unbearably curious. Joe wasn't above using violence to get his way, Davie knew that first-hand, but Jones' style was considerably more vicious. The old man felt that Johnny and others like him in the city were just a bit too 'profligate with the chastisement'. Joe often used words like that, forcing the lads to seek out dictionaries to find out just what the hell he was talking about. Joe Klein had never hidden his distaste for the likes of Johnny Jones, so the two of them sharing a coffee was bound to raise an eyebrow or two.

Davie glanced through a window pitted with city grime and saw the Tailor's familiar figure sitting back in a relaxed manner as Jones, a cadaverous drink of rancid water, leaned over the table top towards him. They made an odd couple. The Tailor was as immaculate as ever and looked as if he'd just been scrubbed with a wire brush, skin pink and fresh and his crop of white hair shining clean. Jones was dressed in an old denim jacket and jeans, a pair of trainers on his feet, his thin grey hair plastered to his skull. A good scrubbing with a wire brush would only reveal another layer of grey skin. He was talking, a long skinny finger stabbing in punctuation at the cracked formica on the table top. The old man occasionally shook his head. Davie wondered for the second time what they were talking about, but, sensing no threat in the room, turned away from the window.

Across the road a group of three young men lingered outside an off-licence. They were in their late teens, roughly the same age as him, for all intents and purposes the same as Davie and his pals. But there was something about them that appeared lifeless, even witless. They had nothing to do and nowhere to go do it, and Davie knew their presence outside an offie was no accident. Inside was cider, and maybe even Buckfast, the fortified wine with a killer kick, but they idled there with an almost studied nonchalance, talking among themselves as their gaze flicked down the road. Davie suspected they were waiting for their banker to arrive.

'You got a match, Bobby?' asked Rab. Bobby nodded, reaching into the jacket of his combat jacket to fetch a box of Bluebells. He was easily the best looking of the three, a thick head of blond hair and handsome features making many a local girl think of a young Robert Redford. There had been one or two guys who misguidedly looked at his long, golden locks and had come to the conclusion that Bobby was somewhat less than masculine. Bobby soon disabused of them that notion. He lacked the sheer power of Rab and the killer instinct of Davie, but Bobby Newman was more than capable of handling himself when the occasion called for it.

'Ta, mate,' said Rab, taking the small box and pushing open the drawer to peek inside. Then he said, 'You got a fag to go wi them?'

Bobby sighed. 'Jesus, Rab – you ever buy your own?'

'What do you think I keep you around for? Your sparkling personality?'

Bobby shook his head and handed over a packet of Embassy tipped. 'I'm tellin you, Rab, I don't know how long I can afford to stay pals wi you.'

'You'd be lost without me, wee man, and you know it,' said Rab, sticking a cigarette into the corner of his mouth and striking a match.

'How'd you work that out?'

'Who'd watch your back? Who'd be there when you needed him? Who'd throw your ugly sister a shag every now and then, keep her sweet?'

Bobby took the cigarette pack back and thought carefully about what Rab had said. 'Listen, ugly she may be…'

'Oh, she is, believe me…'

'Aye, but if my sister didnae polish your pole you'd never get any action and you'd be even more bad tempered than you are. You're no oil painting, Rab McClymont.'

Rab jutted his prodigious jaw in Bobby's direction. 'Fuck off, ya wee bastard. I'm perfectly proportioned, know what I mean? When I take off my trousers and unleash my weapon they think someone else has walked into the room.'

Davie smiled but kept his eyes on the knot of young men on the other side of the road. He could easily have been any one of them, had it not been for the Tailor. After he left the hospital he'd been taken in by his mother's sister, a nice enough woman when sober, but that, alas, was a rarity. Drunk, Aunt Mamie was nasty and boorish and cared as much for Davie as she did about water in her whisky. That suited him well enough – it left him free to come and go as he pleased, the authorities being satisfied that he was domiciled with a responsible adult. Whether that meant his aunt or the succession of gentlemen friends she had staying with her, Davie wasn't sure. The current 'uncle' was a burly carpet fitter by the name of Ted MacMillan, who for some reason looked at Davie as if he was desperate to have a square-go.

The café door opened and Johnny Jones stepped out, closely followed by Joe. Johnny nodded once to the Tailor, who nodded back politely as he placed his Homburg carefully on his head. Jones' sour expression suggested the meeting had not gone as he had hoped. Jones looked Davie up and down, as if sizing him up, and said, 'You're Danny McCall's boy, right?'

Davie paused for a moment. 'Yeah.'

Jones nodded and licked his lips, his tongue sliding out from behind yellowing teeth. 'I knew him, your faither. He was a handy guy to have around. You a chip off the old block, son?'

'I'm nothing like him.'

Jones smiled, knowing instinctively that he'd touched a nerve and the sadist in him enjoying it. 'That's no what I hear. I hear you're just like him...'

'Leave the boy be,' Joe warned.

Jones smiled, but it was really little more than a tightening of the facial muscles. He held up both hands to placate Davie. 'Nae offence, son.' He turned to Joe. 'Just sayin you've got a good boy here, or so I hear.'

'Fine, Johnny,' said Joe, 'but this is something I already know. Thank you for your time.'

Johnny's gaze slid from Davie to the Tailor. 'You think about my proposition, Joe. It could be good for all of us.'

'Thank you, but it is not something in which I would wish to engage.'

'Just think about it, okay? It'll make us a bundle.'

'Very well, Johnny – I will think about it,' said Joe, polite, but clearly unwavering.

Johnny nodded and with a final look at Davie and a glance at the others, he turned and walked off down the street. He had no one with him in the café, secure in the knowledge that Joe the Tailor bore him no particular ill-will aside from the fact that he loathed everything he stood for. Joe watched him swagger away and sighed. 'Such an unpleasant man,' he said. 'I am so glad I need have nothing to do with him.'

'Aye – he gives scumbags a bad name,' said Bobby, making Joe smile.

'Wait here, boys,' said the old man. 'I must have a word with Luca before I go.'

There was talk that Luca Vizzini had once been a gunman for the Sicilian Mafia. Apparently he'd fled his homeland when an assassination attempt on a judge went badly wrong and the man's baby daughter was killed instead. The old Dons, outraged that such a simple job had been so badly bungled, put a price on Luca's head and he was forced to leave in a hurry, eventually fetching up in Glasgow. Here he led a quiet sort of life, running Joe's café. Or so the story went. How Joe first met the man had never been discussed, and Davie didn't know how much truth there was to the tale anyway. But whenever he met the little Sicilian with the ready smile, he sensed something more behind his welcoming nature.

Davie turned his attention back to the boys across the road as they prepared to greet a bulky young man striding towards them with a small mongrel dog on a lead at his feet. The dog stopped to sniff something in the gutter and the boy jerked violently on the lead to bring him to heel again. Whatever it was the dog wanted to investigate proved too tempting though, and he hung back, trying desperately to reach it. His master yanked the lead again, hauling the animal off its feet. A plaintive yelp rose over the traffic sounds and Davie straightened up off the wall as the boy leaned over and snarled something at the creature. The dog lay on its back, looking up at him with tail tucked between its legs as if to protect its manhood. The boy lashed out with one booted foot, kicking the dog in the ribs. The animal's yelp shrieked across the road and Davie's body tensed.

'Easy, Davie,' Rab said, softly. With those two words, Rab was signalling that now was not the time. Jones had climbed into a Ford Escort, but it had not yet pulled away.

'I know, Rab,' said Davie, his eyes never leaving the boy with the dog on the opposite pavement. He'd joined his pals now, a wide grin on his face, as if he was proud of subjugating the dog. 'Jones still sitting there?'

'Car's no moved. Got a coupla boys in there with him.'

'That'll be Boyle and his mate.'

'Sinclair?'

'Aye,' said Davie, watching the youths opposite crowd into the off sales, the dog tied to a lamppost, where it sat, still quivering, nervously eyeing anyone who walked past. Not even the presence of Clem Boyle was enough to distract Davie. There was bad blood there, everyone knew, but no one was quite sure why the red-headed youth had such a problem with Davie McCall. Davie didn't much care, either.

'Fuck me – Jones, Boyle and Sinclair in the one motor,' said Bobby. 'Where's the RAF when you need some precision bombing, eh?'

'We cannae leave Joe, Davie,' Rab interjected, knowing full well where Davie's attention was focused.

'I know.'

Rab's gaze flicked across to the dog, and even he felt a bit sorry for it. 'No matter what, Davie.'

'*I know.*'

The dog kicker and his pals surged out of the shop doorway, carrying a plastic bag filled with bottles. Dog kicker jerked the lead from the pole and together they all walked up the street. The dog clung unhappily to his master's heels, occasionally glancing up at the others as if hoping for a kind word or glance. None of them paid any heed.

'Bobby,' said Rab, nodding in their direction. Bobby knew immediately what was needed and set off in their wake at a swift pace, dodging between the cars as they slowed for traffic lights further along. Rab didn't think Jones would be brazen enough to try anything here, but right now it was their job to watch Joe's back. Bobby would find out where those lads were going and he and Davie would catch up with them later. He glanced at his pal, who was watching the guy with the dog intently.

God help him, Rab thought.

4

LUCA STIRRED HIS COFFEE, his round, pock-marked face thoughtful as he considered what his old friend had told him. 'And how much does he want for this caper?'

'£100,000 from each of us,' said Joe. 'A total of £1 million.'

Luca nodded and continued to slowly rotate the spoon, though the sugar he had dropped in earlier was well integrated with the liquid. Joe watched the brown coffee swirl in the cup and waited. It was a fine roast, kept especially for Joe's visits, and its pleasant aroma filled the café.

'A hundred grand ain't much,' said Luca. 'The profits would be much greater.'

'True, but there is the moral question.'

Luca shrugged. 'Morals are for other people, not for the likes of you or me, Joe. We put aside morals when we killed our first man.'

Joe nodded to acknowledge the truth of the words, experiencing an involuntary flash to a winter day in Poland. It was 1940, the day he killed his first man; a German soldier. The soldier had slaughtered Joe's family – mother, father, little sister – and Joe had shot him with his own rifle, the bullet lifting off the top of the man's head. That single act had set the then Josep Wolfowitz on a journey which took him from fighting with Polish partisans who were unaware that he was a Jew, to post-war Warsaw, to a spell with relatives in Ayrshire and then, ultimately, to Glasgow. Along the way he changed his name, first to Joseph Adamski, and then to Joe Klein. Joe had killed many men over the years, but even now, 40 years later, he still returned to that first one. Forcing the image from his mind, he said, 'I do not like drugs, though.'

'It is a commodity, like any other,' said Luca, ever the pragmatist. 'And Glasgow is wide open for the market.'

That had been Jones' proposition. Each of the city's top criminals would put £100,000 towards a joint venture to bring large quantities of heroin to the city. Jones claimed to have established contacts in Turkey, where the poppy was grown and there was a flourishing legitimate trade in opium – but many growers were willing to sell to less savoury buyers. He had found a lab in France where the raw opium would be transformed first into morphine, then heroin. From there, thanks to links with criminal organisations in London and Manchester, it was brought into the UK. Glasgow was ripe for the trade. Margaret Thatcher had been in office just one year and her government was intent on cutting public spending as the country headed into recession. Opportunities were limited. Bitterness was rising, and young people out there were searching for a means of escape from the sheer hopelessness of their lives. Johnny had told him, 'It's gonnae be massive, Joe, and if we all work together, it'll make us a bundle.'

Luca knew first-hand that there were riches to be found in the narcotic trade. He hadn't left Sicily under a cloud – he knew of the rumours and he enjoyed promoting them – but under his own steam. Young Luca wanted to see the world. That desire had taken him to New York, where a second cousin had introduced him into the Genovese family. It was 1956 and he was, at 21 years of age, a foot soldier for the most powerful crime family in the Five Boroughs. Small and stocky even then but with a confidence that belied his youth, he swiftly learned not just English, losing much of his native accent, but also the way of *La Cosa Nostra*.

At 22 he killed his first man, a two-bit hustler from upstate New York who had conned the wrong old lady. She was the aunt of Luca's *capo regime*, his immediate boss, and Luca and another young blood called Sal Bonaventure were ordered to ensure the grifter grifted no more. Luca and Sal picked him up at his fleabag hotel on the lower west side and drove him to Jersey, where they put a bullet in his skull and then cut out the lying tongue that had smooth-talked the old lady into parting with her savings. They took two grand from his pockets, to be returned to the conman's mark, and left his corpse in a field for a farmer to find.

That luckless little con artist, whose name Luca could not now even recall, was not the last man he killed. Over the next ten years, he took out twelve more men under orders. He never questioned why. One of them was his former accomplice, Sal Bonaventure, who, in 1965, turned rat. Luca lured him out with the promise of hooking up with two girls and put one in the back of his head then cut out his tongue and left it lying on his chest. The irony of their first kill together was not lost on Luca.

But in 1966, Luca made a mistake. He didn't kill the wrong man, as the Glasgow rumours would have it, but instead got the wrong girl pregnant; the red-headed wife of a prominent Brooklyn boss, to be exact. When the inevitable happened and she announced that she wanted to keep the child, her husband was bound to find out. It didn't matter that he had been somewhat lax in his marital duties for over a year because his pecker was being seen to regularly by a cocktail waitress from Alabama, variety being the spice of life. Luca knew there would be no reasoning with the man, and so he hopped the first steamer out of New York harbour and escaped to Scotland, where he had another cousin in Glasgow.

He met Joe the Tailor in 1968, when he'd been in Glasgow for just under two years. Joe owned a string of bookie shops and a couple of illegal gambling houses in the city centre. Rumour had it that he was the principal banker behind any major heist in Central Scotland, but no one had either been able to prove it or had wanted to. He also had a lucrative line in extortion, prostitution and many other means of making an illicit fortune. Fond of roulette, Luca had visited Joe's club one night. He liked him immediately. Joe was ten years older, but a friendship formed, cemented by Luca's swift action one night in 1969, when a hard man in the employ of Norrie Kennedy, Joe's old enemy from Blackhill, tried to muscle in on the gambling house. Luca took off his boot and beat the man senseless – God bless Cuban heels – then dragged him to the door and threw him down the 38 stairs that led from the second floor to street level. Luca couldn't be certain, but he thought the guy hit every single one.

They became friends, the Polish refugee and the Sicilian émigré. They shared mutual interests in music and chess, although they were so well-matched in the strategies and bluffs of the game that their encounters more often than not ended in stalemate. A few months after they first met, Joe bought the café on Duke Street and asked Luca to run it as a full partner. The Sicilian accepted the offer. He felt safe in this backwater city and he needed to put the sins of his past behind him. He was then 34 years of age and he wanted to settle, maybe find a nice woman, set up a home, raise children. He eventually found the nice woman, an Irish girl named Beatrice, and in 1972 they were married. They bought a house, thanks to Joe, and tried for children. But none came. Luca thought God was punishing him for his transgression in New York – not only had he got a married woman pregnant, but he'd run out on her, leaving her to face her husband alone. He never found out what happened to the kid and sometimes at night he thought about going back or at least contacting some of his old buddies. But he never did. That was his past life, and this was his new one. If he was to live that life without children then so be it. So Luca Vizzini settled down to his new life and he never, ever, looked at another woman. The café turned a healthy profit on its coffees, teas, filled rolls and fried foods. The brisk takeaway business was popular and Luca began to introduce more and more Sicilian dishes to the menu, although he knew they would never replace the city's fondness for hot pies, sausage rolls and chips. He looked on Glasgow as his home, and as time passed, he felt it safe to take the occasional trip back home to Sicily.

So Luca was wise to the ways of the criminal world and he knew that, despite the old adage, crime did pay, and drugs paid the most. Glasgow really was ripe for the picking, but he knew his old friend wouldn't take to the new business readily. So he wasn't surprised when he saw Joe shake his head and sigh with finality.

'No, my friend, it is not an enterprise in which I wish to take part. I am not a greedy man. I have enough with my other endeavours. Even my legitimate operations show a profit. I am satisfied.'

Luca shrugged. 'Then if you're satisfied, that's enough. I only hope that Jones sees it the same way.'

'Why should he not? I am no danger to his business.'

'You're known for your... eh...' Luca looked for the right word, '... your altruistic tendencies. Your dislike of narcotics is well known and, I don't know, they may get the idea you'll stand in their way somehow.'

'Nonsense,' Joe said with a dismissive wave of his hand. 'I have moved against monsters in the past – rapists, pederasts, killers of women – but not this kind of thing. I may not like drugs, but if someone wishes to involve themselves it is no business of mine. As long as they do not interfere with me, I will not interfere with them.'

Luca smiled. 'Joe, you know that and I know that, but these guys? They believe the legend of Joe the Tailor. The way they see it, if you're not with them, you're against them. And they need you on board, Joe. They need your contacts – cops, local politicians, and the like. You've even got a judge or two up your sleeve, or so the legend says.'

Joe shrugged. 'Rumours. Conjecture.'

'Sure, but guys like Johnny Jones? They believe all this. And they're gonna need all the muscle they can get if this scheme is going to work.'

'Then they can build their own contacts list. There are many greedy men out there. All they need to do is look for them.'

Luca sat back and stared at Joe. 'Your mind is set?'

Joe thought about this for a second before nodding. 'Then that,' said Luca, 'is that.'

* * *

They stood or lounged on the piece of waste ground, passing the bottles of cider among them. Cider was good because it was cheap. The dog's lead was tied to the wooden arm of an old easy chair that someone had dumped there months before. His owner sat in the chair, one fist wrapped round a bottle that he wouldn't share with his pals. He'd bought the stuff, after all, and he saw no reason why he shouldn't have one to himself. A good looking lad, but there was a mean glint in his eye and a nasty set to his mouth that rendered him rather ugly. He was the leader of this bunch because he was a bad bastard, pure and simple. Indeed, the dog was not the only creature to suffer at his hands that day, for there was a young girl back in his flat with a black eye and a bruised spirit.

Davie didn't know about the girl, of course, but if he had it would have made what he was about to do even easier. Rab didn't know about the girl either, but even if he had it wouldn't have made much of a difference to him. He didn't particularly give a stuff about the dog. This was Davie's show, and he was there to back up his pal, pure and simple.

Bobby Newman had told them where the youths had settled and after Joe the Tailor was safely in his house in Riddrie, Davie and Rab made their way to the waste ground. Davie didn't say a word as he strode into the thick of the youths and began to untie the lead from the arm of the chair. The dog's owner was speechless for a moment, but quickly found his voice. 'What the fuck you doing, ya bastard?'

Davie ignored him and continued to unravel the lead. The youth made the mistake of putting a hand on Davie's arm in a futile attempt to push him away. Davie said nothing, he seldom did when in this mood. He merely lashed out with his right hand, palm upwards, fingers slightly bent inwards, and slammed the heel of his hand into the boy's nose. Then he did it again. And again. Three sharp jabs in swift succession. Rab was not close by – he had positioned himself at the fringe of the group, his watchful eyes alert for any movement from any of the other lads – but he heard the crunch of gristle shattering under the force of the blows and saw blood spurt from the boy's nostrils. One or two of the other drinkers began to move forward, but Rab merely said, 'Now, now, boys, let's not get frisky, eh?' They looked back at him, saw that he was a big fella, then watched as their erstwhile leader writhed on the armchair, both hands trying to stem the blood from his shattered nose, and thought better of taking any action.

Davie finally slipped the lead from the chair and began to walk away with the dog, which went willingly, as if he knew this was his one chance of freedom. But the dog kicker wasn't done yet, and Rab had to admire him for that. Those three vicious blows to the face would have been enough to stop most guys, but he was up and lunging at Davie. Rab opened his mouth to shout a warning, but he needn't have bothered. Davie spun to his right and swung his left foot round and up, catching the boy neatly in the balls. He stopped as if he'd been pole-axed and his hands darted reflexively to his crotch as his knees buckled and he slumped down. Rab smiled at his bug-eyed expression of pain. Sometimes watching Davie work was better than the telly.

'Stay down,' warned Davie.

'That's my dog,' hissed the boy through clenched teeth.

Davie shook his head. 'Not anymore.' As they walked from the waste ground, Rab glanced behind him to make sure no one was following and saw that not one of the group had yet gone to the aid of their fallen pal. It would seem he had lost some face.

'So, it looks like you've got yourself a dog, Davie.'

Davie looked down at the brown wirehaired mongrel trotting at his feet, the dog's body language already showing a change, as if it knew it was heading to a better life. 'Yeah.'

Rab took a few more paces then said, 'Your auntie will be pleased.'

* * *

Rab was right. Davie's auntie Mamie reacted to the appearance of her nephew with a dog in tow with ill grace. She screamed at him to get the *filthy animal* out of her house, which was rich because she'd been on a four day bender with her boyfriend and the house hadn't been as much as threatened with a vacuum for two days before that. She started on Davie as soon as he stepped into the hall. It was five at night and she was still in the shapeless blue dressing gown she'd had on that morning. And the day before. And the day before that. In fact, Davie had to stop and consider before he could remember when he'd last seen her wear anything else but that threadbare rag. Davie ignored her strident screech and headed for his room but the boyfriend, Ted the carpet fitter, stepped in his way. It looked like he'd drunk just enough to let him think he could take him on. Ted was a big lad but, as Michael Caine once said in some picture Davie couldn't quite place, he was out of shape and this was a full-time job for him. Ted stood at the bottom of the stairs, blocking the way. He wore a greasy Rangers top, was unshaven and his hair hadn't been combed for days.

'Your auntie doesn't want that mutt in here, did you no hear?' His words were slightly slurred but there was no missing their belligerent tone. Davie sighed. The world was full of arseholes and it seemed he had the only pair of rubber gloves.

'Ted,' he said quietly, 'you've been itching for this for a while. But don't do it...'

Ted smiled and Davie caught a whiff of cheap whisky mixed with bad breath, not an appetising mixture. The dog sensed a threat and began to growl. Ted ignored it.

'You think you're so fuckin tough, Davie boy. You think you're just the fuckin hard man. Oh, I've heard the stories. The fuckin bogey man, you are. Joe the Tailor's pet rottweiler. Well, let me tell you, Davie fuckin McCall, you don't frighten me. I don't care who you work for. And you know what else? I don't care who your fuckin da was...'

Davie's patience had already begun to wear thin at the mention of Joe the Tailor, but bringing Danny McCall into the equation was a step too far. He punched Ted in the guts and stepped back as he doubled over. Perhaps he had been something in his day, but now Ted was a tub of lard and he went down hard. Davie grabbed him by the back of his t-shirt and jerked him out of the way. The carpet-fitter careered across the hallway and slammed into the front door. The dog was barking now – a deep sound that came up from his guts and belied his size. Auntie Mamie screeched a string of curses that would have made a dock worker blush and rushed to her boyfriend's side.

'You get the fuck out of this house, Davie McCall,' she yelled. 'You get out and you don't come back.'

Davie shrugged and gave the dog a gentle tug on the lead as he moved up the stairs. It was time to move on anyway.

* * *

Rab stayed in a third floor red-sandstone tenement flat on Sword Street, jutting off Duke Street straight as a blade. Joe owned it and the two other flats in the close, so Rab had a good deal on the rent. When the big man opened the door to find Davie standing there with a suitcase and the dog at his feet, amusement flickered across his face and he said, 'Auntie Mamie was pleased then?'

Davie allowed him a slight smile. 'I need a place to crash for a while.'

'You and the dog?'

'That a problem?'

'No to me. I hope someone's housetrained, though.'

Davie looked down at the dog at his feet. 'I dunno, I hadn't thought about that.'

Rab stepped aside, 'Wasn't talking about the dog…'

Davie smiled again as he and the dog stepped into the hallway. 'Thanks, Rab – I appreciate this.'

Rab closed the door. 'No problem, son,' he said. 'That's what friends are for.'

5

NORRIE KENNEDY WAS a happy man.

It wasn't just because he'd had a skinful at the pub. It wasn't just because he'd had a great time that night, belting out old Frank Sinatra standards. It wasn't just that he'd knocked them dead with renditions of 'I've Got You Under My Skin' and 'Luck be a Lady' like he was in a Vegas lounge – and fuck 'em if they weren't happy and would've rather heard the band covering old Eagles numbers. He loved Sinatra, had done ever since he was a boy. Even when his pals were going on about Elvis and later, The Beatles, he still bought Sinatra records. He had a vast collection, not as big as that bastard Joe the Tailor it was true, but extensive all the same. He'd never been to the Jew boy's house down there in Riddrie but he'd heard that he had shelves and shelves of recordings by Sinatra and Dean Martin and Sammy Davis. Bastard had even met Ol' Blue Eyes – he'd been told there was a picture of them together, taken at a show in London back in the 1960s. Norrie didn't know how the meeting had come about nor did he care. He didn't want to think too much about Mister Joe bloody Klein anyway because it would spoil his mood.

The reason for his happiness that night was that he'd finally divorced his nagging harpy of a wife and he was free to set up house with the lovely Louise, a petite blonde barmaid at a pub he owned in Castlemilk, who he'd been shagging for the past two years. She was 30 years younger but that didn't worry him. He didn't care if she was only interested in him because having it away with a big time crook gave her a thrill or because he had the cash to buy her nice things. She got his juices flowing like no woman had in a long time. And he was deliriously happy.

It was 11.30pm on a Wednesday night and Norrie knew his wee Louise would have finished her shift and would be back at the house. From the street his home didn't look like much, but inside it was palatial. His son and daughter used to live with him and his wife, but they'd both moved on, thank God. His son was a limp-wristed wee fuck who wanted to be an artist and his daughter was a clone of her mother. He was glad to see the back of them. But Louise... ah, Louise. All she wanted was to have money spent on her and to be fucked royally, a duty Norrie was more than delighted to fulfil. Even at the age of 60 and with a drink in him, Norrie could still get it up. He hoped she was in bed waiting for him. Even now, as he walked along the dark street, he could feel a tickle at his groin. He glanced back down the road to ensure his men were far enough back because he was developing a hard-on that wasn't going away anytime soon. They knew to let him have his space, but were close enough to wade in should any fucker try anything on. Norrie could handle himself, but Hell, what's the point of being what the papers called a Glasgow Godfather if you didn't have minders?

To take his mind off his libido, he gazed up at the sky and wished he could see the stars properly. That was the problem with living in the city – light pollution. He loved to see the stars. That was why he had a house at Luss on Loch Lomond. He could go out at night and look up and see the whole fucking universe. He planned on taking Louise up to the Loch in a couple of weeks and together they'd stand at the water's edge and look at the lights twinkling in the sky. That would be magic, he thought. Just me and her, together, looking at Heaven's majesty. He'd read that in a book; *Heaven's majesty*. He could visualise the two of them standing outside the wee cottage, hand in hand, staring in awe at the light show above. Then he'd take her inside and shag her bandy.

He could see the house up ahead and Louise's wee Metro City parked out front. She was home. She was home and waiting for him. A big smile broke out on his face. Norrie Kennedy was a really happy man.

He was still smiling when the bullet flew out of the darkness and slammed into his right shoulder. He didn't hear the gunshot and he barely registered the pain before lead burrowed into flesh and lodged against his shoulder blade. He heard another cough as he staggered back and then something punched him on the chest. The bullet scythed through his lungs and erupted from his back in a spray of flesh and blood. Still he didn't fall, but his legs caught the top of a low garden wall behind him and he sat down heavily. He remained there, arms lying limp on his knees, as if he was taking a rest. He managed to raise his head and saw the silenced pistol poking out of a red Ford Cortina. The barrel bucked slightly as another bullet was sent winging towards him and caught him in the throat. His head snapped back, blood spurting from his artery, and his body tumbled backwards into a small garden. He lay on his back, the pain miraculously gone now, but he could hear a strange gurgling noise. It took him a few seconds before he realised the noise was emanating from his neck.

He looked up at the night sky and wished he could see the stars, just one last time. But all he saw were black clouds. He thought for a moment that something dark winged across them. Birds, big black birds, flying at night and he wondered why.

Then he died, his eyes still open, still hoping for a glimpse of Heaven's majesty.

Norrie's men had started running when they saw him staggering back, thinking at first that he had just taken a drunken tumble. But then he fell backwards into the garden and the dark red motor gunned away from the kerb. The notion of a shooting didn't enter their head at this stage. After all, this was Glasgow, not Chicago. It wasn't until one of them slipped on a pool of blood on the pavement that they realised that Chicago had come to Glasgow.

* * *

The dog lay on the floor in front of the gas fire, head between his front paws, and he slept. He was oblivious to the discussion going on, though it was about him. Davie, Rab and Bobby Newman were debating possible names. Bobby had come over earlier, bringing Chinese food with him to celebrate Rab's new flatmate.

'I saw this John Wayne film once,' said Bobby, sipping from his can of Carlsberg. 'He had this dog and he just called it "Dog".'

Davie shook his head as he jerked open a can of Coke. Bobby and Rab were both drinking beer, but he never touched alcohol. Of all the things he'd learned from his Dad, that was the most important. 'Every dog deserves a name,' he said.

Rab was stretched out on the couch, his eyes on the telly in the corner, where a God-awful movie was about halfway through. They weren't really watching, but Rab liked the actress who starred in it and hoped she'd get her top off quite soon. 'I had a dog when I was wee,' he said, balancing his Tennents Lager on his chest. 'Big fucker, he was – an Alsatian.'

'German Shepherd...' said Bobby

'What?'

'That's what they call them now, German Shepherds. They only called them Alsatians because of the war and that, didn't want anything German, you know? But now they're called German Shepherds.'

Rab turned his head to stare at Bobby, who was sitting in an armchair to his right. 'As I was sayin before Barbara fuckin Woodhouse here gave me my lesson for the day...'

Bobby smiled and raised two fingers.

'Anyway,' said Rab, 'we called him Shane, is what I was going to say.'

'That wee dog's no a Shane,' said Bobby. 'He's more a Chico or a Pepper.'

Rab grimaced. 'Pepper?'

'Aye, Pepper, because he's brown.'

'Why no call him shithead and be done with it? Pepper? Jesus! I can just see Davie walkin down the road shouting "Pepper, come to daddy!" He'd have the shit kicked out of him in no time.'

Davie saw a smile tickle Bobby's lips. They all knew no one around here would dare try to kick the shit out of Davie, but nothing need be said. Davie's reputation wasn't exactly something the three pals discussed between them. It was just something that existed.

'I'm going to call him Abe,' said Davie, getting up from the room's second armchair and moving over to scratch the dog's ear.

Rab watched him. 'Abe? Why Abe?'

Davie shrugged. He didn't want to tell them it was after Abraham Lincoln, who had freed the slaves. This wee dog, although he didn't know it, had freed Davie from his drunken auntie and his life in her house. So he'd call him Abe. And as if in agreement, Abe rolled over at Davie's touch and let him scratch his belly.

* * *

When Norrie Kennedy met his maker, the street had been quiet, no traffic to speak of, no pedestrians. Now a long stretch between the dead man's house and beyond was blocked off and traffic diverted. At the barriers, uniforms kept the media and onlookers at bay. News of the murder had spread through the streets like spilled water. Print photographers snapped at everything that moved and TV crews filmed whatever they could. Meanwhile, the public watched the murder circus with ever-increasing levels of boredom, for, not being directly involved, there was little of interest. As the old police saying goes, *there's nothing to see here*. But they remained at the cordons anyway, hope springing eternal that they might catch a glimpse of a bit of blood. This was big, so it was – Norrie Kennedy blown away just yards from his front door and in front of his boys, too.

Blue flashing lights sparkled below the street lamps and bounced off the windows of the nearby houses. Frank Donovan stood over the smear of blood and noted how the flashing light reflected off it. His boss, Detective Inspector Jack Bannatyne, was leaning across the body in the garden, his hands in the pockets of his long overcoat, pulling it closer to his body so that it didn't waft against the wounds. The body hadn't been moved and still lay half in the small garden, two legs draped over the small wall. It looked to Donovan as if he'd simply been pushed over, which of course is exactly what the bullets had done.

Gentleman Jack was something of a legend in the Glasgow force, a no-nonsense thief taker with an admirable contempt for authority and, on occasion, a not-so-admirable contempt for the rule book. As long as it stood up in court, Jack Bannatyne didn't much care *how* evidence was gathered. Donovan, now Detective Constable, thank-you-very-much, had learned a lot over the past year on Bannatyne's team. The only downside was that he seemed to constantly be paired with Jimmy Knight.

He could see Knight further down the street, talking to Kennedy's two minders. Even from this distance and in this light, Donovan could see they looked pretty stunned. Knight was chewing something – he was always chewing something, or smoking those wee cigarillos he liked so much – and Donovan saw him nod, then motion a nearby uniform over to take charge of the only known eye witnesses to the killing. Knight walked back towards him, pulling his sheepskin jacket tightly to his body to ward off the chill.

'What did they see, Jimmy?' It was Jack Bannatyne's voice, from behind the wall.

'The usual, boss,' said Knight. 'No much. Dark red car, sped off in the direction of Blackhill. No sight of the shooter, no sight of anything.'

Bannatyne moved away from the body and walked through the small gate, nodding a greeting to the police surgeon as he passed by on his way to inspect the body. 'Believe them?'

Knight scratched his cheek, which was, as usual, shadowed by a heavy growth. No matter how often he shaved, the Black Knight always had stubble. 'I think they're telling the truth, boss. I think they're pretty shocked by all this. No used to guns, these boys. Knives, chibs, chains, bottles, aye – but no guns. '

Bannatyne nodded. 'Okay, let's get the canvass started. I'll get some uniformed help and I want every door on the street knocked and every person spoken to. Work in pairs...'

Don't say it, thought Donovan.

'One talk, one listen and watch...'

Please don't say it, thought Donovan.

'Anyone dodgy, huckle them down to Baird Street...'

Maybe he won't say it, thought Donovan, his hopes rising.

Then he said it.

'Jimmy, you and Frank work together. You make a good team. You start with the blonde girl in Kennedy's house. She only just got in before it happened so maybe she saw the shooter's car arriving.'

'Sure, boss,' said Knight, smiling at Donovan.

'Yes, boss,' said Donovan, hoping his tone didn't sound as sullen to Bannatyne as it did in his head.

'And find DS Docherty, tell him to pick up Joe the Tailor and some of his boys, invite them in for questioning.'

'You think they've got something to do with it, boss?'

Bannatyne shrugged. 'It's no the Tailor's style, but you never know. There was no love lost between him and Kennedy. They've been feuding for years. It won't do any harm to give them a pull, light a wee fire under them.'

Knight's face brightened in the street lights. 'You want us to lift them?'

'No, we'll invite them in for a wee chat. Got nothing to link them to this yet. Tell them... *ask* them to come in tomorrow. They'll come. Joe the Tailor knows better than not to.'

'Right, boss,' said Knight, grinning.

'Aye, boss,' agreed Donovan.

Bannatyne nodded and moved back into the garden to talk to the police surgeon, who was there to pronounce Kennedy dead, as if the bullet wounds and the blood all over the scrubby wee bit of grass weren't evidence enough. Knight moved closer, his smile broadening. 'You hear that, Frankie boy? We make a good team. What've I been telling you for years, eh?'

'Yeah, Jimmy, I know.'

'You're going to enjoy this. I caught sight of the lassie earlier, Kennedy's squeeze, and she's a wee stoater. Blonde – and no bottle job, either. I'm telling you, when this is over I'll pay her a wee visit myself. I mean, if she could shag Kennedy then she'll shag anyone, right?'

Inwardly, Donovan sighed.

6

BAIRD STREET POLICE STATION was a featureless block of brown brick sitting within shouting distance of the surging M8. As Joe sat in a bare little interview room he could hear the sound and fury of the traffic as it sped east towards Edinburgh and west towards Greenock.

Joe, Davie and Rab had been politely invited to 'assist the police with their inquiries' and placed in separate interview rooms on the ground floor. Joe knew why he was there, of course. It was inevitable he would be pulled in when Norrie Kennedy was shot. He also knew that Bannatyne would keep him waiting, so he made himself as comfortable as the cheap plastic chair would allow and let his mind wander. He didn't think long on Kennedy, a man for whom he had little time when he was alive, nor did he think of Johnny Jones and his plan. Instead he thought of Rachel. Little Rachel, beautiful Rachel. His sister had been dead for 40 years, but he thought of her often.

She was eight years old when she died at the hands of the German soldier, dark-haired, dark-eyed like her mother, whereas Josep Wolfowitz was blond and blue-eyed. He didn't look like a Jew, which had helped when he joined the band of Polish partisans and adopted the name Adamski. Anti-Semitism was as rife within their ranks as in the enemy's, and Joe wanted to kill Germans, not countrymen. And kill them he did, with a knife, with a gun, with his bare hands. He became such an enthusiastic killer of men that even his own side grew wary of him. He killed for vengeance; he killed to cleanse his own conscience. He blamed himself for not being there when the soldier had arrived at their farm.

He thought about the last time he had seen Rachel. He had been wandering the forests with little to eat for days. In the midst of a blizzard he collapsed and waited for death to come. Rachel had been dead for two weeks and yet, there she was, walking towards him. *What was she doing out here,* he wondered, *without a coat? That's a silly little summer dress she's wearing.* As she bent over him, he asked her where she had been, but she smiled and stroked his forehead.

Hush now, Josep, she said, *sleep*.

I don't want to sleep, he said.

Sleep, she insisted, *everything will be all right soon.*

Where are Mama, Papa? said Josep. *Are they waiting*?

Yes, said Rachel, *but it's not your time, not yet. Sleep, and when you awake you will be safe.*

And then he felt her lips brush his forehead, light and soft like the gentle caress of a single snowflake, and as she straightened her soft voice faded and her pretty little face merged with the growing darkness, and he slept. The partisans found him soon after and nursed him back to health, but he could still hear her voice in the snowfall and feel the touch of her lips.

The sound of the interview room door opening brought him back to the present day.

'Mister Klein.' Bannatyne was polite as he sat down opposite Joe. Detective Sergeant Docherty took a seat beside him, flipped open a notebook and clicked a ballpoint pen. They both looked very grim.

'Inspector Bannatyne,' said Joe, his blue eyes twinkling with amusement.

'Sorry to keep you waiting,' Bannatyne lied.

Joe shrugged. 'It is of no consequence. I know you are a busy man.'

'You'll know why I've asked you here, of course?'

'I presume because Mr Kennedy was shot last night. I know nothing about it.'

'You can understand why I'm asking you about it though?'

Joe shrugged again. 'There was no love lost between us.'

Bannatyne gave him a wry smile. 'That's putting it mildly. He tried to run you over with a white transit five years ago.'

'Allegedly.'

Bannatyne nodded. 'True, we couldn't prove it.'

'As far as I'm aware, it was a drunkard who was never traced.'

Bannatyne ignored that. 'You waited a long time for payback, didn't you, Joe?'

Joe shook his head, a slight smile on his lips. 'I really do not mind police officers jumping to conclusions – for some of you it is the only exercise you get – but believe me when I tell you that I had nothing to do with last night's events, Mister Bannatyne.'

'Then who did?'

'I have no idea.'

'Come on, Joe – there's not much that goes on in this city that you don't know about. You're the elder statesman of the underworld...'

'I am a businessman, nothing more.'

'Aye, and I'm Chief Constable.'

'Really? Congratulations on your promotion.'

Bannatyne, despite himself, smiled. He realised he'd been leaning forward so he sat back, forcing himself to relax. 'Give me something, Joe. This is bad. Guns going off on the street? It's not the Glasgow way.'

Joe sighed. He was fully aware of the gravity of the situation but he wasn't going to give the police anything to work with. That *was* the Glasgow way. 'I cannot help you, Mister Bannatyne. Mister Kennedy's death was regrettable, but it would be hypocritical of me to say that I mourn his passing. He was not a pleasant man, as you know.'

'And you are? You're a crook and a pimp, Joe. You bankroll major crimes. You lead young men into temptation. You're no better than Norrie, if you ask me.'

Joe smiled. 'Thankfully, I did not ask. Otherwise, you might have said something hurtful. Now, if you are finished with me I'd like to leave. I am here voluntarily, after all.'

Bannatyne nodded. 'You know the way.'

The two detectives remained seated while Joe stood up and straightened his coat before heading for the door. Bannatyne said, 'This is the start of something, isn't it, Joe?'

Joe opened the door but did not turn back. 'I sincerely hope not, Mister Bannatyne.'

* * *

The only difference between Interview Room Two and Interview Room One was the number on the door. It had a similarly scarred wooden table and identical cheap plastic chairs, as well as the same crime prevention posters on the walls. A cobweb in a high corner may even have been spun by the same spider. Davie had been in rooms like this before and he wasn't fazed. He'd never met the two cops sitting opposite him, though. One was a big guy with a shock of thick black hair and a wide chin sporting a good growth of dark stubble, which reminded him of Big Rab. He had dark eyes and a powerful physique under his grey jacket and white shirt. He gave off an aura of total confidence and complete authority, and Davie knew this one wouldn't blink an eye if he felt the need to raise a hand or two. He'd introduced himself as Detective Constable Knight, and from somewhere Davie recalled stories of a cop the boys called the Black Knight, an absolute bastard who was quick with his fists. The other cop, who Knight had identified as DC Donovan, was a bit smaller and quieter in his ways, but not stupid. His brown eyes watched Davie carefully. He was also unshaven. Davie surmised they'd been up all night.

'So,' said Knight, 'you're Davie McCall, eh?'

Davie remained silent but he held Knight's gaze steadily, knowing the man was on the prod and knowing what was coming next. Knight didn't disappoint him.

'I've heard tales of your da. Big Danny McCall. He was a terror, I hear.'

Even though he had expected it, Davie felt the usual stab at the mention of his father's name.

'Killed your maw, didn't he?' Knight went on, 'Battered her to death. Nasty that, very nasty.'

Davie shifted a little in his chair and immediately regretted showing discomfort. He knew that Knight was looking for his Achilles heel. He didn't want him to know he'd found it.

'Aye, it was a shame. Heard she was okay, your maw. A nice woman who just had terrible taste in men. You were there when it happened, weren't you?'

Davie stared back at him. The other cop looked uncomfortable but said nothing. That was bastard cops all along, Davie thought. They stuck together even when something was out of order.

Knight's lips tightened. 'Cat got your tongue, son?'

Despite himself, Davie blurted, 'That why you wanted me here? To talk about my maw? You caught him yet, have you?'

A faint smile puckered Knight's lips and Davie knew he'd lost a point by responding. 'Naw, son, your da's well in the wind, so he is. Never see him again, no if he's got any sense. All I'm trying to do is get a feel for you and your life, that's all. He was quite a guy, your da, by all accounts. Never met him myself but you hear stories, you know? He was a dangerous man. You want to follow in his footsteps, Davie?'

'Not particularly,' said Davie, and it was true.

'Then why do you work for Joe the Tailor? Your da was a bone-breaker for him and we hear you're the same.'

Davie said nothing. He forced himself to sit back in his chair and appear relaxed, but the truth was this big, dark-haired cop had got his goat too easily. He listened to his own breathing and heard the air roaring in his ears. He told himself to calm down, slow down, pull back. Gradually, the roaring dulled and finally stilled, and he knew he was back in control. As he stared back at Knight something passed between them, an understanding of sorts. Davie saw the man give a slight shrug as he sensed that he had dragged himself back from some brink. Knowing now that pushing him any further in that direction would be useless, he took another tack.

'You know a guy called Norrie Kennedy?'

'Aye.'

'You know he was shot last night?'

'Aye.'

'Know anything about it?'

'Only what I heard on Radio Clyde this morning.'

'Where were you between 11 and 12 last night?'

'In my flat.'

'Oh, aye – you're sharing with Rab McClymont now, that right?'

Davie nodded. News travels fast.

'Down Sword Street, right?'

Davie nodded again.

'How's that working out, eh?'

Davie shrugged. 'Just moved in a coupla days ago. It's only temporary, 'til I get my own place.'

'Joe'll help you with that, I'm sure. He's very... eh... *helpful* with his young boys, isn't he?'

Davie smiled slightly, knowing that Knight was trying another route to get his back up. He was disappointed in the big cop. He thought he would have been more subtle than goading him about his manhood.

Knight smiled back. 'Why the smile, Davie? Something funny?'

'Well, you, for one thing. You're so intent on trying to piss me off. Let me save you some time because I can't be arsed sitting here all day swapping banter, okay? I don't know anything about Kennedy gettin done. Neither does Rab, who's around here someplace too, and neither does Joe. Kennedy wasn't a well-liked guy and he's obviously pissed off the wrong person. So, that's it. Can I go now?'

Knight grinned and glanced at Donovan, whose face remained impassive. 'Well, we're honoured, Mister McCall. We'd heard you seldom string more'n two words together. Aye, son, you can go.'

Davie stood up but Knight was still talking. 'But remember this, we're no having guns going off in our streets, even if they do take out scroats like Norrie Kennedy. These are our streets, no yours or Joe the Tailor's, okay? If we find out you and your pals had anything to do with this, we'll come looking for you. And believe me, we'll no throw the book at you, we'll beat you black and blue with it. Understand?'

Davie looked down at the two cops and he knew that Knight meant what he said. He nodded towards Donovan. 'Does he ever say anything or is he just a cardboard cut-out?'

Donovan looked up and Davie saw a hard look in his eyes. 'I speak, son, when there's someone worth speaking to.'

Davie looked into Donovan's eyes and saw that this guy wasn't like his partner or any other cop he'd ever met. They liked to talk tough, though God knows Knight was no idle boaster, but this guy listened and watched and learned. Davie knew he'd have to keep an eye on this one. 'Good to know,' he said and left the room.

Davie walked down the corridor and pushed through a set of heavy double doors into the public reception area. Joe was seated on one of three low chairs, leafing through a copy of the Strathclyde Police magazine he had found on a low table in front of him. He looked up as Davie appeared.

'They still got Rab?' Davie asked.

Joe nodded, his eyes dropping to the magazine again. 'They do like their little games.'

7

THE LAST THING Rab McClymont expected was to run across Jimmy Knight again so soon. After all, it had only been earlier that morning that the big cop had issued his lecture on the dangers of firearms. When they left Baird Street, Joe had headed off with Davie to the small office he kept in a back room of a pub he owned, dropping Rab off in Duke Street. Rab stopped at the bookies to put a bet on what turned out to be a donkey and was walking back towards Sword Street when he saw the big, dark-headed cop up ahead. Rab veered off the busy main road up a side street, intending to take a more circuitous route homeward. He was hardly scared of the detective, but he knew well enough to keep clear of the law whenever possible. So Rab weaved his way through a warren of back alleys and side streets until he reached Sword Street. He entered his close, climbed the stairs to the second floor.

He found Knight leaning against the doorframe, a big grin on his face.

'Took you long enough,' said the cop.

Rab glowered at the man, fumbling in his jacket pocket for his key. 'What the fuck d'you want now?'

'A word, son, in your shell-like.'

Rab snorted. Why did these guys always try to speak like the guys in *The Sweeney*? He pushed his key into the lock and twisted it, saying, 'Where's your pal?'

'What I've got to say to you isn't for anyone else's ears. Know what I'm saying?'

Rab paused as he pushed open the door. Now he was intrigued. 'How d'you know there's no one in here?'

Knight smiled. 'Your pal Davie's with Joe, Bobby Newman's

still assisting us with inquiries. Apart from a few hairies you slip it to now and then, there's no one else that comes here. We're on our tod, son, don't you worry.'

Rab shrugged and stepped inside, holding the door open for the big cop. 'I'm beginning to think you fancy me, keeping tabs on my pals an' that.'

Knight stepped past and gave a small chuckle. 'Oh, and you're no wrong. But no that way...'

The detective sauntered down the narrow hallway, glancing into the two bedrooms as he walked by, then veered left at the end into the living room. When Rab reached the living room, Knight was in the same armchair Davie had sat in the night before, his feet up on the low coffee table and firing up a short cigar. Rab said, 'Make yourself at home, eh?'

'I always do,' said Knight, blowing smoke towards the ceiling.

Rab sat on the settee. 'Okay, so what do you want? I don't want you here any longer than I have to. It's bad for my clean-living image.'

'I'll get right to the point then. I've been watching you for a while now. Doing a wee bit of digging. You're a smart guy, Rab, everyone knows that. You're very much the Tailor's number one boy.'

Rab opened his mouth to reply but Knight held up a hand to silence him. 'Just shut the fuck up and listen to me. I don't want to be here too long, either, and you'll know why when you hear what I've got to say. You're on the way up, son, and so am I. And we can help each other.'

Rab knew then where Knight was heading and didn't like it. 'I'm no a grass.'

'Aye – you are. You'll all grass if the right buttons are pushed. And what I'm offering you is a business arrangement. A detective is only as good as his arrests, and a good tout can make all the difference.'

'I don't need your money, Knight.'

Knight smiled. 'It's no just money I'm offering, son. I'm offering security. See, I'm gonnae go far in the Job, you know? I'm destined for big things. If I'm right, so are you. We can help each other, know what I'm sayin?'

Rab sat back into the couch and looked at the big cop. He knew exactly what Knight was saying.

Knight's next words confirmed his suspicion. 'But a cop's salary isn't very much, you know? And I've got expensive tastes. I've got a wife and I'd like to buy her a nice house, nice clothes. And here's the thing – I like women. And they like to have nice things bought for them. So, you and me, we'll go into partnership. I don't expect much at first, but you're gonnae go far, as I say – especially with my help. Information's good but cash is better, know what I mean, son? So, you'll get to indulge in your nefarious schemes and I'll take a wee skim off the top.'

'And what do I get?'

'You already know that, Rab, old son. I'll have your back. Any of my colleagues start sniffing around your operation, I'll be there to warn you. If business is really good, I'll be able to divert their attention elsewhere. I'll keep you two steps ahead of the law. I'll be the best pal you've ever had, Rab.'

'And what if I don't live up to your expectations?'

'I think you will. I'm an excellent judge of character.'

Rab knew instinctively it made sense. 'Maybe there's something in what you say. But I don't grass on Joe or Davie, understood? They're off limits.'

Knight inclined his head in agreement. 'Okay. We've all got parameters, I understand that.' Rab didn't know what 'parameters' meant but he let it go. Knight went on, 'So we're in business then?'

Rab considered. When he finally nodded, Knight smiled broadly and stuck out his hand. Rab stared at it for a second then slipped his own big fist into it.

'We're gonnae be good for each other, Rab,' said Knight. 'We're gonnae go far, you and me...'

* * *

Johnny Jones was whistling as he climbed the stairs to his second floor flat in Castlemilk. The meeting had gone well with Harry King, Norrie Kennedy's erstwhile second-in-command, who was well up for taking part in the heroin venture. He had four top men on board, three from Glasgow and one from Ayrshire, because the rural market was not to be ignored. Another six, mostly from Glasgow but maybe one from Greenock way, another from Dumbarton, and he would be ready. It wasn't an easy thing to bring them together, but the promise of millions proved very persuasive in putting aside old rivalries.

He heard the phone ringing as he reached his front door. His boys were in there but they knew better than to answer that line. They sat in the living room, Sinclair reading the *Daily Record*'s front page about Norrie's murder while Boyle watched an Open University programme about farming. The phone was in Johnny's bedroom, its insistent, shrill ringing filling the flat. He picked up the handset, knowing full well who it would be. 'Aye?'

'Is he on board?'

'Of course. Norrie was an old fossil, but Harry's no fool. He knows this is the future.'

'I'm still not happy about Norrie's death.'

'I told you, it was nothing to do with me.'

'Then who?'

'Fucks knows – Norrie had enemies, you know? Maybe Harry took him out 'cos he wasn't interested in our deal. I told you, Harry knows the score.'

There was a silence on the other end of the line as the boss thought about it. 'Harry King's a ruthless little shit, certainly,' he said finally. 'Okay, we move on to Big Jim Connolly next. He's a certainty to buy in, I think.'

'And what about Joe Klein?'

'We leave him for now.'

'He's dangerous.'

'Not to us, if we leave him alone. We need him on board.'

'He'll never do it...'

'He'll see sense.'

'I don't think so...'

'Listen, I don't need you to do the thinking, just the talking. You'll get a hefty chunk of change out of this, don't worry.'

Jones sighed. 'Look, I know Joe the Tailor, he's a one man band. He doesn't like being part of anything.'

'I told you, we need him and he'll see the sense of what we're doing. He likes cash. And we're going to make a fortune out of this.'

Jones was unconvinced, but he knew better than to continue arguing the point. Joe Klein would show his hand eventually, and then the Jew boy would go the same way as Norrie. 'Listen, we need to send a message to the others, you know? Big Jim'll be fine, sure, but I think we should give some of the other boys a wee poke in the right direction.'

'What was last night?'

'Told you, fuck all to do with me. But whoever did it maybe did us a favour, you know? Maybe what we need is a wee example, just to focus their minds.'

Jones could hear him breathing into the phone as he considered this. 'What do you suggest?'

'Barney Cable, he'll no even return my calls. We've got a history.'

Jones' history with Barney Cable was long and complex. Barney had once grassed on one of Jones' backroom boys over a freelance post office job in his area. The lad had failed to cut Barney in, a sign of respect expected whenever someone did some work in his fiefdom, and Barney had ratted him out. Cable had never liked Jones anyway, not since Jones had once made an obscene comment or two about Cable's wife. The two clashed and Jones had come off worse – he still bore the scar on his temple where Cable had smashed a beer bottle on this skull. To Barney's mind it was a fitting punishment for such disrespect, and he had told all and sundry that Jones was a low-life scumbag not fit to breathe the same air as decent criminals. To Johnny it was all a debt waiting for payback. Apart from that, Barney Cable was a Roman Catholic and Jones was a staunch Orangeman who walked in the parade every year with his sash draped proudly across his chest. Like other Glasgow crims, he also raised funds for the UDA and in return had been rewarded with an honorary rank in the paramilitary organisation. He had never actually hefted a weapon for the cause, but he would do it proudly. He didn't like Tims, especially one who had publicly bad-mouthed him.

'Okay, we set an example. But no witnesses, no civilians, understand?'

'Wouldn't have it any other way,' said Jones. 'We've got to show these guys just who's boss, you understand that?'

'I understand it, Johnny, but I hope you do. Remember who the brain behind this business is. You'd still be blowing safes in post office back rooms if it wasn't for me.'

'Aye,' said Johnny, not at all happy with his tone. Okay, so he'd come up with this plan and he'd researched the trade routes and made all the contacts, but Johnny was doing all the fucking work this end. On the other hand, if there was one man in the city who scared the shit out of him, it was this guy.

Johnny stood listening to the dial tone for a second before he realised that he'd hung up. *Fucker,* he thought. *One day you and me'll have a conversation, pal, and then we'll see who's boss right enough.*

8

HENRY GRANT WAS a small youth with thick, brown hair that tumbled down to his shoulders. When he talked, his head darted from side to side as if he was trying to head a football.

'So my da says to this guy, he says, "Look, pal, see if you don't fix that fuckin washin machine right now, and I mean fuckin pronto, I'm gonnae take that toolbag of yours and stick it so far up your jacksey it'll take a team of fuckin mountaineers to find it." My da's dead funny when he starts, so he is, so this guy says to my da, he says, "But, Mister Grant, the machine's just too old to be fixed," so my da says back, he says, "I paid good money for that machine and I expected it to last a lifetime and I'm no quite finished breathin yet." That's what he said, my da, "I'm no quite finished breathin yet," seriously, he's a laugh riot at times, my old man, just comes right out wi' them, so the guy says, he says, "Aye, okay Mister Grant, I'll dae what I can but I'm no promisin" so then he starts working on the machine and sure as fuck he got it to work again and my da says it's amazin what a man can do when he's properly motivated...'

There was a reason they called Henry Grant 'Mouthy'.

'Jesus, Mouthy,' said Rab, 'stop to take a breath, for God's sake! What have you got, lungs the size of Billy Smart's circus tent?'

Mouthy's forehead wrinkled as he considered this. 'I dunno, Rab, I think they're just normal size lungs but you know what? I always did have a lot more puff than other kids when I was wee, you know? See at gym, you know climbin the ropes and the wooden horse stuff and that, well, they'd all be out of puff a long time before I was out of breath, maybe it's something psychological, what do you think? That's what I think anyhow, something peculiar to me, it's my gift, you know?'

Rab shook his head at Davie, who smiled. 'You ever noticed that Mouthy here talks through his nose, Davie?' Rab asked. 'It's because he's worn his fuckin mouth out.'

'Ach, Rab,' said Mouthy, his voice sounding hurt, 'you know I just rabbit when I'm nervous. I'm no like you, or Davie. I cannae just sit here calm like before I go to work, you know? I get nervous and my mouth starts...'

'You must get nervous a lot then, son,' said Rab.

They were sitting in a stolen transit van opposite the gates to a wholesale warehouse that traded specifically with the fleets of ice cream vans that cruised the city streets. But they weren't interested in ice cream. The building behind the gates was packed to the rafters with boxes of sweets, crisps and cigarettes just waiting to be liberated and sold on for profit. There were lots of independent van owners in the city who were happy to buy some dodgy gear at knock-down prices. It was the kind of free market economy that did their profit margins the world of good. Now they were waiting for the nod from the inside man, a security guy with cash problems.

'We still goin out drinkin tomorrow night?' Rab asked and Davie shrugged. 'Come on, Davie son, it'll do you good. Okay, you don't drink but when was the last time you had a shag?"

Davie thought about this. The last time he'd had sex had been three months before when he'd been seeing Morag. They'd been out a few times and they'd done it in his room one rainy Sunday afternoon. They went out a couple of times after that but she'd quickly lost interest. Morag had assumed that by having sex she was getting closer to him. The sad truth was, no one got that close to Davie McCall. Girls fancied him – he was good-looking, the bluest eyes this side of Paul Newman – but there was a coldness, a distance in him that inevitably drove them away.

'Can't remember,' said Davie in reply to Rab's question.

'See? That's no healthy. You come out wi your Uncle Rab the morra night and we'll get you sucked and fucked no problem. So where d'you want to go?'

'How about down the town to the jigging?' Suggested Mouthy.

'No in the mood for dancin,' said Rab, but both Davie and Mouthy knew that he couldn't dance a step and the sight of his big body jerking around with no sense of rhythm was unlikely to stimulate a young lady's libido.

'The Triple Decker, then? Talent's no quite as high class, a wee bit more studenty, but you'll still get a drink and a shag. Maybe even a wee drop of dope, you know?'

The Triple Decker was a multi-storey pub across from the city's Drama College. It was popular with students, hippy types and anyone looking for a bit of hash.

'Fuck no,' said Rab, 'they lassies all want to talk too much before they give it up, want to probe your inner man. They don't understand it's their inner woman I want to probe. No, fuck the city centre pubs, we'll go up the West End. Guaranteed to find a generous lassie or two up Byres Road, you know?'

A security guard emerged from the side door of the warehouse and walked to the gate. Davie sat up, instantly alert, and Rab said, 'Aye, aye – here we go.'

The security guard looked up and down the street, then once behind him before he unlocked the gate. He waved them across as he swung the metal and wire mesh gates open, and Rab started the motor and coasted across the road into the delivery yard. The security man pushed the gates closed behind them and then appeared at the passenger's window beside Davie. He was a squat man in his mid-50s, his uniform draped over a lumpy form like an old blanket. His thin grey hair was combed over his balding pate, doing its best to hide the freckled skin beneath. He looked nervous.

'You'll need to be quick, lads,' he said. 'My supervisor could turn up at any minute. He's doing his rounds tonight.'

Rab said, 'Fuck sake, man, why didn't you tell us that before?'

'I only just found out, one of the other guys at another site phoned me to tell me. The bastard likes to try and catch us sleeping on the job or to see if we're off site. So he springs these visits on us.'

'Fuck sake.' Rab climbed out of the van and the security guard stepped back to let Davie and Mouthy pile out the passenger door.

'You'll have to load the gear through this door here. I haven't got a key to the loading dock.'

Rab's expression darkened. 'Anything else you haven't told me before? Like maybe there's fuck all in this place?'

'No, no!' said the man, backing away slightly, suddenly more afraid of this hulking young man than the impending visit of his boss. 'It's packed tonight, you can have your pick. Just be quick about it, okay?'

Rab sighed. 'Right, Mouthy, you hang around by the gate and keep an eye out for this bloke coming. While you're waiting, cut that security chain, make it look like we broke our way in. You see any lights down the end of the road there, you tell us. And pull your mask on. You, too, Davie.' As he spoke, Rab produced a ski mask from the pocket of his denim jacket and hauled it on. Davie followed suit.

'Right,' said Rab, 'Davie, you take the sledgehammer out the back and batter fuck out of that lock. And you,' he jabbed a finger at the guard, 'show me inside. Move quick, lads, we're on the clock here.'

They moved swiftly to follow his instructions. Rab and Davie's friendship had always been a level partnership, but on a job Davie was happy to follow Rab's lead. Davie hefted the heavy sledgehammer out of the rear of the van, leaving the doors wide open, then swung it with force at the lock on the side door through which Rab and the guard had disappeared. Behind him he could hear Mouthy cursing under his breath as he struggled to cut the security chain. Davie tossed the hammer back into the van, threw Mouthy a glance to make sure he was managing, then trotted into the building.

It was dark inside but Davie could make out rows of metal shelves busy with boxes and plastic-wrapped goods. The glint of a torch along one of the rows told him where Rab and the guard stood and he made his way towards them.

'We'll need to humph the stuff out by hand, Davie,' said Rab, clearly irritated by the whole thing. 'Fuckwit here's no got the keys to the forklift.'

The guard looked uncomfortable. 'I never thought you'd need them.'

'You don't have the keys to the loading dock, you don't have the keys to the forklift, your boss could drop in on us at any moment. Tell me why the fuck I don't give you a kicking right now?'

This made the man even more distraught. He stepped away, glancing at Davie as if for support. 'I'm new at this, you know that! I'm only doing it 'cos I need the cash. I'm taking a big risk helping yous out, so I am!'

'Aye, but I'm beginning to think you're no value for money, know what I'm sayin'?' said Rab, shaking his head. He turned to Davie. 'Start getting this loaded...' he jerked his head to the boxes of cigarettes on the shelf behind him '... and I'll see what else is worth liftin.'

Rab strode off down the row, the guard beetling along behind him, while Davie started hauling boxes off the nearest shelf. He piled a few on the floor then began to carry them out to the van. After a few trips he had a good few cartons of fags stowed away when Rab pushed his way through the door with his big hands wrapped round the handle of a manual forklift trolley stacked high with boxes of sweets and crisps.

'Found this in a corner,' he said. 'Saves humphing the bloody things.'

'Where's the guard?'

'Tied him up in his office, just in case.'

Davie helped him stack the boxes into the back of the van and they were heading back towards the warehouse when Mouthy whistled and began pointing frantically down the road.

'Get the fuck outta sight,' Rab hissed to Mouthy, 'and pull your mask on.' Mouthy looked around and spotted a pair of tall bins. As he scuttled behind them he pulled a woollen ski mask from the pocket of his bomber jacket and hauled it over his face. Rab and Davie climbed into the van and started it up, intending to move it somewhere, anywhere that wouldn't be seen, but their timing was off because the car was already turning into the gate, the headlamps illuminating the still-open back of the van.

'Fuck!' said Rab, looking in the wing mirror. Davie glanced at his own wing mirror and saw the car was simply sitting there in the gateway.

'What's he waiting there for?' Rab wondered.

Davie saw a shadow move from behind the bins and edge towards the car. Mouthy stepped up to the driver's window, something in his hand pointing at the interior, and the door slowly opened. A tall, incredibly skinny man unfolded himself from the small car, his hands above his head.

'Rab,' said Davie, 'I think Mouthy's tooled up.'

'Fuck's sake!' Rab said as he climbed out of the van and Davie slipped from the passenger seat. The tall supervisor was walking towards them, flanked by Mouthy, who held an automatic pistol in his right hand. Davie felt an itch in his stomach at the sight of the weapon. He didn't like guns.

'He was trying to radio someone for help, or something,' said Mouthy. 'I stopped him.'

The man was in his mid-40s and looked scared to death. His face was white, his hands shaking. 'I didn't speak to anyone, honest.'

Rab sighed and grabbed the supervisor by the arm. 'Get inside,' he snapped and propelled the man forward. He glared at Mouthy and whispered, 'What the fuck you thinking about?'

Mouthy shrugged and followed the supervisor through the door. Rab stepped ahead of them and led them all up a short flight of stairs to a tiny windowless office. Inside, the guard sat in his chair, trussed and gagged. His eyes widened when he saw his boss then bulged when he saw the gun in Mouthy's hand. Davie could guess what was going through his head – *this wasn't how it was supposed to happen, they didn't mention guns, he agreed to let them in and they would make it look like they'd forced their way through but they never said anything about shooters*. Davie had a great deal of sympathy for his point of view.

'Sit down behind the chair, on the floor.' The supervisor did as he was told as Rab plucked a ball of thick string off the top of a filing cabinet and began to unravel it. 'I'm gonnae tie you up now. Don't struggle, don't make a noise, or it'll go badly, understand?'

The man nodded. 'You guys do know who owns this place, don't you?'

'Don't give a fuck, pal,' said Rab.

The man swallowed. 'Well, it's Barney Cable, you heard of him?'

Rab kept wrapping the string around the guy and the chair legs but he glanced up at Davie. All Davie could see was Rab's eyes behind the dark mask, but he knew the big guy well enough to know that there was a stab of fear there.

'His name's no on the books, you understand,' the man went on, 'but he owns the place all the same. Just thought you'd like to know because he'll no be best pleased at you guys ripping him off.'

'Shut it,' said Rab, snatching a cloth from the top of the desk. He stuffed it into the man's mouth and stood up.

'C'mon,' he said and the three of them filed out, leaving the two security men back to back in the office, one in the chair, one on the floor. Once safely out of earshot, Rab punched Mouthy on the shoulder, sending him flying.

'What the fuck was that for?' Wailed Mouthy, rubbing the shoulder.

'Who the fuck told you to bring a gun?'

'I thought we might need it. It's alright, Rab, it's no even loaded. I never bought any bullets.'

'We didn't want any guns on this, Mouthy! It was just supposed to be a quick in and out, nae fuss.'

'Well, it's just as well I did, isn't it? Cos that guy was calling the cavalry and I don't think he'd've been stopped by a sharp look frae me!'

Rab saw the logic in this but was angry nevertheless. 'And fuckin Barney Cable, for fuck's sake! This whole thing was tits up frae the start.'

'It's no my fault, Rab, neither it is,' Mouthy whined, 'I just thought we needed a wee bit of hardware, know what I'm sayin? For insurance, like. Davie? Right? Makes them more pliable, you know? Right, Davie?'

He looked imploringly towards Davie, his eyes signalling an unspoken appeal for support, but Davie could only shake his head. Guns were bad news. Sooner or later they go off and that does no one any good. Mouthy visibly deflated and looked down at the pistol in his hand, as if seeing it for the first time. Then Mouthy's face lightened as he had another thought.

'Aye, but it's no my fault that we did a Barney Cable place, is it? You cannae blame me for that. I never planned this job. I never knew this was a Barney Cable place so I'm in the clear there, right, lads?'

'Mouthy,' said Rab, looming large over the smaller youth, 'shut your fuckin mouth and let me think or I'll take that gun and shove the barrel so far up your arse you'll taste metal, got it?'

Mouthy looked as if he was going to argue the point but a dark look from Rab made him clamp his jaws shut. A breeze swept up the street and caught the chain gate, making it swing open with a slight clang. Mouthy glanced in its direction as if he was looking for where the wind had come from. But there was nothing there, just the Glasgow night and the fence moving slightly.

'Right,' said Rab, 'get the rest of this onto the van and we get the fuck out of here. We've done the job now, and even if we leave the stuff here Barney Cable'll come looking for us anyway. We might as well get hung for a sheep as a goat.'

Mouthy looked back at him. 'I don't think you're saying that right, Rab. I don't think it's 'sheep for a goat', I think it's might as well get hung for a sheep as a lamb. Goes back to when you could get hung for stealing they things, you know, so they said might as well steal something big, you know? Cos a lamb is only wee and...'

'Mouthy...' Rab shook his head, knowing that the gun was the least of their troubles now. The fact that Barney Cable owned the business was the real problem. Joe would go nuts if he knew what they'd done, but there was no point crying over it now. Rab hefted a box of Embassy Regal and dropped it into the back of the van while both Davie and Mouthy moved to help him with the rest.

'I was just sayin, Davie, you know?' Mouthy said. 'Cos I don't think he said it right, sheep for a goat...'

Davie smiled and shook his head as he hauled a box of Mars bars to the van.

9

JOE THE TAILOR SHOOK HIS HEAD in sympathy as Barney Cable told him about the robbery. A cup of Luca's best coffee sat on the table in front of him while Barney had a pot of tea and a scone made by Luca's wife. Her scones were hugely popular with customers, who had been known to walk the length of Duke Street to sample them. Barney had never tasted them before and, though

Sheila did a very decent scone, he had to admit that these were pretty good. But he wasn't here to talk about baking, he was here on more serious business. The café wasn't busy – it was still early on a Saturday morning – but even so, Joe hadn't had the heart to ask Luca to close it again. So he had Bobby Newman sitting at the nearest table to keep prying ears away. Rab and Davie stood outside, watching the street and, in Rab's case for all the world was concerned, enjoying a casual smoke.

'They found the van burnt out down Parkhead way,' said Barney. 'It'd been nicked from round there, too. That's why I'm here, Joe. I thought you could put the word out, you know? Help me find these wee scroats.'

Joe nodded. 'Of course I will, my friend. This sort of behaviour cannot be tolerated.'

Barney nodded gratefully and popped the last bite of his scone into his mouth. Joe was a good man, an honourable man, and he would help him out here. They wee bastards were as good as caught.

'And how is the lovely Sheila?' Joe asked. 'And Melanie?'

Sheila was Barney's wife, Melanie his daughter, and he doted on them. 'Both fine, Joe, thanks for asking.'

'She is a beauty like her mother, your Melanie, no?'

'Aye, gives me all sorts of headaches, that. The boys frae the scheme are always round her. I've had to give a couple a wee slap, just to get them to mind their manners.'

Joe smiled. 'Just so, it is not easy being the father of girls, I would imagine, but the father of a beautiful girl…' He ended with a shrug to show how difficult that must be.

'Aye but she's a good girl, is Melanie. Bright, you know? She knows she's better than most of they scumbags. I don't need to worry too much.'

Joe nodded, sipping his coffee, and Barney knew there was something more on the man's mind. He had known Joe Klein for

20 years, always as a friend, never a rival. He was only a few years older, but Barney looked up to him and the Tailor, despite being a Jew, was unofficial godfather to Melanie.

'You have heard from Johnny Jones, I assume,' said Joe.

'Aye, that weasely wee fu– ' Barney stopped himself. He knew Joe deplored foul language and he always did what he could to moderate it around him. It was hard work; swearing came as easily to Glasgow's gangland as shit on a sewage worker's wellie. 'Anyway, he's a wee slime ball.'

'Are you joining his venture?'

'I've not even spoken to the bas– to him. He's sent me a couple of messages and I've got the gist of what he's up to from some of the boys, but I can't bring myself to even talk to him.'

'Will you take part?'

Barney thought about it for a moment. 'There's cash. I hear someone out Edinburgh way is making millions. Brings it in himself from Afghanistan, or Pakistan – one o' they places that end in 'stan'. Got a whole network – runners, couriers, the lot. Glasgow's kinda wide open for it. And if we don't do it, someone else will. I'd be daft to knock it back. The only thing is, I don't like Johnny Jones, don't trust him. Wouldn't trust him as far as I can throw him, the lanky fucker... sorry, Joe.'

Joe inclined his head. Barney was forgiven. 'I have already turned down his offer.'

Barney was surprised. 'Knocking back a lot of cash, Joe.'

'I know, but I, too, have reservations about joining forces with Johnny. And I have problems with dealing in drugs.'

'Aye, I know what you mean, but it's gonnae be big, Joe. Maybe you should get in now.'

Joe sighed. Barney leaned forward, and though they hadn't been talking loudly and there was no one at any of the tables beside them, he dropped his voice further. 'You think Johnny had Norrie done?'

Joe shrugged. 'I have no firm evidence...'

'But you think he did it, don't you?'

Joe shrugged again. He had no desire to falsely accuse any man, not even Johnny Jones, of murder.

Barney sat back again. 'If it was Johnny, he won't stop there. Had Norrie knocked him back?'

'I have no idea. Mister Kennedy and I were not on speaking terms but I believe he had reservations. If you have not yet responded to Johnny's offer then I must also caution you to be careful, my friend.'

Barney smiled. 'I can handle Johnny Jones, don't you worry.'

'It's not Johnny that worries me.'

'How do you mean?'

'The scheme to import this product is, on the face of it, a fine scheme, well planned, well thought out. I do not believe Johnny Jones came up with it.'

Barney considered this, then nodded. 'Know what you mean. He's a sly bastard – sorry, Joe – but he's no mastermind.'

'There is another player behind Jones, someone far more intelligent than he. You are right, Jones we can handle. But a mysterious backer – and one sufficiently ambitious to concoct something of this magnitude? That, my friend, is what worries me. Whether you join the venture or not is, of course, your decision. But until we know who this person is, we must be on our guard...'

* * *

Rab glanced through the café doors at Joe and Barney Cable in conference. He shifted nervously from one foot to the other. 'You think he knows it was us?'

Davie pulled the corners of his mouth down to show he didn't know.

'We shouldnae've torched the van in Parkhead, should we? Too close to home.'

Davie shrugged to say, *who knew*?

'Maybe we shouldnae've taken the gear after all, maybe Barney wouldnae've bothered his arse if we'd left it. What do you think?'

Davie bobbed his head slightly from side to side, *it could've gone either way.*

'Good to talk to you, Davie, you're always so fuckin reassuring, so you are!'

Davie smiled, glanced back into the café, and said, 'No point worrying, Rab. Just see what happens.'

'See what happens? See what happens? I'm shittin bricks here and you say "see what happens"?'

'Worrying about it doesn't go any good, Rab. Okay, we did the job and we shouldn't have, or at least we should've done a bit more checking, but what's done is done, okay? Wait and see what happens, then we react.'

Rab looked into the café again and at that moment Joe looked up and his eyes met Rab's. Right then, right there, Rab knew that Joe knew exactly what they'd done.

He turned his head away sharply and said, 'Joe knows.' Davie glanced at him and Rab looked his way briefly. 'Joe knows it was us, I can tell.'

Davie frowned and looked over his shoulder at Joe, but the old man's attention was back on Barney. Bobby, sitting at the next table, saw Davie looking in and he gave him a small wave. Luca was taking cash from a woman at the counter.

'How can you tell?'

Rab sighed, a deep exhalation that started somewhere down at his feet. 'I can just tell, that's all. Joe's got ways of knowing things. It's fuckin supernatural, but he knows things sometimes. And he knows we did it.'

'You sure?'

'I saw it just now, in his eyes. He knows.'

Davie thought about this. Joe had never bothered about them doing small jobs, as long as they were careful. And even if they weren't, he had some good lawyers he could call – and some bent coppers. But this time they hadn't been careful, hadn't done their homework. Preparation is everything, Joe had always told them, but they had still screwed up.

'I'll tell him,' Rab said. 'I'll no wait for him to say anything to me, I'll come clean. He'd prefer that, I think.'

Davie could see the logic in Rab's thinking. If Joe did know he would want them to be honest with him. If he didn't, he'd still want them to stand up and be men. He'd be unhappy, but he would never throw them to Barney, Davie was certain of that. Reparations would have to be made – and knowing Joe's sense of honour, they would be severe – but no physical harm would come to either one of them or Mouthy.

'Then I'll stand with you,' said Davie and Rab glanced in his direction. Davie looked back and nodded. Nothing more need be said between them. That's what friends were for.

10

KNIGHT AND DONOVAN were in an unmarked car on the corner of Douglas Street and St Vincent Street watching the young woman plying her trade. Soft rain caressed the windscreen and gently embraced the pavement, but she seemed impervious as she stood with her coat open to show off a full figure under a tight t-shirt. She was red-haired but there was nothing natural about the colouring and her face was heavily made up, Knight knew, to cover the signs of acne suffered during her early teenage years, which was why they called her Plooky Mary on the street. She was a tart, but she was also a tout – and a good one. Knight had a charge of assault hanging over her head which he wielded whenever he needed information, and with very little surfacing on the Norrie Kennedy murder, he needed all the help he could get.

So he and Donovan this damp Saturday night decided to visit The Drag, the network of streets running between Anderston Cross Bus station and Sauchiehall Street, to see if any of the working girls who plied their trade there had heard anything. They'd already hit three of the girls they knew and came up with nothing, so Plooky Mary was their last chance.

They climbed out of the car and walked across the road towards her. She'd clocked them as they drove up, of course, her hooker's instincts on the alert. She knew the big dark cop too well, but the smaller one was new to her. He looked okay, but you could never tell with police. The Black Knight was a bastard good and proper, though. She'd given another girl an open face with a steel comb the year before but she'd never been charged with it. He had all the statements and an eye-witness, but he said he'd hold it back as long as she did a turn for him now and again. Mostly that meant steering some information his way, but now and again it meant a shag. Generally that was okay by her; if she wasn't doing it with him it would be someone else, and he always slipped her a tenner or so. But there had been a couple of times he'd taken her to a room and he'd tied her up and slapped her about. He'd been in right dark moods those nights and sure, he'd given her 20 quid each time but that wasn't enough for being slapped about, not nearly enough.

'Mary,' he said as he stepped onto the pavement, a big smile on his face. She was relieved, no pain from him tonight. 'Slow night, eh?'

'It'll pick up, Mister Knight. It's early yet.'

He jerked his head to his mate. 'This is DC Donovan. Frank, this is Mary, one of the best girls on the street.'

The cop called Donovan nodded politely to Mary and she nodded back. She caught him eyeing her up and down, taking in her figure. They all did that, probably weren't even aware of it. A glance up and down, the legs, the hips, the breasts. They all did it, all men, cops, lawyers, sheriffs, even the do-gooders who tried to help them off the streets. She didn't mind the looks. She knew she had a good figure and given what she did for a living, a man looking at her was the least of her problems.

'So what's the word, Mary?' Knight asked, lighting up a wee cigar.

'About what, Mister Knight?'

Knight shrugged, blew some smoke into the air. 'Norrie Kennedy. I know you'll have heard something.'

'Nothing, Mister Knight, it's really quiet over that.'

'C'mon, Mary – you're the ned's favourite tart. They all come to you for a bit of the old slap and tickle. There must be some sort of pillow talk about the Kennedy thing.'

She had intended to deny all knowledge, but she hesitated. She caught the look in his eyes, and knew she'd made a mistake. He was a sharp bastard, was the Black Knight, and that slight pause and the guilt that had flashed across her face telegraphed that she'd heard something. He smiled, his eyes dropping from her face to her breasts straining against the white t-shirt. She closed her coat self-consciously. Some looks she couldn't take.

'Frank,' said Knight, 'me and Mary need to have a wee chat in the motor. Go for a walk or something, will you? Around the block a couple of times should do it.'

Donovan opened his mouth to object, but evidently thought better of it. He wanted nothing to do with whatever was going to happen. He pulled his coat collar up against the wet kiss of the rain and walked up the hill.

Knight smiled, stuck his wee cigar between his teeth and reached over to grasp Mary's arm, pulling her towards the car. 'I don't know nothin, honest Mister Knight,' she said, dragging back a little.

Knight took the cigar from his mouth and said, 'Get in the car, hen. Don't fuck me about.'

Mary looked up and down the street but, apart from the other cop walking away, there was no one. Knight had been right – it had been a slow night and it was only getting slower. He pulled her towards the car and opened the back door, jerking his head to tell her to get in. He slammed the door behind her then walked round the back and climbed in. He twisted in the seat to face her, one arm on the parcel shelf, the other propped against the rear of the passenger seat.

'Okay, Mary, it's just you and me. What've you heard?'

'Mister Knight, I...'

'Mary,' he said, stopping her dead. He stared at her, eyes boring deep into her mind. Even his eyes were dark, she noticed, deep, dark pools that emitted no light – like those black holes in space she'd read about that suck everything in and don't let it go again. Knight's eyes were like that – they took everything in and gave away nothing. She sighed.

'Sibby Colston,' she said. 'Speak to Sibby.'

'Sibby's no a trigger man, he's a wee tea leaf.'

'Aye, but he knows something,' she said. 'He was with me the other night and he said something about Kennedy.'

'What'd he say?'

'Some pal of his *made his bones* with the killing, something like that.'

'Made his bones? He say that?'

'Aye, Sibby's a big reader, into books about the Mafia and that. Made his bones, he said.'

'He say who?'

She shook her head and Knight shifted in his seat impatiently. 'Honest, Mister Knight, that's all he said! See Sibby – he'll burst for you no problem. He's no a hard man.'

Knight looked into her face for what seemed like an eternity before he nodded, satisfied that she had told him all she knew. He sat back in the seat and stared forward.

'That me, Mister Knight? Can I go now?'

He didn't answer at first, didn't even move, then he turned to her and smiled. It wasn't a warming smile. 'There's something else you can do for me before you go,' he said and pulled back the flaps of his coat. She saw his hand moving down and heard the zip of his fly.

'A wee favour, hen...'

* * *

The first time Davie set eyes on Audrey Burke, she was standing at the head of the stairs leading to the upper bar of The Curlers on Byres Road. She was with two friends and they were looking for somewhere to sit in the crowded lounge, which was filled with enough cigarette fumes to smoke haddock. Despite Rab's vow to avoid students, the bar was filled with them, some carefully dressed in slightly tatty casual wear, others simply because that's all they could afford. Downstairs was where you went if you wanted to throw a dart or two or talk about politics and sport. Upstairs was where you came to chase fanny. When Davie, Rab, Bobby and Mouthy had arrived earlier, they looked around and concluded that most of the women there had been chased – and caught – many times before.

Then Audrey arrived, dressed in a suit so white it hurt the eyes, her soft blonde hair thick and tangled to her shoulders. Davie couldn't keep his eyes off her.

And then Sinclair had moved in.

They had spotted Boyle and his mate as soon as they arrived. They had debated moving somewhere else, but it was Rab who said, 'Fuck em. If they start something, we'll finish it.'

Rab was in a good mood. Earlier that afternoon, he and Davie had come clean to Joe about their antics of the night before. Joe hadn't been pleased, but he was by no means surprised by the news and Rab knew they had done the right thing. How the old man had known they were responsible, Rab would never know. As he told Davie, Joe the Tailor had a way of knowing things. He warned them against any further freelancing without checking with him first and then promised he would make it right with Barney somehow. He asked them if they had sold on the gear – which they hadn't – and told them to keep it safe so it could be returned. Perhaps if Barney got his merchandise back on the quiet, he would be satisfied with making a killing on the insurance. Barney would accept Joe's word that the young men had no idea they had transgressed against him. There would be a solemn undertaking that they would help Barney at some point in the future in some way and that, as they say, would be that.

So it was with a lighter heart that Rab forced Davie to change out of his customary jeans and trainers and into something more presentable in order to head up the West End. Davie chose a pair of slightly flared, high-waisted black trousers and a dark jacket over a white shirt. Rab forsook his usual bulky army surplus jacket and denims for a stylish black two piece with a very faint cream pinstripe. He shaved his chin as closely as the razor would allow, but still looked like someone had coated his jaw in black paint. Mouthy turned up at Rab's flat wearing a three piece suit and a lightly coloured floral shirt with a matching tie. His thick head of wiry hair was, for once, neatly combed and he smelled strongly of Brut, prompting Rab to comment that if the pub ran out of alcohol they could always just lick his cheeks. Davie could steer a car but he had no license, so Bobby Newman agreed to be their designated driver, not being much of a drinker anyway. He was wearing a pair of tight, flared fawn trousers and a brown-flecked jacket over a cream shirt. The idea was to be well turned out without appearing too dressy.

Davie was as smartly-turned out as was possible for someone who paid no attention to fashion but, even so, he felt like a tinker as he looked at the girl. She was, he thought, simply stunning. Sinclair thought so too, because he was on his feet like he was on springs and inviting her and her pals to join him and Boyle at their table. She looked unsure, but her pals agreed readily. Davie, sitting at a corner table, narrowed his eyes as unease washed over him. He recalled what Bobby had once said about Boyle and Sinclair – that they didn't chat girls up, they relied on a half brick and a back alley.

Before she arrived, he had been thinking about peeling away from his pals and heading home. But as he watched her settle at the table, he decided to stay.

11

'C'MON, FRANKIE BOY – lighten up, for God's sake...'

Knight had on his most placating smile as he steered the car through the streets towards the Gallowgate. The roads were quiet at this hour on a damp Saturday night, so they were making fairly good time. But Donovan was not happy with his partner's extra-curricular activities.

'Jimmy, it's no on,' Donovan said, the anger stretching his voice thin. 'If the boss ever heard of you copping freebies from a tout he'd have your balls in a vice.'

'Ach,' said Knight dismissively, 'I'll bet he's had a few good ones on the house in his day. He's no squeaky clean, is Bannatyne.'

'Have some consideration for me then.'

Knight glanced sideways at his partner. 'How? Did you want a go at her? You should've said, man!'

Donovan sighed. 'Naw, I did not want a go at her.'

'Oh, sorry – forgot! You're happily married, aren't you? Although to my mind that's one of they whatchamacallits – an oxymoron...'

'Jimmy, we're supposed to be working together. Now, I don't care what you get up to when you're alone, but I'm telling you – don't involve me again.'

There was a silence in the car for a moment, then Knight said softly, 'Or what, Frankie boy?'

'What?'

'Or you'll do what? Rat me out? Clype on me to the boss? Cos let me tell you, that wouldn't be advisable.'

Donovan gave the other man a long, hard stare. 'You threatening me, Jimmy?'

Knight smiled again. 'Just saying how it is, my friend. You might be fuckin holier-than-thou, but it doesnae do to be telling tales. The Job frowns upon it, if you know what I mean. And you don't want to be frowned upon, do you, Frankie? Cos you'd soon find yourself up shit creek without the proverbial. Out in the streets alone at night, with no one to back you up. Not a good place to be, son.'

Donovan fell silent. Most cops were honest – maybe the odd bottle of whisky here and a free meal there – but it was unacceptable for one of their number to stick his neck out and inform on the others. The force was a brotherhood, and brothers stood by each other. They knew who the rotten apples were, but seldom was there anything done about it. Donovan had serious doubts about Knight's honesty, illicit sex aside, but he was not about to take it any further. Nevertheless, Knight's threat brought the bile to his throat and he wanted to reach out and smash his smiling, dark good looks into the steering column.

Donovan was still silent when Knight pulled the car up outside a four storey, red sandstone tenement on London Road, near the site of the Barras street market, and turned the ignition off. Knight nodded towards a ground floor flat and said, 'This is it – Sibby Colston's place.'

Knight had told him everything he needed to know about Sibby Colston. His Christian name was Simpson, but it had been shortened for whatever reason to Sibby, rather than the usual Simmie. It didn't bother him because he didn't like the Christian name Simpson, which to him sounded a bit poofy. And the last thing Sibby Colston wanted was to sound poofy. He hated the shirtlifters, the very idea of what they did to each other horrified him. That was why, when he saw Knight and Donovan pulling up in the street, he must have decided that flight was his best option. Donovan had just stepped into the closemouth, Knight at his heels, when he saw a young man pounding towards the rear door and the back court.

'Sibby!' shouted Knight as they took after him, clattering down the three steps that led to the big door leading to the rear of the tenement. The back courts here were separated by lines of railings about three feet high and Sibby had already propelled himself over the first set when they came out and was haring off into the darkness.

'He's a nimble wee fucker, I'll give him that,' said Knight. 'Frankie boy – you're fitter than me. I'll get the car...'

Before Donovan could protest, Knight had doubled back and was through the close. Donovan sighed and began to climb the railings, seeing the young man up ahead laying his hands on the next set and springing over them in one bound.

I'll never catch him, Donovan thought, but all the same he leaped over the fence and ran on to the next one. Knight was right – he was the fitter of the two and he took the next fence with ease. But Sibby was evidently in better shape, for he was already over the third and last fence and heading towards another back door.

'Sibby!' Donovan shouted. 'We only want to talk!'

But Sibby wasn't prepared to listen, let alone talk. He pushed open the door and vanished into the back close. Donovan hauled himself over the third fence and shouldered the door open, hearing the young man's footfalls echoing round the tiled passageway as he headed for the street. Donovan came out of the closemouth and saw him sprinting across the road in the direction of Glasgow Green. If he reached the safety of the park they'd lose him, Donovan knew. There was no sign of Knight or the car, so he took off after the young thief, hoping his wind and legs could keep up. In his mind he was still cursing Knight for his threat and the anger it created helped fuel his exertions.

Further ahead he saw Sibby running alongside the park, unable to leap over the fence because it was too high. But he seemed to know where he was heading and Donovan wondered if he knew of a hole in the railings somewhere. If Sibby managed to get into the park he'd be away – no way would they catch him, not in the park. Donovan tried to find the strength to pick up the pace.

Then he was aware of Sibby slowing down and further ahead he saw why – Jimmy Knight was leaning against the fence, a section from which railings had been taken away at some time immemorial. Knight looked as if he was waiting for a bus. Christ, he was even eating a bag of crisps. Sibby slowed and stopped a few feet away, glancing back towards Donovan briefly as he pounded along behind him. Knight straightened and smiled, holding out his arms as if he was going to give him a hug.

'Sibby, Sibby… that's no way to treat guests.'

Sibby looked from him to Donovan, who had come to a halt and was panting like an old horse. *I need to take better care of myself*, Donovan thought.

'I've no done nothin,' Sibby said and Donovan noted that he didn't sound in the least out of breath.

'Never said you did,' answered Knight, his tone friendly, which made Sibby shift his feet nervously. Donovan hoped he wasn't thinking of making another break for it. He didn't think he had it in him for another sprint. Knight grinned. 'We only want a word.'

'I don't *know* nothin.'

'Ah now – we both know that's not true, don't we, son?' Knight crooked his finger at him. 'Get in the motor, Sibby.'

'What's the charge?'

'Told you, just want a word. But if you push it, I'll think of something.'

Sibby took him at his word and grudgingly climbed into the back of the car. Donovan, still breathing heavily after his run, glared at Knight as he passed by him on his way to the other rear passenger door.

'How'd you know he'd head for here?' He said in a low voice as he opened the door.

Knight smiled, crumpled the now empty crisp bag into a ball and fired it over the fence into the bushes. He walked around the front of the car, not answering until he reached the driver's door. 'Sound copper's instinct, Frankie my boy.' He opened the door. 'Something you should work on maybe…'

Donovan cursed under his breath and gave his partner a dirty look as he climbed into the back seat of the car alongside Sibby. Knight smirked. What he didn't mention was that when he had tried to lift Sibby once before, the little shit had slipped through his fingers by squeezing through that same gap in the railings. This time he was ready for it.

Knight swivelled to turn his attention to the young man in the back seat. 'Now, Sibby, what do you know about the shooting of Norrie Kennedy?'

Sibby looked surprised. 'Fuck all, I – '

Donovan snarled, 'Don't fuck us about, son. We know you know something so be smart. Tell us about your pal who "made his bones" on the killing.'

Sibby tried to bluff it out, his expression a picture of innocence. 'Honest, I only know what I've read in the papers an that. And what does "made his bones" mean?'

That was when Donovan snapped. He wasn't particularly angry at the boy, but Knight had really got his goat. He twisted round in the seat, pulled back his right arm and drove his fist into Sibby's face just below his right eye. He cried out, his hands shooting up to cover his face. Donovan felt pain jagging up his arm from his knuckles but tried not to show it.

'Just give us a rest from this shit, Sibby,' snarled Donovan. 'Who's the pal and where can we find him?'

'You hit me!' Sibby's voice was muffled behind the two hands folded across his face.

'Aye, and I'll do it again if you don't cough up sharpish.'

'He hit me!' Sibby wailed at Knight who just looked back at him with an amused expression. Sibby looked back at Donovan. 'You're no supposed to hit me!'

'We do a lot of things we're no supposed to do, old son,' said Knight. 'Now, I think you'd better start talking before my mate here really loses it...'

Knight flicked his eyes at Donovan and smiled. Donovan didn't return the smile. He hadn't meant to hit Sibby, and now he was feeling guilty.

'Sibby, son, there's a wee job on our books up at Bridgeton Cross – a grocer's got done over. We've still no got anyone for it. It wouldn't be hard for me to find some witness or other who saw you there...'

Sibby's hands came away from his face. 'But I didnae dae it!'

'I know, son, but no one said life was fair, did they? Now, who's this pal of yours and where is he now?'

Donovan knew that Knight was more than capable of fitting the boy up for the robbery. Knight was rock steady when it came to threats – he always followed through – and Sibby would know that. Now, thanks to the earlier punch, Sibby also knew that Donovan was a bit short in the fuse department. As he examined his options, Donovan sensed him reach the conclusion that he was sitting between a rock and a hard case. And because he didn't want to end up in jail sucking off some big man's dick, he told them what they wanted to know. Plooky Mary had been right – Sibby burst no problem.

12

THE GIRL MANAGED to stay in their company for just over an hour, which in Davie's book meant she deserved some sort of medal. Handsome they may have been, and they obviously held some kind of appeal for her friends, but Sinclair and Boyle were no charm school graduates. Davie pegged the other two girls as posh birds keen for a bit of East End rough. But the one in the white suit was clearly uninterested. He'd seen Sinclair put his hand on her arm a few times and each time she pulled it away and edged back, putting more space between them. Occasionally she said something and Davie could tell from her expression that it was something cutting. Sinclair, though, didn't give up. *God loves a tryer*, thought Davie.

Rab and Bobby had returned from a tour of the pub to size up the talent and it didn't take them long to follow Davie's keen gaze. Rab immediately sussed that Davie's interest lay in something other than Sinclair and Boyle. He looked at the girl in the white suit and smiled.

Leaning in to Davie's ear, he said over the blare of Queen's 'Crazy Little Thing Called Love', 'You gonnae go and talk to her or just worship her from afar?'

Davie glanced at his pal, unsurprised. He shook his head. Bobby, overhearing Rab's comment, gave the girl an appraising glance, then turned to Davie and grinned approvingly. 'How no? All she can say is fuck off.'

Davie shrugged and Bobby smiled. 'You know your problem, Davie? You're shy.'

Davie smiled slightly and shrugged again. Bobby was right, there was no way he was going over to talk to that girl. He didn't have the words.

'It'd piss Sinclair and Boyle off no end if you went over there and took her away from them,' said Bobby.

Rab nudged him. 'You want me to come with you, Davie?'

Davie thought about it, then shook his head. 'No, thanks. She's out of my league.'

'That's a load of shite, man!' Rab said. 'Faint heart never won fair fuck. Shakespeare said that.'

'Forget it, Rab...'

'Too late anyway,' said Bobby, and Davie looked back to see her standing up and looping the strap of her handbag over her shoulder. She said something to her friends and then her eyes spat fire at Sinclair. Davie presumed he had finally stepped too far out of line. She walked away from the table and Davie could sense the bastard's eyes roaming hungrily over her as she walked towards the stairs.

'You shoulda gone and spoke to her, Davie,' said Rab. 'You've been looking at her all bloody night. She even saw you...'

Davie felt worry stabbing at him. 'Is that why she left?'

'Fuck no! She clocked you ages ago. She's left because Sinclair and Boyle are fuckwits. And so are you, come to that. She was a looker, right enough, and you never even had the balls to go and ask her if she wanted a drink.' Rab shook his head. 'I don't know what I'm gonnae do with you, mate, I really don't.'

Davie couldn't help but agree. Then he saw Sinclair stand up and head for the stairs. He knew he wasn't going to the toilet and he wasn't going to the bar. He was going after the girl – and Sinclair was not renowned for his gentlemanly conduct. Davie rose, picking up an empty Coke bottle and tucking it under the sleeve of his jacket. 'Go for it, tiger,' Rab said, settling back with a grin.

Davie scanned the street downstairs for Sinclair and the girl. A few feet away stood Hillhead underground station and he checked to it see if they were at the ticket office but the entranceway, bright and shiny after its major renovation the previous year, was deserted. He looked once again down the street but saw no sign of them, so he turned and trotted up to the corner of Great George Street just in time to see Sinclair vanish to the right into Lilybank Gardens. He sprinted after him.

The soft rain had stopped and Byres Road was all hustle, even at that time of night, but the Gardens were silent. The far side was lined by sandstone buildings, by day busy university offices but quiet and empty by night. Davie spotted the girl's white suit in the gloom of the Gardens as she walked across the grass, Sinclair close behind her. Davie quickened his pace, a roar growing in his ears as he moved.

* * *

Audrey was lost in thought as she crossed the grass, slick from the earlier rain. She was pissed off with her friends for their indulgence of those two morons, playing up to their coarse remarks and simpering at their obvious jokes. She probed in her handbag for her car keys and found she was more annoyed at herself for having stayed so long. They had planned to go dancing in the city centre later, but she'd soon realised that they would insist on taking those two. It was a night lost.

She was aware of movement behind her and she turned just as Sinclair reached her.

'You never gave me a kiss goodnight, hen,' he said, lunging the final couple of feet towards her. She had no chance to make a sound before one arm was round her shoulders, the other clamped onto her mouth. He stuck his face into her hair and hissed, 'Scream or anything, darling, and it'll make things worse for you...'

His hand slowly loosened from her mouth and began to slide down her chin and her neck towards her chest. 'Let's have a wee look to see what you've got under this suit, eh, darling?'

It was then, mercifully, that the dark-haired guy she'd seen looking her way in the pub appeared...

* * *

Sinclair was evidently too intent on the girl's body to notice Davie appear behind him, the Coke bottle sliding out from under his sleeve. Davie tapped him on the shoulder, and when Sinclair looked round in surprise, swung the bottle at his forehead. He was aware of the girl's eyes widening as she saw the bottle coming her way, but Davie's aim was true and the heavy base clunked Sinclair just above the nose. He stumbled back, releasing the girl, and Davie stepped in, the bottle swinging again, this time catching Sinclair on the cheek bone with a satisfying crack. Sinclair's hands darted to his face but Davie simply moved forward, battering his head and hands, on some level noting that the solid glass had not shattered, but even if it did it wouldn't matter, because then he would use it to cut and to tear. It was something his dad had told him, a trick the old boys knew – that a good quality bottle was a double weapon.

Audrey watched as he methodically went about the business of beating the other one and, God help her, she derived some measure of satisfaction from it. She had seen him in the pub before, watching her, but curiously had not felt uncomfortable under his gaze. There was something different about him now though. His face was blank as he swung the bottle, no expression, no sign of exertion, nothing. And his blue eyes were so cold, so distant as he lashed out, forcing the creep further from her. It was as if something inhuman had taken over.

Sinclair fell back without a sound, retreating, trying to escape the rain of blows. He hadn't even registered who it was giving him such a beating, all he felt was searing agony as the guy kept battering the shite out of him. He had a carpet knife in his pocket but he couldn't reach it, not with the blows raining down. If he could get it, he'd sort this guy out, no problem, if he could just drop one hand away from his face long enough to reach down into his trouser pocket...

And then he was down on his knees, arms slumping to his side, blood streaming, pain blazing through his body. Thoughts of the blade were gone now, all he wanted was it to stop, just stop, that's all, *just stop the blows coming, please God, all he'd wanted from her was a wee kiss and a cuddle, just make it stop, he didn't deserve this...*

Suddenly it all stopped and he heard the girl give a small gasp so he opened one puffy eye to see his man Boyle standing over Davie McCall.

* * *

Davie, like Sinclair before him, had been too intent on his work to notice Boyle's approach. The roaring in his ears was too loud, his vision focussed solely on the prostrate figure in front of him as he worked, swinging the bottle back and forth. He first realised that he had made a mistake when he felt hands on his shoulders pulling him away. He spun around into a crouch, ready to ward off a new attack, but a fist connected with his nose and he staggered back. Two further rapid-fire punches followed before Boyle grabbed his lapels, stepped in closer and jutted his head sharply into his nose in a stellar example of the Glasgow Kiss. Boyle rammed his knee up into his crotch and a further wave of sharp pain filled Davie's body. He almost doubled over, but Boyle held onto him and drove his knee into his balls a second time. Davie felt the searing agony rage through him and his knees began to buckle. This time Boyle let him go, stepping back before spinning around quickly, his foot swinging up and slamming into Davie's ribs. He grunted and tumbled onto his side just as Boyle's boot connected with his ribs again. A third vicious kick slammed into to the side of his head. The sharp focus that had got him through the attack on Sinclair completely evaporated as his vision erupted with colour and the roaring in his ears was replaced by a sharp, piercing whine. His head snapped sharply to the side and he rolled onto his back. He was still conscious, which was something, he thought.

Boyle turned to his pal and said, 'You okay, mate?' Sinclair nodded, rising unsteadily to his feet, wiping blood from his eyes. 'Then hold on to her – don't want her fetching help.'

Their voices were muffled by the harpies screeching in his head, but Davie moved his eyes to see the girl. She had seemingly been paralysed by the sudden violence and had stood for the few seconds the fight had lasted as if rooted to the spot. Now, as they looked at her, that numbing shock ebbed and Davie saw her move. But Sinclair grabbed her, his bloody hands staining the pristine white of her suit. He pulled her in against him, hands moving around her waist and snaking under her jacket, his groin pressed against her buttocks. A look of utter disgust flashed across her face and her arm shot up as she tried to jab her elbow into his nose. *Good for you*, Davie thought, but Sinclair was ready for it. He blocked the attack with his free hand and twisted her arm behind her back. She struggled against him but Sinclair held her firm, one hand wedging her arm behind her, his other wrapped around her waist. Davie had hurt him, but obviously not enough, because he was still up to sliding that hand upwards to cup her breast while his head nuzzled at her hair and into her neck. 'Just hang about, hen,' Davie heard him whisper, 'My pal'll no be long, then we'll have some fun…'

Davie struggled to get up but found something was holding him down. He had felt like this once before, and matters then had not turned out well. That time he had been forced to watch as his father killed his mother. He heard the sound of glass shattering and he focussed once more on Boyle, who had found the Coke bottle and smashed it on some stone steps leading up from the gardens to the street. Boyle stood over him, looking at the jagged weapon in his right hand for a second before transferring it to his left, and smiling. Davie knew that if he did not get to his damned feet, the pain he felt now would be nothing compared to what Boyle would inflict.

'It's been a long time comin, but I'm gonnae fuck you up big time, son,' Boyle said, placing his right hand on Davie's shoulder as he continued to struggle to get up. 'Danny McCall's boy, eh? You're nothing but a piece of meat now, son, and I'm gonnae carve you...'

'Ach, Boyle, you always did talk far too much.' The quip came from behind them, and Davie saw Boyle's head jerk in its direction. Davie knew that voice well and had never been happier to hear it in his life. Rab stood a few feet away from them, Bobby and Mouthy just behind him. Rab was smiling, albeit with little humour. 'I'd put that down before you cut yourself.'

'Fucker deserves what I'm gonnae give him, Rab – look what he did to my mate...'

Rab turned his gaze on Sinclair and sneered at the boy's swollen and bleeding face. 'Bit of an improvement if you ask me. And let the lassie go, for God's sake, you've ruined her nice suit.'

Sinclair did as he was told, stepping away from her as if she had plague. Boyle rolled his eyes.

'Help Davie up, lads,' said Rab. Bobby and Mouthy stooped to haul Davie to his feet. He tried to not to wince or let the pain that sliced through him show on his face as he hung between them like a wet washing.

'You've still no dropped that, Boyle,' said Rab, nodding at the jagged bottle in his hand. 'Don't make me take it away from you.'

Boyle looked down at the broken bottle as if he had forgotten all about it and let it fall to the ground. Davie knew that Boyle had taken him down thanks to the benefit of surprise, much as he himself had done with Sinclair. Rab McClymont, on the other hand, was big, powerful and an accomplished street fighter. Boyle had lost his edge and he knew it. Davie saw the red-haired boy's eyes move from Rab to glare at him while his left hand unconsciously drifted to a silver signet ring on his right and began to twirl it round his finger.

'Wait a minute,' said the girl, and before anyone else knew it, she had hefted her foot squarely between Sinclair's legs. He squealed and his knees crooked as his hands moved to his groin.

Bobby laughed. 'She shoots, she scores!'

Audrey looked at Sinclair with contempt. 'You ever come near me again, you fucking creep, I'll kill you.'

Rab smiled in approval. 'I think she means it, lads. I'd stay well clear. Now, be good boys and fuck off.'

Boyle supported his pal as they moved across the grass. Rab turned to watch them, not moving until they had turned out of sight.

'We need to call the police,' said the girl. 'We can't just let them walk away like that.'

Rab ignored her and said to Davie, 'You okay, mate?'

Davie had regained enough of his strength to be able to stand on his own but his head throbbed, his chest ached and his balls burned. 'I never saw him coming.'

'Always watch out for the bastard at your back. Still, it's a wee lesson for you, son – you're no Superman. You can get hurt...'

'Superman can get hurt, wi kryptonite,' said Mouthy.

'Aye well, there's no a lot of that about in Glasgow, Mouthy,' said Bobby, smiling.

The girl frowned. 'Is no one listening to me? We need to get the police – and your friend here should go to the hospital.'

'Hen,' said Rab facing her, 'I think you're smart enough to understand that we're no about to involve The Law in anything. And that goes for hospitals, too.'

'But he could be badly hurt. That guy kicked him in the face...'

'Hospitals ask questions that we wouldn't want to answer. And that brings us right back to The Law again. We'll see to Davie, he'll be fine. C'mon, lads.'

Davie stopped beside her as his friends walked across the grass. Rab looked back and halted, too.

Davie asked her, 'You be okay?'

'Yes... thanks – for what you did.'

He shrugged but she reached out with one hand and gently

touched his face. He saw her eyes were green now and they were wet with tears. 'No, I mean it,' she said. 'If you hadn't come along I don't know what would've happened.' He looked down at the ground, sheepishly. The touch of her hand on his skin had felt like an electric shock. 'My name's Audrey, by the way, Audrey Burke.'

'Davie McCall.'

'Thank you, Davie McCall.'

'Okay... Audrey Burke.' He tried to smile but his face hurt.

'Here...' she opened her handbag and rifled inside, coming up with a card. 'Take this, call me. It's got my office number on it.'

Davie took the card and saw the masthead of the *Evening Times*, Glasgow's evening paper, emblazoned in red, alongside her name and the word 'Reporter'. He slipped the card in his pocket and nodded to her. She smiled and he moved off to join his friends.

'See?' said Rab as they walked away, 'How hard was that?'

13

SITTING ACROSS A DESK from Gentleman Jack Bannatyne after a nightshift could be a demoralising experience. He was iron-grey of hair but still firm of jaw. His blue suit looked as if it had been bought that morning from Slater's (the city centre tailor's that was a favourite among cops), his shirt was crisply ironed and was so white Donovan felt the need for sunglasses just to look at it, his light blue tie so neatly knotted at his throat it would win a Boy Scout merit. But both Knight and Donovan knew there was another explanation for their superior's nickname. According to the neds, he was called Gentleman Jack because he always kept his gloves on when he beat a confession out of a suspect.

It was the end of their nightshift and both Donovan and Knight looked and felt downright seedy. Unshaven, tousled, red-eyed and with breath reeking of too much coffee and tobacco, Donovan at least was desperate to get home and fall asleep. But before they could log off, they had to report to Bannatyne what Sibby had coughed up.

'Sibby told us about this guy, Andy Tracy,' Knight said. 'Pal of his, apparently. Anyway, he said that Andy'd been boasting about doing a number on Norrie Kennedy, trying to impress, you know? Build up his rep.'

Bannatyne frowned. 'Heard of this boy?'

Knight shook his head. 'He's a new one on me, boss.'

Donovan was shocked – he was beginning to think that Knight knew every scroat in the city.

'Anyway,' Knight went on, 'we went round to this place where Sibby said the boy was staying but it was empty. Looked like a giro drop to me. Spoke to an old biddy next door and she said she'd no seen him all week. That would be from just before Norrie got done.'

Bannatyne sat behind his desk, his fingers drumming a pile of files as he considered the new information. 'This boy got a record?'

'Usual stuff; gangs, thefts, breaches – nothing that big.'

'Firearms?'

'Did a hotel over once with a shotgun, but he got off with it.'

'How'd he get off with it?'

'Bloody good lawyer who spotted a flaw in the evidence record.'

'God bless Legal Aid, eh?'

'Yes, boss.'

Donovan turned away, his stomach turning at the sight and sound of Knight touching the forelock. Bannatyne was a good copper and a good boss, but Donovan wondered how he could sit behind his desk looking so comfortable with Knight's lips plastered to his arse.

Bannatyne asked, 'This scroat got any known affiliations?'

Knight shook his head. 'Nothing noteworthy, the usual roster of scumbags.'

'Any leads to where he is now?'

'Working on it, boss.'

Bannatyne thought about this for a moment, then nodded once. 'Okay, go home the pair of you, you look washed out. We'll get the dayshift onto nosing around for this boy, you can get back to it tonight.'

The two detectives got up and left. All Donovan wanted to do was get home to his Marie and Jessica, his wife and baby daughter, get as far away from Knight as possible. In the corridor outside Knight said, 'Liked the way you handled Sibby last night, Frankie boy. Never thought you had it in you...'

'Fuck off, Knight,' said Donovan and walked away. He was too tired to think of a riposte with any kind of finesse to it.

* * *

Rab was heading out to fill Joe in on the events of the previous night when Knight whistled at him from a dark blue Cortina parked at the closemouth. Rab looked around him, concerned that someone might see them talking.

'Relax,' said Knight, 'it's too early in the morning for anyone to be about.'

'How'd you know I'd be up?'

'You're an early riser, Rab – that's why you'll go far.'

'Even so, we shouldnae be seen talking to each other...'

'Ach, don't get your knickers in a twist, son. It's natural that I'm gonnae give you a pull every now and then.'

Rab had to agree with this. Being hassled by the filth was an accepted part of The Life and always had been. It was just that their new arrangement made Rab nervous.

Knight asked, 'You heard of a guy called Andrew Tracy?'

'Aye.'

'He part of Joe's mob?'

'Naw, Joe'd have nothing to do with him.'

'Why not?'

'Too unpredictable. Joe doesnae like unpredictable. I say Tracy's too fuckin crazy.'

'In what way?'

'In every way. The boy's a few raisins short of a fruit scone, you know what I mean? He'll dae anything.'

'Would he kill?'

Rab's brow puckered. 'You thinking about him for the Kennedy thing?'

'Maybe.'

'Aye, he's capable of it. Wouldn't bother him one way or the other.'

'Where can I find him?'

'You tried his gaffe?'

'Not been there all week.'

'Spoken to his burd, then?'

Knight's eyebrows raised. Sibby hadn't mentioned that Tracy had a girlfriend. 'What's her name?'

'Sylvia something or other, lives in Parkhead, near Celtic Park. McGuigan, Sylvia McGuigan. She's an old thing, maybe 35, but Tracy likes 'em older. Probably thinks he's fuckin his maw or something. I told you he was crazy.'

Knight drummed his fingers on the steering wheel. 'Right, I'll try her.'

'Am I gettin paid for this, or anything?'

'That's no how this works, Rab son. You're no just a tout. You and me, we're partners. You keep me appraised of stuff and I'll look out for you. We're in this for the long run and the rewards'll come, don't worry. This? This is money in the bank for you, Rab.'

Knight fired up the Cortina's engine and jerked it into gear. He looked out the open window again and smiled. 'Money in the bank, son.'

Rab watched the car move off down the street, which was still deserted, then walked along Sword Street, pondering how often banks got robbed.

* * *

Knight phoned from a call box to get one of the lads in Baird Street CID to have a quick look at the voter's roll for a Sylvia McGuigan in Parkhead. There was only one person with that name listed and the street was near the football ground, just as Rab had said. He next called his wife to tell her he was still working. She didn't ask any questions; seldom did. They had been married for four years and she thought he was a dedicated copper, which in a way he was. By rights he should have gone home to bed, but there was no way he was going to let one of those lads on the day shift accidentally track down Tracy. This was *his* lead and he was determined to follow it through. Sleep was over-rated anyway. He could get by with a couple of hours later that afternoon. He'd be fine.

When he clapped eyes on Sylvia McGuigan, he really couldn't see what Tracy saw in a boiler like her. But then, maybe he wasn't the answer to a young girl's dream himself. She wasn't up for telling him anything at first, apart from the fact she'd not seen Tracy for a while. Knight had a philosophy, though – they had the right to remain silent, but he really didn't advise it. After some firm reasoning, she soon managed to recall the name of one of Tracy's mates, a boy they called Tony Rome. *She couldn't remember his real name*, she told him through clenched teeth as Knight crushed the fingers of her hand in a powerful grip, *they called him that because of his dark complexion*. 'Like a Tally, 'cept he's no one,' she said. On further pressing, she told him Tony lived with his girlfriend in the Red Road flats.

Knight left her a tenner and headed for the Red Road.

* * *

Joe the Tailor lived in a detached house in Riddrie, not quite in the shadow of Barlinnie Prison, but it was perched above him like Castle Dracula in the vampire films. The Big House on the Hill, they called it, and Rab could never comprehend why Joe chose to live so close the place. To Rab it would be a constant reminder of where someone like him was destined to end up. He had never done time in the Big House and he never wanted to either. Borstal had been bad enough.

Rab was never comfortable in Joe's home and it wasn't just because he could sense the high walls of the Bar-L leering down at him. The room in which they sat was like a study, its walls lined by book-filled shelves. He wondered if Joe had read them or if they were just there for show. These books were all hardback, many bound in leather, and they looked old – Charles Dickens and stuff like that. Rab let his gaze roam over the rest of the room. A glass cabinet in one corner housed delicate-looking Chinese figurines and the hardwood floor was covered with three Chinese rugs. A dark wooden desk sat beside a long window which ran from floor to ceiling, looking out onto Joe's back garden, which was green with early summer's bloom. There was music playing on Joe's fancy stereo. Rab didn't recognise the singer but he knew it was one of those old guys that Joe liked so much – Sinatra or Dean Martin. Rab couldn't say which because he had a hard time telling them apart. To his ear they all sounded the same. One wall opposite the desk had a few framed photographs, mostly of people Rab didn't know, people from Joe's past, he assumed. Another showed Joe with Frank Sinatra, both smiling at the camera, both with drinks in their hand and Sinatra's arm around Joe like they were bosom buddies. Rab might not be able to pick out his voice, but he at least knew what Sinatra looked like, having seen his films.

The Tailor had told all his boys that if they heard anything about the murder of Norrie Kennedy they were to let him know immediately. So even if he hadn't been intending to come over that Sunday anyway, Rab would have made his way out to Riddrie to tell him that Knight had quizzed him on Andy Tracy – and that Tracy might somehow be connected to the McKay killing. Of course, he didn't mention his new arrangement with the cop.

When Rab finished telling his story, Joe sat quietly for a few moments. When he finally spoke, it was of Davie's brush with Boyle and Sinclair, rather than Rab's conversation with Knight . Rab was neither surprised nor hurt. Davie was Joe's favourite, he knew that.

'And how is David now?'

'He's alright, Joe. Ribs hurt a wee bit, and his face isn't as pretty, but he's walking. I think he's learned a wee lesson from all this.'

Joe nodded. Rab was under no illusions. He knew the old man was fond of him, but he loved Davie like a son. As he had listened to the description of the beating Davie had taken, Rab had seen Joe's face tighten and he sensed a cold rage building. Someone would pay for what had happened the night before. But not yet, for Rab's other information had to be digested and dealt with first.

'So – this police officer… what was his name again?'

'Knight.'

Joe nodded, filing it away. 'Yes, Knight. A detective?'

'Aye, he was one of the bastards that interviewed us after Kennedy got done.'

'Yes. And this Knight, did he intimate that he had any firm intelligence as to young Mister Tracy's whereabouts?'

'He hasnae a clue, Joe. I sent him over to see Tracy's old burd, that Sylvia one. She'll no know where is he is neither. Tracy's a funny sort, you remember him? Bananas, he is.'

Joe nodded, for he did indeed remember Andy Tracy. He remembered him very well.

14

Despite his looks, the closest Tony Rome came to being Italian was eating tinned spaghetti. A couple of calls from another public phone box told Knight that his real name was Anthony O'Brian, a former choirboy from Possil. Like Tracy, he was strictly small time. Unlike Tracy, he had his head screwed on the right way. Old Sylvia had been right – he moved around a lot but not, as Knight had at first suspected, for nefarious reasons but because he worked with a travelling fairground. Tony Rome was the guy who kept the waltzers waltzing and the dodgems dodging. Knight had to concede he was a good-looking bugger and would lay money on the luck he had with the ladies. His dark complexion was complemented by thick, dark hair while his brown eyes shone with good humour. Knight, no ugly bastard himself, quite fancied kicking him in the face.

He was certainly a lying wee toe-rag, and Knight had a sixth sense when it came to lying wee toe-rags. The lie came off them like a smell. So when Tony told him he'd not seen Tracy for ages, Knight's copper's nose detected the unmistakeable whiff of porkies. Still, the bright flat on the 23rd floor was not the place to stage some unpleasantness, not with the boy's girlfriend sitting in the same room and a baby asleep in a cot.

So Knight thanked him for his time and left but he hung around at the entrance to the flats. It was a pleasant afternoon, so he waited patiently, puffing on a cigar.

After half an hour, just as he was beginning to think either he had been wrong or Tony had moved faster than he had expected, the young man pushed through the glass doors. Knight smiled to himself, thinking *maybe I should take up reading tea leaves*. Tony didn't see Knight standing to his right as he came out, but he did hear him say, 'Going somewhere, son?'

The young man turned around, his handsome features a moving picture first of surprise, followed by shock, followed by a decent attempt at casual. 'Going out for a wee walk, Mister Knight. You waiting for somebody?'

'Waiting for you, Tony, old son.'

'How? I've already told you – '

'A pack of lies, and we both know it.'

Tony backed away a couple of steps but Knight didn't move. He simply stood there, one shoulder leaning against the wall, both hands in his coat pockets. Tony stammered a bit as he said, 'Honest, Mister Knight, I don't know where Andy is.'

'Now, that's just not true, is it?'

Tony took another couple of steps. 'It is so true.'

'Tony, son, if you're thinking of making a run for it, go ahead. I'm too tired to chase you and anyway, you look as if you're a fit wee fucker. So you go ahead. I'll just take a trip back up in the lift and pay Mandy upstairs a wee visit. Have a chat, know what I'm saying?'

Tony's expression darkened. 'She doesnae know where Andy is either.'

'You know? I believe you there.' Knight gave Tony a small smile. It was not a pleasant smile.

Tony's eyes narrowed and his voice hardened. 'You leave her out of this.'

Knight was impressed with the boy's show of balls. 'Well, that's up to you, isn't it? Where's Andy, Tony?'

Tony looked around him, as if searching for allies, but both the main entrance and the space around the flats were empty. Knight could almost hear the thought processes clicking in the boy's head as he calculated the odds. Tony was trying to decide whether this big bastard cop would really do something to Mandy. Finally,

Knight saw the boy's face fall as he came to the unhappy conclusion that he would.

When he spoke, Tony's hard edge was considerably blunted. 'What do you want him for?'

'That's between him and me.'

'You gonnae hurt him?'

'Not if I can help it. But I'll hurt you in a minute if you don't start playing the fuckin white man.'

Tony considered his options and came up with only one solution. 'I cannae tell you where he is, cannae describe it to you, you know? It's away up out of the city. I'd need to show you.'

Knight stepped away from the wall. 'Then lead on, MacDuff…'

* * *

The white van steamed up behind Barney Cable before he and his driver, Peter Morton, knew it. They were on a narrow country road north of the city, heading for Summerston. It took them miles out of their way but Barney liked to get away from the world of grey concrete that seemed to be his life. It was a lovely morning, and though they glimpsed the city through occasional gaps in the hedges, it still felt like a day trip.

Peter was driving, and he swore as the van barrelled up close behind them then veered out to overtake, almost clipping their wing mirror. Barney shook his head as it sped ahead, scraping against the hedges on the driver's side.

'What a dick,' said Peter as he steered the car as far away from the van as he could.

'Did you see him coming?'

'No, bastard steamed up right behind me there.'

'Some folk shouldnae be behind a wheel…'

'White Van driver, what can I say?'

'Is it one of they Pratna vans? Wherever you go, there's a Pratna van.'

The two men smiled together as they watched the van speed ahead before vanishing around a bend. They were comfortable with each other, their friendship based on mutual trust, which was something rare in The Life, where loyalty was on the World Wildlife Fund's endangered species list.

Peter's smile faded and a frown took its place as he edged round a bend and saw the white van sitting in the middle of the road, blocking their way. Peter slowed the car down and said, 'What the fuck are they doing now?'

Barney felt something cold rifling the hairs on his back. He knew this was not right. He sat upright and said, 'Back up, Pete.'

The doors of the van flew open and two figures jumped out. They both had balaclavas over their heads and one waved a sawn-off shotgun while the other aimed a pistol.

Barney yelled, 'Back up!' Peter did as he was told, throwing the gear stick into reverse and jamming his foot on the accelerator. The engine screamed as the car backed away, tyres churning dust from the road. Barney punched the glove compartment open just as he heard both barrels of the shotgun blasting at the car. He heard rather than saw the windscreen crack and shatter, showering them both in tiny fragments of glass as Peter tried to keep the car steady on its backward trajectory. Barney's hand scrabbled inside the glove compartment until his fingers found the pistol under the various documents.

'Fuck!' spat Peter and came to a screeching halt. Barney twisted round in the passenger seat to find a Vauxhall Chevette blocking their way and a third shooter standing in the road, waiting for them. Barney's heart sank. He knew they were sitting ducks inside the car. Their only chance was to get into the open.

'Make a run for it, Pete,' he said, throwing his own door open and tumbling out. The sky was dotted with screeching black crows, startled from a stand of trees by the shotgun blast. Barney straightened with the gun in his fist and loosed off a shot but it went wide.

The shooters threw themselves to the ground anyway and the one with the shotgun dropped his weapon. He heard Peter getting out and trying to run across the road, but the guy behind them fired three rounds. Barney swore he heard the bullets hitting Peter's flesh, a kind of soft splashing sound, and his mate's body jerked a couple of times before pitching forward like a puppet with the strings cut. Barney didn't need to get any closer to know Peter was dead.

Barney yelled, 'Bastards!' The two in front were still kissing the tarmac, so he whirled to fire at the third, who had ducked down behind the rear of Barney's car. 'Bastards!' He screamed again, and fired another two rounds in the direction of the van. Neither shot connected but careened off the road, spraying them both with dust and making them flinch. He spun again and loosed off another round as the bloke behind the car poked his head up. The bullet thudded into the boot and he dropped out of sight again. Barney took the chance to dart across the verge towards a gate to his left. If he could get over that and into those trees just a few feet beyond, he had a chance. That's all he had to do, just get over that fence, and in another five or six feet he'd have some cover. That's all, another few feet and he was in the clear...

The first bullet caught him between the shoulder blades as he put his foot on the bottom bar of the fence. The second bullet bit into his arm and the gun slid from his fingers.

'Sheila,' Barney said, before a third bullet took off the back of his head.

Barney Cable was dead before he hit the grass.

* * *

Tucked away at the edge of a pine forest near Lennoxtown, between the city and the Campsie Hills, the caravan was owned by a local farmer who rented it out with no questions asked. All he knew was that three young lads had been staying there for over a week and that they had been no trouble. He'd been well paid for the rental – cash, which had arrived in the post soon after the booking had been made by phone. He didn't ask any questions because he really didn't care. As long as they didn't shag his sheep, they could do what they liked for that kind of money.

A small track led from the road through the forest to where the caravan nestled, a stile climbed the barbed wire fence to allow access. It was a pleasant enough situation, isolated enough for privacy, close enough to civilisation for supplies, but the three men had been going quietly crazy here. Two of them were brothers from Manchester by the name of McGuinness and were comfortable in each other's company, but they didn't know the other guy very well. They only knew him as Andy, and even in their brief acquaintance, they recognised him as bad news. They had been hired through intermediaries so had no idea who their paymaster was. Andy, though, was a local lad who seemed to know very well who had hired them to make the hit on Cable. They also suspected he was unstable.

The McGuiness brothers were no strangers to violence, but Andy seemed to enjoy gunning that fellow down the other night. To the Mancunians it was just a job, to him it seemed a distinct pleasure. They didn't much like being penned up with him in this caravan and longed for someone to tell them it was all clear to go home. They still weren't clear on why they had to hide out here in what they considered the arsehole of Scotland, but their mysterious employer had insisted on it. So stay they did, listening to Andy telling them stories of jobs he had pulled and men he had killed. They didn't believe a word of what he said but they let him talk, focussing their attention on the small black and white telly. Soon, Andy just became so much background noise, so much static, and they could filter him out easily. They had obeyed instructions and stayed put, apart from trips into Lennoxtown for groceries. Andy had left them briefly a couple of nights before to make his way back into Glasgow. He missed his pals, he'd told them, and he'd only be gone one night. To be truthful, they had been glad to be rid of him, even if only for a few hours.

Andy Tracy was proud of himself. He'd always wanted to kill a man and now he had – and to cap it all he had some money coming. Okay, he had to spend a few days in the back of beyond with these two English wankers but that was a small price to pay. Soon he'd be back in the big city, spending his cash on burds and booze. And when he ran out of the readies, he'd just take another job. He'd been promised there'd be more work to come. Sibby hadn't believed him when he'd told him he'd made his bones but Andy, steeped in Mafia lore, knew he'd become a *Made Man* by pulling the trigger on Norrie Kennedy.

He heard the car on the track through the wood and went to the window. A black Metro City bounced along the bumpy trail, but he didn't recognise it. However, when it came to a stop near the style he did recognise the man who climbed out. *Maybe this was it,* Andy thought, *maybe he was going back home, back to Glasgow. Maybe he's got another job for me.*

The McGuiness brothers were sprawled on the long seats that converted into beds, but they tensed when the newcomer climbed the stile. They looked at Andy, who smiled in reassurance. 'It's okay, lads,' he said, opening the door. 'It's the boss.'

The boss was over the stile and walking towards them. He ignored the brothers and stared straight at Andy.

'You disobeyed me, Andrew,' he said as he moved closer.

Andy's smile froze and then melted from his face. 'How?'

'You went into Glasgow, didn't you? You talked.'

As usual, Andy's first impulse was to lie. 'Naw, no me.'

'Do not lie, boy. The police have your name. They are looking for you. They are on their way now.'

Fear began to gnaw at Andy's stomach. 'Naw, I never…'

The man ignored his protestation of innocence. 'Did you dispose of the car properly?'

'I never said nothin.'

The man sighed and looked instead at the McGuinness brothers. 'Was the car disposed of?'

'Yes,' said one. 'You've got our word on that. Burned out, tossed down an old quarry. It's under water now. They'd find it, right enough, if they knew where to look for it.'

'Good.' Satisfied, he turned his gaze back to Andy. 'And the gun? Did you get rid of it like I told you?'

Andy nodded eagerly. 'In the Clyde, just like you said.' That was another lie, for the gun was hidden away under his small bed in the caravan.

The man nodded again. 'Very well. We have to move you. Pack your things, we leave at once.'

The brothers nodded and moved back into the caravan. Andy tried smiling but received a glare in return. He moved back into the caravan and the boss followed.

As he climbed the small steps to the door, the boss looked behind him, his eyes scanning the field around them for signs of life. He listened for an engine or voices, but all he heard were crows calling and the soft wind sighing through the conifers. He closed the door behind him and turned first to the McGuinness brothers, who had already begun gathering their belongings and had their backs to him. He took his hand out of his coat pocket and aimed the silenced automatic at their backs, pulling the trigger four times. They pitched forward without a sound, the bullets punching through their bodies and drenching the side of the caravan with blood.

Andy had been wondering how he was going to sneak the gun out from under his bed without being seen when he heard the faint pops behind him and he whirled round, but the gun was already trained on him.

'Don't…' said Andy, but the boss merely shrugged, his face impassive behind the pistol.

'I'm very sorry, Andrew,' said Joe the Tailor. 'But you just cannot be trusted, I'm afraid.'

And then he squeezed the trigger for a fifth time. Andy's head snapped back, a red hole appearing at his forehead. He seemed to hang there for a moment, his face bearing a quizzical expression, as if trying to understand what had happened, before he slumped to the floor.

With a final, sorrowful, look at the bodies, Joe turned and left. He drove away from the scene quickly, but not fast enough to raise any suspicions if seen, leaving the caravan to the gentle breeze and the mournful cry of the crows.

15

IT TOOK AUDREY half the morning to pluck up the courage to speak to Barclay Forbes. She was the newest member of the news team, just a few months out of the journalism course at Napier College in Edinburgh. He, on the other hand, was a near legend, an experienced reporter who had covered Glasgow crime for 30 years. He'd been with the *Daily Record* for a time and from there he'd done a stint with the *Glasgow Herald*, but broadsheet ideology hadn't sat well with him and he made the move to the *Evening Times*. He was a tabloid hack through and through, a clear and concise writer with a sense of drama and a clever turn of phrase. His contact book was the stuff of legend, reputed to contain an array of lawyers and cops for whom Forbes 'bought a drink' now and again.

He was a small man, as thin as a posh soup but without the breeding, with a thick head of black hair which had kept its colour for the past 20 years only with the aid of the hair care counter at

Boots the Chemist. Audrey watched the veteran reporter from across the news room that Monday morning, wondering if she should approach him. He sat with his foot propped up on an open bottom drawer, a phone hooked between his ear and his shoulder as he scribbled on a pad in front of him. Occasionally, he smiled as he talked, causing his heavily-lined features to crease into a facsimile of tight isobars on a weather map. A cigarette dangled between his lips and jiggled up and down as he spoke.

Barc hung up and stubbed what was left of the cigarette out in an already overflowing ashtray before lighting a fresh one. Without lifting his foot from its makeshift rest, Barc swung round and faced his typewriter then began stabbing at the keyboard with stilletto-like digits. Occasionally he glanced at the notes on his pad, but mostly he worked from memory and his eyes clicked from keyboard to paper frequently.

Audrey took a deep breath and stood up from her desk. The big room around her was remarkably quiet. Telephones rang, typewriters clattered and people spoke, but there was no frenzied racket, no hardened hacks rushing in with scoops demanding that the front page be held. Of course, it would heat up towards the next deadline later that morning, but it was nothing like the movies. She slowly picked her way towards Barc's desk sitting out on its own away from the others, which was the way he liked it. There was one thing you could never accuse Barc Forbes of, and it was being a team player. She lingered close to his desk, hoping to catch his eye, but he didn't seem to notice as his attention remained squarely on his words. Just as her nerve was about to desert her, she heard his familiar voice rasp at her, 'You're hovering, hen. I can't abide a hoverer.'

He spoke without lifting his head from his typewriter, but when she still hesitated to speak, he looked up at her, sat back in his chair and plucked the cigarette from his mouth. 'Spit it out, hen – what's on your mind?'

'Sorry to disturb you, Mister Forbes.'

'Don't be sorry, as long as it's important.'

'Well, I don't know...'

He took a long draw on the cigarette, blew the smoke out of his nose and squinted at her through the fog. 'Audrey, isn't it?'

She was surprised he knew her name. 'Yes.'

'Hen, you've been itching to come over and speak to me all morning. Now, handsome devil that I undoubtedly am, I don't think you've come to ask me on a date. So that means it's something to do with a story, am I right?'

'Yes... well, no... I mean... I don't know.'

'That's what I like, a girl who knows her own mind. Let's have it then.'

She took a deep breath. 'Do you know of a guy called David McCall?'

His brow furrowed. 'I know of a Danny McCall. Hard bastard. He had a boy, might've been called David. Why?'

Audrey recounted the rape attempt and how Davie had come to her aid. She didn't tell him about the grilling she'd received from her dad when she got back home with her good white suit covered in blood. She had spun him a yarn about a friend's nosebleed and their attempts to stem the flow in the toilet, during which she'd got blood on her hands and on her suit. Her father wasn't a stupid man and he clearly didn't believe a word. But, in the end, he trusted his daughter and knew that she would not get into anything that would worry him. Audrey felt badly for that because she was fairly certain she was about to get into something that would worry him.

The fact was, she hadn't stopped thinking about Davie McCall. It was his eyes that held her, so blue, so clear, and when she closed her own eyes she still saw them. She had hoped he would come over and talk to her in the pub, but he hadn't made a move. On the few occasions she looked back, his gaze shifted and he looked ashamed, which told her he wasn't a creep, just shy.

Barc asked, 'So has this McCall phoned you?'

She shook her head.

'But you want him to?'

She looked away and shrugged. 'Well...'

He smiled slightly. 'Aye. What do you want from me, hen?'

'I just wanted to know if you'd heard of him. You think he might be McCall's son?'

'It's possible. I'm sure his name was Davie. His dad used to work for Joe the Tailor. You heard of him?'

'Gangster, isn't he?'

'Aye, he's about as big as they come around here. He likes to cultivate new talent, if you know what I mean. He's like Fagin; finds young lads with promise and teaches them the ropes. There's been talk that old Joe likes to teach them some other things, too, unsavoury things that would frighten the horses if you did it in the street, but that's a load of bollocks. Boyle and Sinclair I definitely have heard of. Boyle's a bad wee bastard, Sinclair's a follower. They run around with a bloke called Johnny Jones. They're as nasty a pair of neds as this city can churn out. You want me to ask around for you, see what I can find out?'

'Would you mind?'

'Mind? You heard what happened yesterday?' She nodded. 'We've got five dead bodies and the word is they could all lead in some way to Joe the Tailor, and now you come to me with another name linked to the old bastard. Hen, this is serendipity if ever I saw it.'

* * *

Jack Bannatyne was angry and when Jack Bannatyne was angry, he didn't believe in bottling it up. He stood behind his desk and leaned towards Jimmy Knight, who sat in the chair opposite looking even more tired and bedraggled than he had the previous morning.

'I don't need maverick cops on my team,' said Bannatyne. 'Leave that shit to Hollywood, understand?'

Knight nodded, all he had the energy to do. He hadn't had a shave or a shower since Saturday, and here it was Monday. He had spent Sunday chasing around Glasgow, trying to track down Andy Tracy, but in the end all he found was his dead body – and two others. Tony Rome had taken him to the caravan outside Lennoxtown and together they'd discovered the bloodbath inside. When Knight had pulled open the caravan door, he found Andy on his back, eyes staring sightlessly at the ceiling, and the other two sprawled over the caravan's seats. Knight had snapped at Tony not to touch anything, but the sight of the blood congealing on the caravan walls had the idiot throwing up all over the crime scene. Knight didn't know who the other two corpses were, nor did he care at this moment. All he wanted was this arse chewing to be over with so he could go home and get some sleep.

'You want to stay on my team, you learn to be a team player, Knight, okay?'

'Yes, boss.'

'Don't fuckin "yes, boss" me. You gad about like Dirty Harry again and I'll have you bounced back into uniform so fast the blue serge'll chafe your balls.'

'Yes, boss... I mean, sorry, boss. I just didn't want to waste any of the lads' time on what might've been a wild goose chase. I thought I'd chase it down on my own time.'

'Aye, and if you'd told us we could've covered more ground a hell of a lot faster. A phone call to Lennoxtown could've had uniforms up there in minutes and right now Tracy could've been bursting like a wet paper bag in the interview room! But no – you had to be Clint fuckin Eastwood and go it alone, and in doing so you've lost us the one lead we could've had. You should've been at home getting some sleep yesterday! Look at you! Look at the state of you, ready to drop off that chair.'

Knight couldn't argue because he actually was ready to drop off the chair. He'd sent Tony back to Lennoxtown to call the killings in while he waited at the caravan. Tony made the 999 call then legged it back to Glasgow, but Knight didn't much care. He'd find him again if he needed. When the cavalcade arrived from the local station, naturally there were questions to be asked, which Knight elected to answer truthfully. When he was finally allowed back to Baird Street late on Sunday, Bannatyne was getting ready to visit the scene himself. He'd told Knight to wait in the station until he came back. He'd been gone all night and Knight had tried to catch some sleep in an empty cell but the bed there was like a lump of stone. Now here he was in Bannatyne's office getting a verbal kicking.

Bannatyne sighed and sat down, his anger abating. 'Okay, get yourself home, get some kip. We'll take it from here.'

Knight stood up and walked from the room. Bannatyne shook his head and reached for the phone. There was a slip of paper on his desk with a number on it, and he squinted at it as he dialled. He waited until he heard the voice on the other end of the line and said without introducing himself, 'Things are getting out of hand.'

'I know,' said Joe on the other end.

'We need to talk...'

16

If the weather was fine, Audrey often walked from the paper's Mitchell Street offices to the Ramshorn Kirkyard where she could enjoy her packed lunch in peace and quiet. It was one of the city's oldest churches and graveyards, a compact square of graves and slabs surrounded by taller buildings. There was a bench where she could catch some sun as it slipped past the tall Kirk, letting her mind clear. It was warm, even for May, and she had read a report that morning predicting rising temperatures in the days to come. Soon she'd be able to sit here every day if she wanted – later that summer the paper was moving to the old Express building, which sat on the eastern edge of the graveyard.

'They said you'd be up here,' a rasping voice said, and she opened her eyes to see Barc Forbes looking down at her. As usual he had a cigarette in the corner of his mouth, and he was wearing a fawn coloured trenchcoat. All he needed was a trilby with a Press sticker in the band and he'd look like a Hollywood reporter. He held a pack of Embassy tipped cigarettes in his hand and Audrey could see the white spaces on the cardboard were covered in scribbles.

'Your boy Davie's the goods, right enough,' he said. 'Dad was Danny McCall, a hardman for Joe the Tailor, like I said. By all accounts he was also a bit of a drunk and liked to smack his wife and wean around when he'd had a few too many. Drink apparently brought the nasty out in him, and he was a vicious enough bastard when he was sober. You heard the stories about a bloke getting crucified back in the late '60s? Hands nailed to a wooden floor?'

Audrey nodded. The crucified man was a bloody slice of Glasgow folklore.

'Well, Danny McCall's the boy that supposedly did it. Joe the Tailor likes to see himself as some kind of Knight Errant, protecting fair virgins and shit like that. This boy raped the daughter of a guy who paid Joe protection money and Joe sent Danny out to deliver a message. No one knows if Joe told him to do the hammer and nails act or if Danny took it upon himself. Anyway, the boy ended up spread-eagled on the floor of some new-build houses in the Gorbals, nailed to the wooden floor. Workies found him next day. They say his blood had soaked the wood so bad they had to replace the planks.'

Barc paused to take a deep drag from his cigarette and turned the pack to find a new note on the side. 'So, Danny's a bad bastard and he works for Joe the Tailor, who's a nice enough bloke unless you piss him off. But the drink's got a real hold of Danny and one night he rolls home and he starts knocking seven kinds of shite out of his wife, a nice woman, they say, who really didn't deserve what she got. How she ever got mixed up with Danny McCall in the first place beats me, but there's all kinds of stories like that.'

'Maybe he wasn't like that when they met.'

'Aye, maybe. Anyway, the boy – Davie, your Davie – was there. He must be 14, 15, and he tries to stop his dad. But the old man picks up a poker and he lays the boy out, snapping his arm in the process. The boy couldn't do anything but lie there and watch as his mother was beaten to death.'

'Jesus!'

Barc nodded. 'Danny must've realised what he'd done, so he goes round to his boss Joe for help. But Joe won't have anything to do with this. He phones the cops himself and Danny legs it, disappears. There's some that say Joe had him topped and his body's in the foundations of some new office block. Maybe it's true. All I know is Danny McCall hasn't been seen since.'

'And what about Davie?'

'Joe took him under his wing, like I said. He pals around with big Rab McClymont.'

'Rab? I met a Rab on Saturday. He saved Davie.'

'Aye, thick as thieves they are, literally. He's as close to your boy as anyone can get.'

'What do you mean?'

'Your boy's a bit of a loner, hen. He doesn't say much, prefers to let his fists and his feet do the talking. He's like his dad in that way. He's only 18, but he's already one of the scariest guys on the streets. There's more of his dad in him than I think even he'd like to admit.'

Audrey thought about Davie's blank expression as he swung the Coke bottle against Sinclair, how the blue eyes were totally devoid of any kind of heat, as if the mind inside had died and he was a machine just doing its job. And yet, he had waded in to defend her. He had followed them to defend her. Everything he'd done was to defend her.

'You're wondering why he protected you, aren't you?'

She looked back at Barc's lined face and nodded. 'That's Joe's influence,' he said. 'Joe's the father Davie never had. He's intensely loyal to the old man. Well, all his boys are. He also inspires great hatred. Norrie Kennedy and him had been feuding for years, and there's others who would happily see him dead and buried.'

'Do you think Davie had anything to do with the murders?'

Barc sighed and looked down at his fag packet as if the answer was there. 'No, hen – your boy's no the type to use a gun. He's strictly a hand-to-hand guy – maybe a chib, a blade, anything that comes to hand but no a gun.'

She exhaled in relief. She was uncomfortable enough with the violence she saw in Davie, but the idea of him gunning anyone down, even another crook, was unacceptable.

'He phoned you yet?'

She shook her head.

Barc nodded and pushed his Embassy Tipped packet into his coat pocket. 'He will. What you gonnae do when he does?'

'I don't know.'

'He's a good looking bugger from what I'm told.'

She nodded and the older reporter sighed. 'Look, I'm no yer da, so you can tell me to mind my own business, but you want my advice?'

She looked at him and nodded again.

'Keep away from him. I know, he came in like Sir Galahad and, I know, he's no repulsive. But he's a dangerous boy. You're a nice lassie, you've got a life ahead of you, a career, husband, weans, whatever. Davie's got the jail or a grave. He's no for you, hen. He'll bring you down. He won't want to, he won't mean it, but he'll bring you down. Jail or the grave, hen. That's the way it is with these guys.'

She knew he was right. She knew that Davie McCall was not

someone she should allow into her life. But when he phoned later that afternoon, she arranged to see him.

* * *

Street lights rippled and swam on the surface of the river like iridescent fish while, above Joe the Tailor's head, cars thundered over the huge concrete canopy that was the Kingston Bridge. He stood alone, leaning against the railings on the walkway, watching the dark waters slap against the wooden beams below. Daylight was fading, the sky above the city reddening as the sun sank inexorably into the west. He looked across the Clyde at the warehouses and derelict buildings on the opposite bank, crumbling reminders of the city's past prosperity. Glasgow was changing. Its reliance on the river for its fortunes had long since passed. The bridge above him and the traffic which rumbled over it were symbols of the new Glasgow, going somewhere fast. Joe was not certain he wished to go with it. He did not think that the new city was necessarily a good thing. The building of the bridge and its motorway had destroyed communities on both sides of the river. On the north bank, where he was looking, he could see where Anderston once was. It was gone now, just a memory, as were other streets, other homes where people had lived and loved and died. The great industries were dying, too. The shipyards were shadows of their former glory. The ironworks which had glowed with hellish intensity into the night had been extinguished – Dixon's Blazes in the south was now a vast empty gap site, the Parkhead Forge was gone. The old style economy of building and manufacturing was being replaced by financial and service industries. The drug trade that Johnny Jones was selling was another, if illicit, example of this new economy.

Joe longed for the days when the city was bustling, when tramcars ruled the streets and the old neighbourhoods were in one piece. He even missed the thick grey fog that could blot out the sun and banish all but the hardiest behind closed doors. But it was gone forever, he knew, for it had been created by the marriage of the mist that rolled from the water with the thick smoke belching from the myriad of factory chimneys and household fires. Glasgow gave the world a word for this noxious substance; smog. The air was cleaner now, but as far as Joe was concerned, not necessarily sweeter.

There wasn't another soul to be seen on the walkway and he knew he shouldn't be in this lonely place without back-up, but he had agreed that this meeting would take place without the scrutiny of others. Norrie Kennedy was no longer a threat, but Barney Cable's murder proved someone else most certainly was. Joe knew in his heart that Johnny Jones was behind it. He also knew that if there was a hit list, he was on it, and he had an automatic in his coat pocket just in case. It wasn't the weapon with which he removed Tracy and the McGuiness brothers from this veil of tears. That particular firearm had been broken up and the pieces dropped from different bridges crossing the Clyde before he made his way to this rendezvous.

He felt a tinge of sadness as he thought of the young lives he had snuffed out. It had been necessary, however. It was also always the way it would end. The McGuinness brothers had been slated for death in Manchester – something to do with missing money – and Joe had agreed to carry out the contract in return for using them first. Tracy was trouble, always had been, but useful for this one job. All three would have died eventually, but Knight had got just a little too close, so Joe's timetable had to be moved up. Even so, he never took murder lightly.

The walkway was dotted with old capstans, relics of when boats of all shapes and sizes used to tie themselves to the quay, and was long and straight, which was why he knew Bannatyne was approaching before the detective said anything.

'Wasn't sure you'd come, Joe.'

Joe turned to face Bannatyne and smiled, holding his hands out as if to show they were empty. 'Why would I not? I am as concerned about these events as you.'

Bannatyne nodded and moved up beside Joe, inspecting the railing to ensure that it was free of bird shit before he rested the arms of his coat on it. He said nothing for a moment as he gazed at the darkening river. 'I like this time of day, don't know why.'

'It is the light. On a day such as this, the light is...' Joe searched for the right word, '... spectacular.'

'Aye,' said Bannatyne, looking at the buildings on the opposite bank, their walls stained red by the dying of the sun, their windows reflecting the lingering rays like neon. 'What's going on, Joe?'

'I wish I knew,' said the Tailor with a sigh.

Bannatyne turned to face the older man. 'Who's doing it? Who's turning my town into the wild bloody west?'

Joe gave him a slight smile. 'You wish me to turn grass, Jack?'

'Do you know something?'

'I have... suspicions.'

'Then tell me.'

'Why should I? We do not have a relationship, you and I.'

'No, I'm not one of your tame coppers, that's true. Never will be.'

Joe's smile broadened. 'Never is a long time, my friend. Who knows what tomorrow will bring?'

Bannatyne shook his head. 'Joe, I like you. For a crook, you're okay. But you're still a crook...'

'Ach,' said Joe dismissively, 'labels, labels. I am a businessman, that is all.'

'Aye, but your business can hurt people.'

'And what of the tobacco manufacturers and the arms dealers? Do they not hurt people? Yet they are 'respectable.' I provide some innocent fun – gambling, pleasures of the flesh.'

'You exploit people's weaknesses. And let's not forget armed robbery and extortion. You've hurt a lot of people, Joe, or had them hurt. You're an affable sort and you're honourable in your way but you're still a crook.'

'Do you believe I have nothing to do with this?'

Bannatyne paused, and nodded. 'Norrie Kennedy's murder did make me think you had a hand in it, but Barney Cable was your pal. As I said, you're an honourable sort in your way. You'd never hurt a pal.'

'Barney was a good man.'

'Good's maybe stretching it a bit. I'd've put him away in a heartbeat, but he was a dying breed, I'll grant you that.'

'I am afraid you are right there. There is a new wind blowing in the city, Jack. I do not like what I smell on it.'

'Then tell me what's going on. Let me put a stop to it.'

'Do you think you can?'

'I can try.'

'With arrests and the courts, with lawyers and evidence?'

'With the law, yes.'

Joe shook his head. 'Perhaps my way would be better.'

'More guns, more killing? That's never better, Joe.'

'Ha! Without guns and killing where would we be, my friend? Remember, I am Polish. I saw what Hitler did, and without those guns and a lot of killing, he and his kind might yet be here today.'

'That was war, Joe.'

'And so is this.'

'Innocent people...'

'Innocent people die in war, you know that! Every day, somewhere in this world, innocent people are dying, backed by Governments and religion and commercial interests. The difference between those wars and mine is that we ensure that civilians do *not* get hurt. Unlike your "legal" wars.'

Bannatyne sighed. 'I can't let it happen, Joe. Just tell me what you know and let me try to end this carnage.'

'And if you cannot?'

Bannatyne fell silent. He knew a bargain was being offered here. Joe would tell him what he knew and let the law take its course if Bannatyne could make a case stick. But if Bannatyne failed to gather the evidence to send the killers to jail, then Joe's form of justice would take over. Joe wouldn't trouble himself with legal niceties like evidence, corroboration or a jury of peers. Joe would be the judge and Joe would be the jury. The executioner would be some faceless, nameless gunman brought in from outside the city.

'If I can't follow this through, then let the good times roll,' said Jack. Joe stared into his eyes and saw that the police officer meant what hc said. He nodded.

'Johnny Jones.' he said. 'He is putting together some deal for which he needs considerable investment.'

'What kind of deal?'

'That need not concern you.'

'Joe...'

'Do you want this information or not?'

Bannatyne nodded. He desperately wanted to know what Jones was cooking up, but he knew he could bide his time.

'Anyway,' Joe continued, 'Norrie Kennedy did not wish to join and Barney was also hesitant. Neither of them had any love for Mister Jones. I believe that put them in the firing line.'

'What about you? Are you involved in this deal? That why you won't tell me about it?'

'No, I have already declined. I will not tell you because that much of a grass I am not. I am only giving you Jones because I dislike this killing as much as you.'

'Yet you'd happily continue it.'

'Only one more – Johnny Jones. But I am willing to play it your way for now.' Joe didn't mention that he believed there was someone else behind Jones, someone who would also have to be dealt with if the time came.

'What about this Andy Tracy and the other two, the Manchester lads? What's their part in this?'

'I believe Jones used Tracy as his trigger man in killing Norrie Kennedy. The two brothers were back-up and wheelman. There is always a back-up gun, as insurance against the trigger man getting cold feet.'

'So why'd they get done?'

'You were getting close, I believe. I would not have trusted Tracy, and there was no reason why Jones would. He's no fool.' The lies came easily to Joe's lips, especially as they merged so seamlessly with the truth. He had been unwilling to falsely accuse Jones before, but Barney's murder changed matters.

Bannatyne nodded thoughtfully. 'It fits. We found a gun under a mattress in the caravan.'

Joe froze, but his expertise in dissemination prevented any shock from showing on his face.

'The technicians are on it now, checking it against the bullets recovered from Kennedy's body,' Bannatyne said. 'But my nose tells me it's the murder weapon. It was sloppy of them – keeping it.'

Yes, thought Joe, *very sloppy*. The murder weapon couldn't be traced to him, and he now knew for certain that he had done the right thing in removing Tracy from the picture.

'So if Jones is on a spree, who's next?'

'I would imagine that would be me.'

Bannatyne's eyebrows twitched and he unconsciously looked around, taking a slight step away from Joe, who smiled. 'Don't worry, my friend – I do not think it will be tonight.'

Bannatyne nodded and looked again at the water. The light had turned from red to grey and there was a chill rising from the river that had not been there before. He pulled his coat around him.

'But, my friend,' Joe said, 'may I make a suggestion?'

Bannatyne nodded.

'Be quick about gathering that proof. I have no intention of becoming a new notch on Johnny Jones' gun. If he makes a move against me, our little arrangement is over.'

17

DAVIE LIKED TO take late night walks through the city streets. He liked the dark and he liked the quiet. He kept Abe on a lead because he still wasn't confident enough to trust him not to run under the wheels of a bus. Abe didn't seem to mind. He was happy to be out in the fresh air with Davie.

Davie didn't know if it was the painkillers, but the ache in his ribs had lessened considerably in the two days since his encounter with Boyle, convincing him that there was no permanent damage done. He still felt a dull ache whenever he walked, but he refused to give into it. To take his mind off his bruises, he thought of Audrey. It had taken him most of the day to pluck up the courage to phone her and when he finally did he'd had no idea what to say.

'It's Davie,' he'd said when he heard her voice. 'From the other night.'

'I know,' she'd answered, and then went quiet. He knew she was waiting for him to speak but he couldn't think of anything at first.

'So,' he'd said, 'you okay?'

'Yes, thanks to you. How about you?'

'Yeah, fine. He kicked me pretty hard but I'll live.'

There was another silence and behind her he could hear voices, phones, and the clatter of typewriters. He swallowed, wishing he'd written down stuff to say. Might've been easier.

'Anyway,' he'd said, 'thought I'd phone, make sure you're okay.'

'I'm fine,' she'd said and then she waited again. Davie stood with his ear to the phone, staring down at her business card in his other hand, his thumb flicking the edge. In his mind he heard Rab's voice telling him to talk to her, for God's sake.

'Good,' he'd said, wishing he'd at least spoken to Bobby about this. Bobby had the patter that women liked. Davie was useless. *Say something*, Rab's voice was yelling, *just so she doesn't think you're a complete retard.*

'So, listen,' he'd said, 'I was thinking...'

'Yes?'

He licked his lips. 'So I was thinking...' *Okay, Davie, she knows you've been thinking, well done, but what exactly were you thinking? Spit it out, man.*

'I was thinking that maybe we could... em... maybe meet up. Or something. You and me.'

She fell silent again and Davie felt his heart sink. *She's going to say no,* he told himself, *of course she's going to say no. Why the hell would she want to meet up with you? She probably thinks you're a thug, just like Boyle and Sinclair. And maybe she's not wrong. Get used to the idea, Davie, she's going to say no.*

And then she said *yes, she'd love to meet up.*

'Or something,' she said and he could hear the smile in her voice. 'You and me...'

Davie felt a wide smile break out on his face and his heart, already banging away, picked up the tempo. 'Okay,' he'd said, 'Good. Great.'

Davie smiled again as he thought about it. He wondered if he should risk breaking into a jog, just a short one, but as if in warning, a stabbing pain shot through his ribs. *Too soon,* he thought. *A walk is enough for now.*

Duke Street was quiet, only the occasional vehicle sliding past. Davie had two options for his evening stroll. One walk took him westwards, towards the city centre and past the hospital, an eye-catching building that Joe told him was built originally for the city's poor in the days before the NHS. Nearby was the abattoir, a large, ugly, concrete monstrosity which gave Davie the shivers. He had seen cattle being herded up a sloping walkway into the building and had felt pity for them, for they had no idea what lay ahead. Occasionally one would break free and career down Duke Street before it was caught. The sprawl of the Tennents Caledonian Brewery was further on, a blaze of light all night, and then the Great Eastern, a large, crumbling building that Joe told him had been built as a mill but was now a dosshouse.

Joe had a vast repository of facts about his adopted city. He had once taken Davie and Rab on a walk around the perimeter of a small housing estate near the junction of Duke Street and High Street, searching a high stone wall for bullet holes left by the IRA in the 1920s. Back then, it had been the site of the city's North Prison, and Joe told them they had been trying to free one of their men from police custody and had ambushed the van here. Davie smiled as he recalled Joe's excitement when he found a series of holes in the sandstone.

However, Davie did not go west that night. He turned right at the top of Sword Street to head eastwards, the decision made more by Abe's nose than anything else. The shops were closed now and the street yellowed by the overhead lights. In the flats above the shops, lights blazed behind curtains and blinds. Some of the lights flickered as decent folk watched television. Decent folk leading decent lives.

Luca Vizzini was just closing up as Davie and Abe reached the café. He'd pulled the metal grate down over the front door and was locking it when he saw Davie and Abe coming towards him. His dark features broke into a wide grin and he said, 'Hey, Davie, whaddaya hear, whaddaya say?' Davie could still hear a trace of spaghetti and meatballs in Luca's New York accent, even when he was trying for James Cagney. Sometimes he knew the Sicilian exaggerated his native accent because it was good for business and it made him more colourful, which, in a city of grey buildings and grey skies, was always welcome. 'How you doin, kid?'

'Getting there, Luca.'

Luca bent down to pat Abe's head. 'Hey, boy – lemme see if...'

Luca rooted around in his jacket pocket. '... ah, *si*... there...' He produced a piece of chocolate wrapped in silver paper, which he unwrapped and fed to Abe. Luca smiled and nodded in satisfaction as the dog wolfed down the treat. 'Good boy, that's a good boy. So, you going for a walk?' When Davie nodded, Luca went on, 'You know, Duke Street is the longest street in the country?'

Davie smiled. 'Joe tell you that?'

Luca grinned back. 'Yeah. What can I say? He's up there reading the Encyclopaedia and I got my nose buried in Mickey Spillane.'

They shared a smile as they thought of Joe's breadth of knowledge, and how willingly he shared it. Luca's expression darkened. 'It's a shame what happened to Barney, eh?'

Davie nodded.

'And those guys in the caravan. Did you know them?'

'I met Andy Tracy once,' said Davie. 'Don't know the other two. Not local.'

'Ah, *si, si*, they were from down south. Still, terrible business – a helluva thing.'

Luca seemed genuinely distressed by Sunday's events.

'And you had trouble yourself, I hear,' Luca motioned towards the bruises on Davie's face, 'with Sinclair and Boyle?'

'A bit.'

'They were here tonight, both of them. Sinclair was looking like shit, I've gotta say.'

'I got in a few before Boyle taught me a wee lesson,' admitted Davie.

Luca's face turned thoughtful. 'Be careful around Boyle, Davie. He's a no good son-of-a-bitch. I got the feeling they were here looking for you, or Rab. For those guys it ain't over. Sometimes I think they are more Sicilian than me. *Vendetta*, Davie – do you know this word?'

Davie nodded.

'It's not a good thing, and I was raised with it. It is destructive.

It eats everything around it, leaves nothing. Watch your back, kid.'

Luca gave Abe one last pat before turning and walking away to wherever he had his Volvo estate parked. Davie watched him go then resumed his own walk in the opposite direction. It was Abe's low growl that made Davie stop, a soft footfall that made him turn around in time to see Boyle and Sinclair coming out of a close-mouth behind him. The thought that they were waiting for him flashed briefly in his mind, but the look of surprise on Boyle's face confirmed that this meeting was pure chance. Sinclair's face was swollen, his nose taped up, his puffy eyes and cracked lip making any kind of expression virtually impossible.

'Fuck sake,' said Boyle, smiling without any warmth, 'the sights you see when you've no got a gun, eh?'

He looked at his pal and Sinclair mumbled something in reply, but Davie had trouble making out the words through the swelling. Then Boyle's face brightened and he said, 'No, hang on...'

He lifted the flap of his windbreaker to reveal the butt of a pistol at his waistband. Davie felt his flesh chill despite the warm night. He took a couple of steps closer to the wall so that neither of them could get behind him. Abe's growl deepened and his hackles rose like a serrated blade along his back. His head dropped until it was level with his ragged back and his entire body tensed. Instinctively, the little dog had taken a dislike to both young men. Davie tightened his grip on the lead.

Boyle was still smiling, which only served to make him look meaner. 'Out for a wee stroll, Davie?'

'He likes walking at night,' said Sinclair, speaking slowly so the words could get past his swollen lips.

'That right? What are you, son, a fuckin vampire? You scared of crucifixes and garlic and stuff?'

Abe bared his teeth and took a single step forward. Boyle looked down at him for the first time.

'You keep that mutt away from me, McCall, or I'll put one in its heid, so help me.'

Davie gave Abe a gentle tug on his lead and the dog edged back closer to his feet. But his throat continued to rumble as he watched Boyle and Sinclair through intense eyes, every now and then baring his white teeth in a silent snarl.

Boyle dropped his jacket over the gun as headlights picked them out. He watched the car pass them by, then swivelled his head back and forward to see who else was on the street. Davie did the same. He saw two young couples walking arm-in-arm on the opposite side of the street and further back a drunk staggered through the final stages of his preparations for the next day's hangover. Davie glanced upwards to the windows, but no one was looking down on them. If Boyle decided to use the gun there was nothing Davie could do to stop him. The trick would be in preventing Boyle from pulling the weapon in the first place. And that meant Davie would have move first.

'How're the ribs, Davie?'

'Sore.' Davie replied, knowing there was no point in lying.

'Doesnae matter,' said Boyle, shrugging. 'It's all water under the bridge now, isn't it? No hard feelings, eh, Davie?'

Boyle stepped forward and held out his right hand, the large silver signet ring catching the light from the street lamp beside them. To the casual observer, the move would have looked like an overture of friendship, but Boyle was a leftie and the gun was tucked into the right side of his belt. Davie knew that if he took the proffered hand, Boyle would whip out the gun and blast away. Whatever was going to happen, it was going to happen soon. Every muscle in Davie's body tensed, sending pain stabbing through his ribs, but he ignored it. He had to ignore it. He could not let it slow him down.

Boyle let the hand hang there for a few seconds before letting it drop with a shrug. 'Okay, son, that's the way you want to play it, fine.'

He looked away nonchalantly, and at the same time his left hand reached under his jacket. But Davie was already moving, dropping Abe's lead and lunging forward, one hand reaching towards Boyle's wrist, the other already bunched and pulling back. He saw Boyle's eyes widen in surprise and he was aware of Sinclair stepping forward and Abe darting between them and barking, his teeth snapping and it was going down beautifully and Davie knew in his heart he had timed everything perfectly and he felt the blood singing through his veins just as he always did when he knew he was onto a winner...

The screech of tyres beside them brought them all to a halt and a voice called out, 'Everything okay there, Davie?'

Boyle's hand froze under his jacket, Davie's grip still firm around his wrist, and they both turned to see Luca leaning out of the open window of his Volvo.

'I'm fine, Luca,' said Davie.

'You wanna lift somewhere?'

Davie felt the heat returning to his body and the roaring in his ears faded to a whisper. He forced a smile. 'Sure, Luca, that'd be great.'

He let go of Boyle's arm and, without taking his eyes off him, stooped to find Abe's lead. He led the still snarling dog towards the car.

'This isn't done yet,' said Boyle, quietly. 'There's a change coming, Davie, and you and your pals are gonnae be surplus to fuckin requirements. But you and me, son, we're gonnae have a reckonin, so we are. I'm gonnae have you, Davie McCall...' His voice rose to a high pitched nasal whine, '... and your little dog, too!'

Boyle laughed, Sinclair joining in enthusiastically. Davie said nothing as he walked round the front of the car, opened the rear door to let Abe leap in, and climbed into the passenger seat. Luca stared at the two young men on the pavement for a long, hard moment and their smirks slid away as they sensed the malevolence in the man. Then the Sicilian released the handbrake and drove off.

Davie craned his neck to look back and saw the two of them watching the car. Even at this distance, Davie could feel the heat of Boyle's glare, and he wondered just what it was that was eating him.

18

Clem Boyle and Jazz Sinclair had been friends since primary school. Boyle had been a tough kid even then, but then, he'd had to be. He was the youngest of four brothers, each one of them desperate to emulate their father. Colin Boyle was a pal of Norrie Kennedy. They'd been brought up together in Blackhill and together they had kicked, punched and slashed their way through their teenage years and into early manhood. But Colin didn't have the ambition or the cunning of his childhood mate, so while Norrie climbed the greasy pole of criminal achievement, Colin had to be content with hanging around near the bottom rung catching what rewards slid his way. Norrie never forgot his old pal, though, and made sure he was involved in whatever jobs called for his particular talents. Those talents included the ability to administer pain and a willingness to use a firearm – talents that stood Colin Boyle in good stead as a blagger. There was always room for a young guy with a shotgun in his hand and the ruthlessness to fire it. Boyle senior was one of four masked men who knocked over a British Linen Bank in Anniesland in 1966, making off with £65,000 in cash. They crippled an old man who tried to stop them, blasting his legs then prising the one pound note out of his hand that he had intended to lodge in his savings account. Colin had pulled the trigger and he'd been known to say that the old bastard deserved it for getting in the way. Two years later, he blinded with ammonia a security guard who had refused to open the rear door of his van to let his guys relieve it of the payroll being delivered to a steelworks near Motherwell.

With the proceeds of these jobs, Colin bought a comfortable semi-detached in Baillieston and raised a family with his wife Mira, a red-headed, freckled Irish lass with a temper to match her colouring. Colin loved all his sons, but it was the youngest, Clement, that he doted on. The other three boys were aware of this and never missed a chance to torment the lad, for he had inherited his mother's red hair and freckles, which was a constant source of humour for his siblings. They loved to make fun of his name – he was named after his great-grandfather – and so he came to hate anyone who dared use it, preferring to go by just his surname. As he grew older the freckles faded and the hair colour darkened and he developed into a good-looking enough young man. But even then, his brothers took endless delight in ribbing him.

Colin Boyle died in 1975. He was kicked to death by Danny McCall.

It didn't matter to Clem Boyle that by all accounts it had begun as a fair fight and, in fact, his father had started it. All that mattered to him was that Danny McCall beat his father to the ground and then proceeded to kick his head in. Colin Boyle lay in a coma for six weeks before he finally passed away in a bare room in the Royal Infirmary, his wife at his bedside, holding his hand. Only Clem and Gerry, the oldest son, were present at the funeral with their mother. One brother was in Peterhead Prison for murder and the other doing time in Wormwood Scrubs for a bank robbery in Putney. At the graveside, Boyle gripped his father's signet ring in his hand, his only tangible link to him, and told his brother, 'One day, I'm gonnae get Danny McCall and I'm gonnae do him. He's gonnae pay for what he did.'

The young Boyle never got the chance; two years later, Danny murdered his wife and vanished. But Davie McCall was still very much in evidence.

Colin Boyle had been a criminal and a vicious one at that, but Clem Boyle had at least grown up with two loving parents. Jazz Sinclair had no such luxury. His father had deserted his mother when he was three years old, and from then she had gone through a number of men. The young boy lay in his room at night being serenaded from the next room by the throaty groans of the men as they climaxed. He became used to the many rows she had with her boyfriends, and the occasional slap as one or other resorted to violence to make their point. He had no brothers or sisters, no real friends, no friendly aunts or uncles with whom to take refuge. There was just him and his mother and the men she insisted he call 'uncle'.

His given name was James, but he had taken to signing himself as Jazz by the time he reached primary school. Clem Boyle, who was placed beside him on the first day, saw him scribble his name on a piece of paper that was being passed round the children.

'That's a funny name,' said the young Boyle.

'It's short for James,' said the young Sinclair. 'What's yours?'

'Boyle.'

'Boyle what?'

'Just Boyle,' he said, holding out his hand. Jazz looked at the hand then eventually shook it. From that moment on, they were pals, and Jazz was grateful for it.

Over the years, Sinclair learned how to handle himself well enough, but he never sought out confrontation. Boyle was different – he revelled in a fight. Sinclair avoided trouble if he could, but being friends with Boyle so often brought the need to face up to it. Sometimes, though, he wondered if his friendship with the red-haired firebrand was healthy. Boyle had never lifted a finger against Jazz, but there was a side to his pal that scared him. Jazz often thought about the night Boyle had stuck his knife up some lad's arse. He'd stood by as Boyle hauled the boy's pants down and rammed the blade up there. He didn't know why Boyle felt the need to do it and he'd never had the nerve to ask him about it. It was just something Clem had done because his blood was up. But it had scared the hell out of Jazz and sometimes he woke up hearing the boy's screams and seeing Boyle's face as he did it, his eyes dead and cold and distant.

Then there was the murder of Barney Cable. Sinclair had gone along with it because, to be honest, none of it seemed real. The preparation for the ambush had seemed like they were talking about a film or something. But when he and Boyle had burst out the back of that van, he'd suddenly realised that it was all for real and he'd hit the ground as soon as the bullets began to fly. He'd cowered there, praying he wouldn't get hit, while Boyle had got to one knee and taken aim at Cable's back as he'd climbed the fence. Even firing the shotgun had been a mistake – his finger twitched as he leaped from the van and landed badly on the hard concrete, jarring his injuries from the night before. It had been pure luck that the double rounds had smashed the car's windscreen. But Boyle seemed to be in his element.

Sinclair was ashamed that he hadn't been more assertive that day and he vowed that if he ever got the chance to make up for it, he would. That's why, that Wednesday night, he went with him to follow McCall. He knew Boyle had a beef with him, knew it was something to do with their dads, but he never asked for details. The fact that they'd set their sights on that blonde burd in the pub and she'd been taken away from them by Davie McCall added another layer of resentment.

McCall had no idea that he was being shadowed that night, Sinclair knew that. They had followed him all the way from Sword Street, where he took a taxi into the city centre and the Dial Inn, a pub across West Regent Street from the Odeon Cinema. They parked their car and watched as McCall waited outside the pub. The picture house loomed like a giant warehouse to their left and McCall stood on the right hand side of the road, glancing occasionally around him. It was another warm spring evening and McCall was wearing a blue denim jacket, blue jeans and a white shirt. His hair was combed neatly and he looked clean and crisp. Boyle noted with satisfaction that he still favoured his right side, limping ever so slightly as he paced back and forward. McCall was nervous, which was a sight neither of them had seen before.

Jazz commented, 'He's kinda jumpy the night, is he no?'

Boyle nodded then seemingly realised why McCall seemed so skittish. 'I'll bet he's meetin a lassie, that's why!'

Jazz frowned. 'You think it's her frae Saturday night, like?'

'Well, it's no any of the hairies from up our way, no meetin here.'

Jazz's frown deepened. He had really fancied her and now McCall was getting in there. 'Bastard!'

Boyle dug his elbow into his pal and nodded towards Renfield Street. Sure enough, the girl was walking towards McCall. If anything she looked even better in the daylight than she had in the smoke-filled gloom of the pub. She was wearing a dark, pin-striped trouser suit that accentuated her curves. Her long blonde hair tumbled down around the collar of a white blouse.

'What the fuck does she see in a scroat like Davie McCall?' Jazz wondered.

Boyle remained silent. McCall sticking his nose into their business that night was one thing, but seeing the cow afterwards was just rubbing their faces in it. Even more than before, Clem Boyle hated Davie McCall.

* * *

As soon as he saw Audrey, McCall felt a smile break out and something catch in his chest. When she smiled, he felt a curious warmth spread through him. He didn't know what that was either.

'I wasn't sure you would actually come,' he said when they were settled in the downstairs bar, both with a soft drink in front of them. She was driving, Davie never drank. The barman had given a short, disgusted shrug when he ordered. Someone had fed the jukebox and when Davie carried the drinks to their table Madness were singing *My Girl.*

She laughed. 'Why wouldn't I come?'

McCall shrugged. 'Well, we met in kinda strange circumstances.'

'That's one way of putting it,' she said, sipping her fresh orange and soda, her eyes sparkling over the rim of the glass. She put the glass on the table top again. 'To be honest, I wasn't sure I'd come either.'

McCall said nothing, but his hand turned the glass slowly round on the table.

'I've heard some things about you, Davie McCall,' she said, and he nodded slowly. He was not surprised. Someone in the paper was bound to have heard of him or his father.

'Some of it might even be true,' he said.

'But you helped me the other night, and that means something.'

'And is that the only reason you're here? Because you feel you owe me?'

She thought about this and sipped her drink again. She didn't answer until she had carefully laid the glass down again, as if she was afraid of breaking it. 'No,' she said. 'I'm here because I want to be.'

McCall nodded and said, 'Good.'

* * *

Boyle had been watching the door of the Dial Inn for 30 minutes when something penetrated his concentration and he glanced at the car radio.

'What the fuck's this we're listening to?'

Sinclair took the cigarette from his mouth and said, 'Radio Clyde.'

Boyle screwed up his face and snarled, 'I know that, for fuck's sake. What the fuck's the song?'

'It's Keith Michell.'

'Who the fuck's Keith Michell?'

'The actor bloke – played that fat king on the telly. He's singing *Captain Beaky*.'

Boyle said flatly, '*Captain Beaky*.'

'Aye, he's a pigeon, or something...'

'Switch it the fuck off. I'm no sitting listening to a song about a fuckin bird.'

Sinclair did as he was told. 'It was number one,' he said in his defence, as if it was his fault that it was on the radio station's playlist.

'I don't fuckin care if it went fuckin platinum, it's shite,' said Boyle, turning his attention back to the pub door. 'Fuckin '*Captain Beaky*'...'

The sat in silence for a few minutes until Davie and the girl emerged and crossed the street towards the Odeon box office on the corner of Renfield Street and West Regent Street.

'They're going to the pictures,' said Jazz.

'Looks like it.'

'We gonnae wait here till they come out?'

Boyle thought about it. 'Naw. We could miss them, so there's no point. I just wanted to see where the fucker was going, that's all, and who he was meeting. We'll let him have his date wi that bitch for now.'

Boyle started the car and glanced into the wing mirror before pulling out and heading south towards Castlemilk.

19

JOHNNY JONES WAS alone in his flat watching *Coronation Street* when Bannatyne and Donovan paid him a visit. He was an avid fan of the soap, having caught the bug from his wife who had followed it from its earliest days. They had watched it together, right up to when the cancer took her, and now that she was gone he kept up the tradition, her framed picture facing the telly. That way he could at least pretend, if only for half an hour a couple of times a week, that she was still with him. That was why he made sure he was alone whenever the show aired.

So when the doorbell rang during the commercial break, he felt a flash of irritation burn through him. He contemplated ignoring it, but whoever was out there was insistent and seemed to be leaning on the buzzer. Jones sighed angrily, pulled himself out of the armchair and walked quickly down the hallway, intending to send whoever it was away with a flea in their ear. He jerked open the door, a snarl freezing when he saw who it was. Bannatyne he knew, but the younger copper was new to him.

'Johnny,' said Bannatyne, a big smile on his face, 'we need a word.'

'It's no convenient the now,' said Jones.

Bannatyne's smile broadened and in that instant Jones knew the cop was aware of his *Coronation Street* tradition and had chosen the time specifically to find him at home and alone.

'We'll not take long,' Bannatyne said, brushing past him and heading down the hallway towards the living room. As he walked he said over his shoulder, 'This is DC Donovan, one of my team. Frank, this is Johnny Jones.'

Donovan nodded as he stepped over the threshold and closed

the door behind him, but Jones barely glanced at him. Instead, he moved swiftly after Bannatyne. 'Hey, you cannae just walk in here.'

Bannatyne stood in the centre of the living room sporting an exaggerated puzzled expression. 'We can if you invited us in.'

'But I never invited you in.'

'Could've sworn you invited us in. Did you hear Mister Jones invite us in, DC Donovan?'

'Distinctly heard him say, "Come in, lads",' said Donovan.

Bannatyne smiled back at Jones. 'There you are. You need to do something about your short-term memory, Johnny old son.'

Jones sighed, knowing better than to argue the point. 'What you wantin? I'm busy.'

Bannatyne glanced at the television in the corner. 'Aye, well, Elsie Tanner will need to wait for now. I want to talk to you about Norrie Kennedy.'

Jones sat down in his armchair. Bannatyne stood on the rug in front of the gas fire while Donovan lurked near the door. Jones knew Bannatyne was trying for a psychological advantage by staying on his feet, but he was an old hand at this and didn't give a toss. 'Don't know anything about it, already told you.'

'Yes, you did. But I didn't believe you.'

'Cannae help what you believe.'

'I believe you had him killed.'

Jones give him a dismissive smirk. 'Told you, cannae help what you believe.'

'You know the lad that got himself shot up Lennoxtown way?'

'Aye, read about it. Terrible, so it was.'

'We found a gun in the caravan that linked him to the Kennedy job.'

'So what you talkin to me for? He obviously did Norrie.'

'A source tells me you hired him to do it. And my source says that you had something to do with Barney Cable's murder, too.'

Jones began to laugh. 'Give us a break, Bannatyne. Who the hell do you think I am? Al Capone? I don't kill people. You know me, I'm a safeblower, a scallywag. A bit dodgy, aye, but I'm no fuckin gangster.'

'I think you're coming up in the world, Johnny. I think you've got ambition. My source tells me you're up to something, something big, and Norrie wasn't playing ball so you took him out of the game. I've got lads out hitting all the known armourers in the city and if we link that gun to you, we'll come for you.'

Jones shook his head. 'I'm telling you, Bannatyne, it's no down to me. Who's your source anyhow?'

Bannatyne smiled. 'You don't expect me to tell you that, surely, Johnny?'

'Well, whoever he is, he's giving you a bum steer. I wouldnae listen to him. Load a shite, that.'

Bannatyne nodded and glanced at Donovan. 'Maybe so, but you're on a warning, Johnny. All this is getting out of hand. Six killings this month. Makes Strathclyde Police look bad and we don't like that. Makes people wonder who actually runs these streets, you know? So let me make this perfectly clear...' Bannatyne stepped closer to Jones and leaned over him. 'We run these streets. Not you and your kind. The sooner you understand that, the better.'

Jones stared back steadily at the detective, the corners of his mouth tugging down appreciatively. 'Nice speech, Bannatyne, wee bit rough, but with a wee polish you'll be able to deliver it at the police college and get a standing ovation. But see, wi me? It means fuck all. I had nothing to do with Norrie Kennedy's murder, nothing to do with those lads up in Lennoxtown, nothing to do with Barney Cable. You want to pin them all on me, go ahead and get the proof. But here's the thing – you'll need to fit me up for it cos, and I think I'll get a t-shirt printed up wi this on it, I had fuck all to do with any of it. Now, if you're finished threatenin me, I want to get back to my programme.'

Jones squinted past Bannatyne to focus on the screen. The

detective straightened and stepped out of his way, jerking his head towards Donovan, who nodded and stepped into the hallway. Bannatyne listened for the front door opening and then he leaned back in to Jones.

'Joe the Tailor sends his regards, Johnny,' he said quietly.

He left Johnny watching the final few minutes of the Street. Jones didn't take much of it in, though, because his anger had begun to rise.

* * *

When Boyle and Sinclair arrived at Jones' flat they found him in the armchair where Bannatyne and Donovan had left him. He was staring at the television screen, but they could tell by his expression that he wasn't really watching it. The young men knew that something had happened and they stood in the centre of the room without saying a word, waiting for him to acknowledge their presence. After a couple of minutes Sinclair glanced at Boyle and raised his eyebrows, wondering if they should say something. Boyle shook his head and motioned his pal to sit on the settee. Sinclair did as he was told and Boyle took up position on the arm of the second armchair. Jones was yet to move or even look at them. He simply stared at the screen.

Finally, he said quietly, 'Had a visit from that fucker Bannatyne.'

Sinclair felt fear flicker in his stomach. 'What'd he want?'

'Says I had something to do with the Norrie Kennedy thing, the three lads up in Lennoxtown and Barney Cable...'

At the mention of Barney Cable, Sinclair felt his fear grow into full-blown panic. He glanced fearfully at Boyle, but his friend appeared unconcerned.

'Seems to think I'm some kinda one-man Murder Incorporated,' Jones went on. 'And I'll tell you something else – someone's been filling his heid wi these lies.'

Sinclair swallowed and asked, 'Who?'

Jones' next words came out in a snarl. 'That fuckin wee Jew boy Joe fuckin Klein, that's who.'

Boyle spoke in a steady, clear voice. 'So what do we do now?'

Jones' eyes flicked towards Boyle. 'He's stepped over the line. We're gonnae fuckin put one in his heid.'

20

WHAT DAVIE REMEMBERED most about life with Danny McCall was the drunken rage and the violence, but even that was mostly a blur, fragments of memory jumbled together to make a disjointed whole. The only thing that was vivid in his mind was the terrible night when Danny McCall had finally crossed the line from wife beater to murderer.

Davie didn't know why his father had come home to their tenement flat in Oatlands in such a rage that night. He was, of course, drunk. It was a stormy night and the rain hurled against the windows of the three-room flat alongside a strong wind, but the living room-cum-kitchen was warm and cosy thanks to a raging coal fire in the grate. Davie was watching a western with Gary Cooper and Burt Lancaster and the first thing Danny McCall said when he came in was an order to 'get that fuckin shite switched off.' Davie was enjoying the movie, but he did as he was told, for he knew better than to answer back or argue the point. Danny McCall threw himself into an old, worn armchair and glared at his wife, who was standing in the corner ironing clothes lifted from a plastic basket at her feet. 'You gonnae make me somethin to eat, or what?'

Davie's mother sighed and laid the iron down on the edge of the ironing table. 'We've got some gammon in the fridge.'

Danny McCall's eyes turned cold. 'Gammon? That all you gonnae offer me? Gammon?'

'I never got to the butcher's the day.'

'How no? You too busy or what? You got such a busy fuckin day on your hands that you couldnae get out and buy your man some decent grub? You got some sort of business empire to run or something? Eh?'

He was on his feet now and Davie saw the fingers of each hand tightening into a fist. The young man knew what was coming next. 'I'll run down the chippie for you, da,' he offered, hoping to distract his father. 'Get you a fish supper, how's that?'

But Danny McCall didn't even look in his direction. 'Don't want a fish supper. I want there to be something in my house ready for me when I get home. A chop, or a steak maybe – something nice and tasty. But no, my dear wife's been too busy to see to my needs. So what I want to know is, what the fuck's she been doin wi her time? Eh? Tell me that.'

Mary McCall shook her head and leaned on top of the ironing table. 'Danny,' she said, her voice weary, 'I can't do this anymore.'

Danny frowned. 'Do what?'

'This!' said Mary. 'You, your anger, your drinking. I can't do it anymore, Danny. I've had enough.'

'Really?' There was an exaggerated look of surprise on his face. 'So tell me, my dear – what are you going to do about it?'

Mary paused and Davie saw the colour draining from her face. Later, when he thought about it, he became certain that he saw a look of determination harden her gaze, as if the need to challenge her husband had been building for years. Joe told him that when he made inquiries himself, he discovered that Mary had confided in a neighbour that it was only concern for her son that had kept her tongue still. She knew she should have left her man long before but she hadn't, partly out of the hope that the old Danny – the one she had loved and married – would return. But that night she knew that the old Danny McCall was long gone and she couldn't stand it any longer. She had to do something.

'We're going to leave,' she said quietly. 'Me and Davie. We're going.'

'The fuck you are,' said Danny, stepping forward, fist balled and ready, but he stopped when his wife surprised him by snatching up the hot iron, the closest thing to her, and held it in front of her like a shield.

'No, Danny,' she said, her teeth gritted, eyes slitted in a determined squint. 'Not again. You take one more step and God help me. I'll brain you with this.'

Danny McCall was at a loss for words. He looked from his wife's face to the iron in her hand and then to their son, who was equally as stunned. He shook his head almost sadly and stepped back to the open fireplace. He stared at the flames for a moment or two then stooped and picked up the heavy metal poker. It was long and pointed and had a sharp hook jutting out near the end.

'Okay, darling,' he said, 'you want to play, let's play…'

Davie had never seen his father move so fast. He launched himself across the room, knocking the iron out of Mary's hand with the poker while his left slapped her across the face. She cried out and slumped back against the wall. Danny raised the poker again to bring it down on her head. Davie was at his father's side before he knew what he was doing, reaching out to grip his arm. But even with a drink in him the older McCall was too fast, lashing out with a back-handed blow then whirling and pushing the boy across the room until his back was against the wall. He jerked his knee upwards into his son's groin and Davie felt agony surge through his body. He began to slump as Danny, still using his left hand, clubbed him to the floor. Davie tried to curl into a ball but his father kicked his legs back again and stood over him. Then he raised the poker above his head. Davie looked up, tears streaming down his face as much from the anger and frustration at not being able to do anything as it was from the pain. He looked into his father's eyes, blue like his own, and saw nothing there that he recognised. The father's face was expressionless as he looked down at his son. There was no rage, there was nothing. Something dark and violent had taken over. For a fleeting second Davie sensed that Danny McCall was somewhere else and that this creature with the poker poised above his head was a demon that existed only to cause pain.

Then Danny McCall brought the heavy metal poker slicing down.

The jagged agony shooting up Davie's right arm was like nothing he had ever experienced before. It was then superseded by the second and third. His father seemed to sense that, for he stopped his fourth blow in mid-swing and stared down at his son for a second. Through his pain, Davie saw something seep back into Danny's eyes, a warmth that melted the ice. The older McCall looked at the weapon in his hands and then at his son, opening his mouth to say something. But no words came. Then, mercifully, Danny slumped off to the side with a grunt, and Mary McCall was standing there, iron in hand, the power cord dangling free.

A great weight held Davie down, and all he could do was watch as his mother moved closer to his father, who was still shaking his head groggily. Danny's hand went up to his wound and came away with blood. He looked at it in a puzzled manner and then his attention returned to his wife as she swung the iron once more. This time Danny was ready for it. He ducked under her arm, stepped in and punched her in the stomach. It was a deep blow and air burst from her throat in a gasp as she doubled over, the iron slipping from her hand. Danny grabbed her by the hair and swung her across the room, sending her tumbling over a wooden chair that was partially pulled out from the small kitchen table. She rolled across the floor, colliding with the tall standard lamp that was the room's only electric light. It swayed then toppled, and the bulb exploded with a pop. Now the room was lit only by the glow of the fire, a strange, unearthly light that sent shifting shadows dancing on the wall. Danny kicked her head. Davie heard her groan again and saw her hands jerk up to her face. Danny McCall kicked her again and her head snapped to the side and the hands fell away, although Davie could see she was still moving, her legs jerking as if she was trying to get up. Danny stepped over her until he was straddling her, and raised the poker once more.

'Dad – don't,' said Davie, but his voice was weak. 'Dad – please don't,' he said, a bit louder now. Danny McCall hesitated, the poker above his head. He looked over at his son and Davie thought just for a second that he saw something human there. But as the son stared into the father's eyes for the final time, that flicker of humanity guttered and died.

'Dad – please...' pleaded Davie, but his father was no longer there and he knew it. Danny returned his icy gaze to his wife and brought the poker arcing down. As Davie finally tumbled into unconsciousness, he knew that final image would be etched in his memory for good; his father, standing over the body of his mother, lit by the red glow of the firelight and the sound of rain battering against the windows punctuated by the thud of hard metal on soft flesh.

* * *

Davie thought about that hellish night and of what his father had become as he walked the east end streets, Abe at his heels. His deepest fear was always that whatever lived inside Danny McCall lived within him, too. He justified to himself that the people he hurt deserved it, but he knew that was not strictly true. It was one reason why – Joe and Rab apart – he did not forge close friendships.

But Audrey was different.

Something about her had gripped him. He didn't know what he was feeling or why he was feeling it, but for the first time he didn't feel compelled to push her away. He had sat through the film watching Dustin Hoffman trying to bring up his young son without the aid of a self-centred Meryl Streep and had enjoyed it, even if it wasn't exactly to his taste. He had enjoyed it because Audrey sat beside him, although he was tense and nervous and afraid that their arms would touch on the shared rest between them. Then, about halfway through, she moved, snaking her arm though his to take his hand in hers, and he felt all the tension ebb away at the touch of her fingers, cool and smooth, and they sat for the rest of the film just holding each other's hands.

Later, as he walked her to the car park where she had left her car, he began to grow nervous again. She was talking about the film, saying how much she hated Streep's character, but he was thinking ahead. He desperately wanted to kiss her but he didn't know how to go about it, even though they walked hand-in-hand through the city centre streets. She had taken his hand again, so that meant something, he told himself. In the end, she took the first step. They had reached her car and went though the clichéd ritual of the first date. She told him she'd had a good time and he said they would have to do it again, and of course she agreed. She gave him a small smile then stepped closer, her hands resting gently on his waist as she leaned forward and kissed him. For a brief second Davie didn't know what to do, but instinct kicked in and his hands moved under her jacket and round her body, experiencing pleasure at the feel of her firm skin under her blouse. Her lips were cool and soft and she pulled him closer as they stood there for a short time. Then they parted and she smiled again as she reached up to wipe away a trace of lipstick from his mouth.

'If you don't phone me, I'll phone you,' she said, then climbed into her car and drove away, giving him a small wave through the window as she did so.

It took Davie a full minute to realise he was grinning like a fool.

21

BARNEY CABLE'S FUNERAL should have taken place sooner than it did but his body, and that of Peter Morton, were held back by the police for 'investigative purposes'. They never explained what those 'investigative purposes' were – police never like to explain anything – but finally, after two weeks, they agreed to release the corpses for burial.

The night before the belated funeral, Davie sat with Joe in his study, staring at a chess board made up of ornate Chinese figures. Joe had taught Davie the basic moves years before, but the intricacies of the game still eluded him. His mind couldn't quite process the stratagems and feints that were required to wage this game of war. He was a straightforward move-and-take player while Joe often sideswiped him by showing a willingness to sacrifice a valuable piece in order to gain an advantage a few moves down the line. Still, though, Joe played Davie as often as possible in the hope that the young man might soak in the lessons of life that were taught on the black and white squares. He had never told Davie, but Danny McCall had been a superb player, more than a match for Joe. They had passed many an evening in this room, pitting their wits against each other. The older McCall was a ruthless player and the audacity of many of his moves often left Joe floundering.

Frank Sinatra was singing about the wee small hours of the morning on Joe's fancy stereo as Davie stared at the board. Joe waited patiently, his face giving nothing away. Davie knew the old man was up to something with his Bishop, but he couldn't work out what. He reached forward and touched his Rook, planning to fire it across the board at Joe's piece, but something made him hesitate. He sensed he was being set up, but wasn't sure how.

'Tell me about your girl,' Joe said eventually.

'What do you want to know?'

'Do you like her?'

Davie nodded, withdrawing his hand from the Rook without moving it and studying the board again. There was a trap here, he could feel it.

Joe asked, 'Her name is Audrey?'

Davie nodded. Named after Audrey Hepburn, she had told him, because her father had fallen in love with the actress after he saw her in *Roman Holiday*. His pet name for her was 'Funny Face', from a musical the actress had starred in. Her father was an engineer and had wanted her to go into teaching, but she had harboured a desire to become a reporter since her early teens. Her father could tell it was what she desperately wanted to do and let her go her own way. She could always win him over, she'd said, while her mum was a harder nut to crack. She was a secondary school history teacher and was well-used to the wiles of teenage girls. Audrey told him she had a brother three years younger who was going to university to study Law and a black and white cat she called Bustopher Jones from some poem. She told him all this over the course of three further dates while he had told her very little of himself and nothing at all about the night his mother died. There had been times she had left the door open for him to speak about himself, but he had thus far refused to step through it. He hadn't spoken of it to anyone apart from Joe. However, there was a growing part of him that wanted to tell her.

He wondered if this was what love felt like. He had no real frame of reference. He'd loved his mother, certainly, but this was different. He was, he knew, emotionally naïve, but thoughts of Audrey, of seeing her, of touching her – they made him feel at peace. He liked the feeling. He wanted it to last forever.

Joe sensed the depth of feeling. He said, 'You must be careful, David.'

Davie looked up and saw concern in Joe's eyes. 'Why? Because she's a reporter?'

'No. Because you may hurt her.'

'I'd never hurt her.'

'Not physically, certainly. But you could hurt her in other ways. Your world is not her world, you must know this.'

Davie looked down at the chess board, but he no longer saw the game. 'What if I changed?'

Joe sat back in his chair. 'Do you think you can?'

'Do you think I can?'

'I am unsure whether any of us can really change what we are.'

'But we can try.'

Joe thought briefly of his own life, of how the violent actions of one German soldier had changed *his* destiny. He thought of his family, of little Rachel and the last time he saw her, or at least thought he saw her, in that snow-covered forest. He thought of the men he had killed in the war and those he had killed in peacetime. He thought of the path he had chosen and from which he had never veered. Could he have changed at some stage? Could he have become something else? Or was that path set from birth? All his adult life he had plotted and schemed. But he was wearying. Could people like him change? Could Davie? When Joe looked at the young man he often saw the father looking back, they were so alike. How much of the father lived in the son, he wondered?

'Yes,' said Joe, gently. 'We can try.'

Davie moved his Rook to take the Bishop, just as Joe had plotted. He had sacrificed the piece in order to achieve checkmate within two moves, the first of which was to send his Knight to within striking distance of Davie's King. Joe reached out to place a fingertip on his Knight, then withdrew it slowly and moved his Queen instead, thus ruining his carefully planned strategy.

That night, Davie won his first game of chess.

* * *

A convoy of cars followed the two hearses from Drumchapel through the streets to the sprawling graveyard at Lambhill. It was a beautiful morning, the heat that had been building steadily for days reaching a new high, which somehow made the events even more poignant to Joe. He and Luca sat in the back of the Rover while Rab drove and Davie stared out of the passenger side window. No words were spoken, everyone sensing that Joe had no desire to hear any idle chatter.

When they reached the gates of the cemetery a bank of reporters and photographers waited, and Davie's thoughts turned to Audrey. But he knew the gangland funeral was to be covered by Barclay Forbes. Davie had never seen the veteran reporter but he saw someone he thought fitted the description Audrey had given him.

'Fuckin parasites,' muttered Rab as he steered through the gates. 'There's nothing they'd like better than to have us kill each other off in time for their fuckin deadlines.'

Davie glanced at his friend and said, 'They're no all like that.'

Rab shot a look back at Davie and gave him a shrug, as if to say he wasn't so sure.

The sheer number of vehicles meant they had to park a fair distance from the plot and the four of them walked up a gentle incline to where a knot of Barney's family and friends already gathered. They positioned themselves a respectful distance from the open grave, but close enough to hear the priest speak a few words of comfort over the coffin, his voice punctuated by sobs from Sheila and Melanie Cable as they held each other's hands. Barney's mother, Beatrice, stood stiff and straight nearby, staring with unwavering intensity at the coffin which housed her son's body. Harry King – Norrie Kennedy's one-time lieutenant – was present with a couple of his boys. So was Big Jim Connors and two of his lads. They both bore mournful expressions, though they were no doubt plotting how they were going to move into Barney's territory. A little further away, as if they were not part of the funeral party, he saw Bannatyne and the two cops, Knight and Donovan. He craned his neck to spot the police photographers but couldn't see them. At least they had the decency to keep themselves hidden.

Joe had assured them that there would be no unpleasantness at the funeral and Davie had let his guard down. He was annoyed with himself that he neither saw nor heard Johnny Jones and Clem Boyle move in behind them. The first he, Joe or Rab knew of their presence was Jones' rasping voice when he said, 'Funerals are always sad, eh, Joe?'

Joe displayed no surprise when he turned, but Davie knew him well enough to spot irritation tightening his jaw. 'You are not welcome here, Johnny.'

Jones gave him a small, stiff smile. 'Got to pay my respects.'

'You are not welcome here,' Joe repeated and turned his back on the man again. Jones's eyes deadened, and Davie watched Boyle, who stared back with a sneer on his lips. The two eyed each other while their respective bosses talked. The thought that this was the first time he'd seen Boyle without Sinclair niggled at Davie's mind.

Johnny leaned into Joe's ear and whispered, 'I know you fired me in with that bastard Bannatyne, Joe. That wasn't right, neither it was.'

Joe remained silent but his eyes flicked across the crowd to where Bannatyne stood with Donovan and Knight. Joe saw Bannatyne watching them intently and gave the detective slight nod.

Jones hissed, 'I'm no gonnae let that pass. You're a fuckin grass, Joe Klein, and I'm gonnae let everyone know it.' Joe whirled so quickly that the skinny man stumbled back slightly in surprise, his face paling just a little and his disdainful smile faltering. Boyle took a step forward, as did Davie, but Rab was closer and he laid one hand on Boyle's chest, fingers splayed. It was relatively gentle but there was no mistaking the threat in his eyes.

'Take that fuckin big mitt off me, McClymont,' Boyle warned, his voice loud enough to attract attention from the people at the graveside. The Priest faltered in his speech and looked their way, as did Sheila, Melanie and Beatrice. Knight and Donovan looked at their boss, but Bannatyne shook his head. Rab removed his hand from Boyle's chest in an exaggerated fashion and held it in the air. Joe looked from them back to Jones, who had recovered his composure and was smiling again.

'I suggest you leave, Johnny,' said Joe quietly. 'You've already disrupted proceedings quite enough.'

'Aye, we're going, so we are,' said Johnny, his voice low. 'Just wanted to say what had to be said.'

Jones flicked his eyes over Luca, who stared back at him, face impassive. Jones turned and walked away. Boyle glared at Rab for a second, then turned his attention back to Davie. 'Soon, Davie boy,' he said. 'Soon.'

A few minutes later the graveside service ended and the mourners drifted away. Beatrice Cable stepped into their path, her body as straight as an iron bar and just as unyielding. She looked directly into Joe's eyes and said, 'My son told me you are a good man, Mister Klein.'

Joe shook his head, 'That was kind of him, but I fear I am not a good man, Mrs Cable.'

Beatrice reassessed her words. 'An honourable man, then. He said you were a man of your word.'

'I like to think that is true,' conceded Joe.

'Then give me your word on this, Mister Klein. Give me your word that the men responsible for my son's death will pay for what they have done. Tell me they will pay in blood and that their families will feel what I am feeling now.'

Joe sighed, 'Mrs Cable...'

'Your word, Mister Klein. An eye for an eye, it says in the Bible. A life for a life. Give me your word.'

She stared at him, her gaze unwavering, but Davie saw something tremble at her chin. And when he saw her eyes glistening, he knew her iron was beginning to melt. Joe saw it, too, and finally he nodded. 'You have my word.'

22

BY THE TIME Joe Klein reached home that evening, he felt physically and mentally drained. He rejected any notion that he was growing old, but at 55, he knew that his young friends already saw him as such. Even some of his not-so-young friends looked on him as the old man. He often wondered if it was his years in the forests and mountains of Poland that were catching up with him. The cold and the damp were never far away then, seeping into his flesh and bones as he slept rough in caves and leaky barns, alternately avoiding and then stalking Germans. Whatever it was, he was weary. The past few weeks had been particularly stressful and he knew he could do with a break. Planning the murder of Norrie Kennedy – and Joe did not think of what he had done as anything less than murder, even if Kennedy was a prime candidate for being put down – and then the hasty mopping-up made necessary by his poor choice in contractor had taken their toll. Then there was the business with that little rat Johnny Jones. What had started off as an unappealing business opportunity had grown into something that could engulf the entire criminal world. Barney Cable and Peter Morton had paid the price, and Joe knew it wouldn't stop there. It couldn't stop there. He had promised Beatrice Cable that the guilty would pay and Joe Klein was indeed a man of his word. He had even started the ball rolling, making a few phone calls from a public call box. Such arrangements were not made on an easily traceable landline.

Despite what he might tell cops like Bannatyne, Joe didn't see himself as a businessman. He was a criminal, a crook – what Luca would call a hood. It was a choice he had made years before and he had never regretted it. Yes, he had a number of legitimate interests and they brought him a nice return, but these were merely blinds for the real money makers. Joe Klein had never been much for self-analysis but he did wonder how different his life might have been had that German soldier not slaughtered his family. He probably wouldn't have travelled to Warsaw, would certainly never have arrived in Scotland, never have taken up residence in Glasgow. No, as a Polish Jew in wartime he was more likely to have been herded with his sister and parents onto a cattle car and taken to Dachau or Treblinka where they would have been reduced to names on a meticulous Nazi death list, just a tiny fraction of the six million poor souls who died because they were Jewish, or gay, or gypsies, or communists. Joe didn't think about the past too much, but he did often think of Rachel. It would have been nice had she lived. She had been on his mind more and more recently, and, sometimes, when he was alone in his house, he was sure he felt her presence, just a wisp of something at the corner of his consciousness, a shadow on the edge of his peripheral vision. But he had no time for such nonsense. The dead were dead and they had no further contact with the living. To believe otherwise would have driven him insane. He had killed too many men to consider an after-life.

He locked the front door behind him and walked into the kitchen, where he opened the fridge door and stared inside. He was hungry but didn't want to eat, which he admitted was a strange sensation. He decided instead on a small glass of milk, just to line his stomach. He could think about making himself something later. He had become, over the years, a cook of some distinction, at least among the few people for whom he prepared food, that being only Davie, Rab and Luca these days. His kitchen was large and boasted every gadget and implement he needed. It was a large room with a long picture window looking out onto his rear garden, a mature stretch of grass stretching off to a high stone wall dotted with bushes and a couple of ash trees. A top-of-the-range, wall-mounted gas oven and hob were situated on the far wall of the kitchen amid more working surfaces and oak panelled cupboards and drawers. The centrepiece was an ancient solid wood table he had bought at an auction. It was a hefty piece of furniture, scored by decades of use and it looked somewhat incongruous in the middle of his hi-tech and gleaming work surfaces, but it reminded him of his home in Poland, of meals shared with his family around just such a table. Like everything else in Joe's home, it was spotlessly clean.

He carried his milk to his study, thinking he would sit for a few minutes listening to music.

He placed the glass on his desk and turned to the stereo system on the bookshelves. The hi-fi was one of his luxuries, a sound system for which he'd paid a considerable amount of money. The speakers – four of them – were expertly situated around his room in order to 'maximise his listening pleasure', as the salesman had put it. He had bought the system from an up-market outlet on Bath Street. The store supplied only individual pieces of kit that came together to form a whole for the more discerning listener. Joe had paid extra to have an engineer come to his home to set up the system and site the speakers, because it was important that everything be perfectly aligned. Joe loved his music – Sinatra, Martin, Davis – the music of his era. He had nothing against rock and pop, though he abominated disco, but he loved the crooners and the fullness of sound from a big band. He powered the amplifier then turned to the rows of albums on a custom-built set of shelves beside it. He ran his finger along the spines, finally selecting a double Sinatra album, *A Man and His Music*. Carefully, lovingly, he eased the second disc from the sleeve. He placed it on the turntable and pressed start. As usual, he felt the thrill of pleasure as the stylus hit the vinyl with a soft thump and Sinatra's voice began to fill the room.

He walked back to his desk and settled himself down in the soft leather chair. He took a sip from his milk and laid it down on the blotter before finally sitting back, closing his eyes and letting Frank's voice drift over him. Joe exhaled deeply and felt the tensions of the day leave with his breath. He opened his eyes and let his gaze travel across the selection of photographs on the far wall, finally lighting on the one of him with Old Blue Eyes himself. If Joe had such a thing as a prized possession, it would be this. He had seen Frank perform in Glasgow in 1953 but had not actually met him. This photo had been taken in London's Royal Festival Hall in June of 1962 after Frankie's show. Joe was introduced as the owner of a string of pubs in Central Scotland, which was, in fact, true. There was, of course, no mention of the brothels, the money-lending, the extortion or the armed robberies he funded. Joe often wondered if Frank would've batted an eye if he had known, given the shady shoulders he was reputed to have stood upon in the United States. Frank had his arm round Joe's shoulder in the picture and they were both grinning at the photographer, their hands filled with whisky glasses the size of half pint mugs. Joe seldom touched strong liquor but he had made an exception that night. When Frank Sinatra offered you a drink and poured it with his own hand, you did not turn it down. Even now he could feel the pressure of the singer's hand on his shoulder and he smiled.

The picture was slightly askew, which was troubling. He had a woman come in four mornings a week to clean, but this was the only room in the house from which she was denied entry. This was his sanctuary and he did all the cleaning, polishing and vacuuming himself. He was unlikely to have left that photograph, his prize photograph, slightly off-centre. He tried to think of when he had last touched it but he was too tired to recall. Of course, it was possible he had brushed against it and not noticed. In the end, it didn't matter – though he did resolve to ask the cleaner if she had entered the room that morning.

He gazed across the surface of his desk, which he himself had polished that morning. He saw a smudge on the right hand corner that he must have missed, which wasn't like him. He thought about fetching the polish and a soft cloth but decided it could wait. He wasn't that obsessive. He took another sip of the cool milk and it was as he was placing the glass down again that he saw the top right drawer was not fully closed. He reached out and slowly pushed it snug into the desk with the tips of his fingers.

He spun his chair towards the French doors and looked out onto the garden. The sun was beginning to set, bathing the bushes and the ash trees in a pale pink glow. As he watched, first one then another black bird landed on a branch and seemed to stare towards him. Crows, he thought, or Jackdaws, more likely. Not Ravens, he'd never seen a Raven here. Joe looked to the sky and saw dark clouds gathering against the red sky. The weather would break soon and a storm was coming.

* * *

Jazz heard the music floating through the rooms and up the stair to where he sat in a dark cupboard. He had broken in earlier that afternoon and had wandered round Joe the Tailor's house for hours before he saw the car pulling up outside. That big bastard McClymont had been driving and for one panicked minute Jazz thought he was coming in with the old man, but he relaxed when he saw him head down the drive and Joe walk towards the door alone. Jazz had run up the stairs to settle in the cupboard. It seemed to be a storage area, and not one he thought the Tailor was likely to enter. The young man sat on the floor and listened intently to the sounds of movement on the floor below.

He wondered if he should have done the business as soon as

the Tailor had walked in, just waited behind the door and put a couple in him before he even knew what was happening. Yes, that's probably what he should've done because then it would all be over now and he'd be away. But he hadn't and now he was growing nervous. The gun suddenly felt very heavy and he could feel his palm sweating. He hadn't noticed how heavy it was when Fat Morrie, the armourer, had put it in his hand. Perhaps it was something to do with that thing screwed onto the end, the silencer. It was big, a lot bulkier than the ones he saw on the telly, and it had cost him extra, but he knew it was necessary. Even though Joe's house was larger than Jazz was used to and had a fair bit of garden around it, a couple of gunshots would echo up and down that street like a bloody explosion. Morrie had no idea what Jazz wanted the gun for – he never asked – but he warned Jazz that if it should go off he shouldn't be surprised at the noise because the silencer doesn't suppress everything, just enough to ensure the neighbours didn't wet themselves. Morrie had warned Jazz that he'd have to get close to the target before he pulled the trigger.

Jazz laid the weapon on his lap and wiped his hand on his trousers. Up until now, it had all seemed somehow abstract. He had thought about killing Joe the Tailor almost constantly since Johnny had mentioned it, but like the planning of Barney Cable's murder, it hadn't seemed real. But now, here he was in Joe's house, gun in his hand, and suddenly it was a reality.

He knew Boyle and Johnny would be wondering where the hell he was, and smiled in the darkness. They would shit themselves when they heard what he'd done. He knew they didn't think much of him but with this single act, just a couple pulls of the trigger, he would become something else in their eyes. This would make him a man. So though he felt fear fluttering in his belly, he knew he would go through with it. *This was a game changer*. This was going to be the making of him.

He hefted the gun again – Christ, when did it become so bloody heavy? – then rose as softly as he could and with a shaking hand pushed open the door.

Sinatra was still singing as he eased himself down the stairs, the weapon stretched out before him. He couldn't recall if any of the steps had creaked earlier and prayed that he would make it down without any noise. Reaching the hallway below, he stopped and listened. The music was coming from the old man's office and he moved slowly in its direction. Jazz had been in there earlier, sitting in the big chair at the dark polished desk, poking around Joe's things. He'd been sitting there when he caught sight of the picture of the old man with the singer and he'd gone over and lifted it off the wall for a better look. That had impressed the hell out of him, it really had, Joe meeting Sinatra. A new track began and Jazz recognised *All the Way*, one of his mum's favourites, and he had to stop himself from humming along. He smiled as he moved because it couldn't be more fitting. He was going to go all the way with this. He crept towards the open door and glanced in. The room was washed in red as the sun sank, as if there was a neon light outside. He could see the big, dark wooden desk beside the French doors that led out to the garden and a half empty glass of milk on the blotter. The big chair was turned away from the door and facing the garden. Jazz couldn't see him but he knew Joe the Tailor was sitting in it, probably looking out at the dying of the light. That was something his mum used to say about the sunset, the *dying of the light*. He took a deep breath, held it, and stepped into the room, the gun raised ahead of him, his hand shaking. *Just do it, Jazz son*, he told himself, *another few seconds, get it done and get the fuck out there...*

He didn't hear Joe move behind him, but he did feel his fingers clamp over his mouth, then something hot burning its way into his back. He tried to turn but the old man was too strong for him and anyway, the pain jolting from his back was too intense. Something was jammed in there, he could feel it between his ribs, and it was still going in. The gun slipped from his fingers and he suddenly felt very tired. Pain raced through his body and his legs began to buckle. He wanted to say something, but the hand was too tightly wedged across his lips. All he could manage was a muffled mumble as he slid to the floor. As he fell, whatever it was that had been in his back slid from his body, but the pain was still there and it was still travelling but then it began to subside and he felt cold, so very cold, and then he felt nothing at all.

Joe stood over the young man's body for a full minute. He recognised him as one of Jones' lads, and judging by the bruising on his face, he was the one Davie had battered. He felt the familiar sadness wash over him, realising with a sigh how young he was. Just a boy, really. But Joe, of all men, knew what damage 'just a boy' could do. He took a handkerchief from his pocket and wiped the blood from the knife.

He stepped over the body, picked up the phone and dialled Luca's number.

* * *

Luca hunched over Jazz's body, his face impassive though his mind was working feverishly. This was a not-unexpected turn of events, but he was still somewhat shocked. He recognised the boy, of course, but he felt none of the sadness that Joe felt. Instead, anger caught at his throat. He moved back, careful not to step in the dark blood that pooled out from under the body and seeped into the thick pile of the Chinese rug.

'He's just a kid,' he said.

'Sent to do a man's job.' Joe was sitting at his desk, sipping a whisky. He had poured it straight after summoning his old friend. He would have no more than one, for that was his rule.

Luca reached out a gloved hand and picked up the silenced automatic from where it lay on the rug a few inches away from Jazz's hand. 'Did you have to kill him?'

'Old habits die hard,' said Joe, and Luca nodded, understanding. When threatened, men like them often killed first and thought later. It was in their blood, something both he and Joe had come to terms with a long time ago.

'The rug will have to go,' said Luca matter-of-factly. Joe sighed and stood up to join the stocky Italian. It was a pity. He liked that rug.

'Where did you park?' Joe asked.

'Just outside,' Luca answered, but it was a lie. He had left his estate car further up the road, parking outside a row of shops, before walking down the darkened street to Joe's house. The road was comparatively busy, but he knew no one in a passing car would pay the slightest bit of attention to a man walking alone. When news of this broke he was confident no motorist would come forward with a description.

'Very well,' said Joe. 'We had better get this done then.'

'Sure,' said Luca as he raised the pistol to waist level and fired. He was only two feet away from Joe and there was no chance he would miss. He could've fired from ten times that distance and still be confident of hitting. The bullet took Joe in the centre of his chest and he staggered back, the whisky glass dropping to the floor, its contents splashing his shoes. He was still on his feet as he stared in surprise at the spreading dark red stain on his shirt, and then he slumped backwards against his desk, leaning on the top for support. He looked back at Luca, his eyes questioning.

Luca took a step or two away to widen the distance from Joe, just in case there was life in the old dog yet. 'You shoulda taken up Johnny's offer, Joe,' said Luca, the slight break in his voice the only sign that this was not easy for him. The question in Joe's eyes died as he realised the truth.

'Yeah, you were right, Joe – Jones don't have the brains to come up with a scheme like this. Those trips I made to the old country? I made some detours, setting up the pipeline from Turkey, the lab in Paris, the import network to here. Jones is just a front, a buffer, someone to talk to the guys around here, draw them in, and the guys down south, your pals, Joe.'

Joe slumped onto the desk top. 'It is a dirty business,' he rasped.

'It's a fuckin gold mine, Joe, but you just don't have the sense to see it. You're like the old Moustache Petes in New York – out of date, out of time. They wanted nothing to do with drugs either, until they were forced out, one way or another.' At that Luca waved the gun slightly to emphasise that some ways were more permanent than others. 'Edinburgh showed you the way but you were all too dumb to see it. The cash from narcotics makes your take look like chump change.'

'... people's... misery...' muttered Joe as he clung to the desk, desperate to remain upright. But he was fighting a losing battle. He could feel what little strength there was in his legs beginning to ebb.

'Fuck their misery,' spat Luca, suddenly angry. 'Those suckers wanna pump it into their veins, it's their choice. It's not like we're gonna go out and force people to get hooked. There's a demand out there for what I'm gonna supply, Joe. You see it in the States, you see it in London. Simple fuckin economics, Joe – supply and demand. Sooner or later, someone was gonna do it here. It might as well be me. It's what Mrs Thatcher wants – free economy. Entrepreneurs. You coulda been along for the ride but you had to develop morals, for shit's sake. And what's up with that, eh Joe? Where'd a guy like you get so all high and fuckin mighty? You ain't so lily-white you can afford to look down at an opportunity like this. You're a fuckin pimp and an extortionist, for God's sake. You've stolen and you've killed and you think you can say that this business is somehow beneath you? Jesus fuckin Christ, Joe, wake up and smell what you've been shittin.'

Joe found his legs no longer had the strength to hold him and he slid down the side of the desk into a sitting position. He couldn't feel the pain now, just a deep, penetrating cold that he hadn't experienced since the blizzard in Poland all those years ago. Something was floating past his eyes now, something white, and he realised it was snow. He could feel it on his flesh. Luca's voice was muffled and he had difficulty in making out his words, but he no longer cared. He knew he was dying this time, knew it with a certainty he had never felt before. He considered praying but decided against it. He would not know how to pray and anyway his sins were too great, too great.

And then he saw her: little Rachel, just as she had been in 1940. She was standing behind Luca but he could not see her. He never would. She was smiling and beckoning to him. He reached out to her and she took his hand. Her touch was warm and inviting and he felt her tug at his fingers, encouraging him to rise.

Come, she mouthed.

It is time, Josep.

Come.

Joe Klein smiled as he slipped away and became Josep Wolfowitz once more. He rose and took Rachel firmly by the hand and they walked past Luca, Rachel giggling with delight at being reunited with her brother.

Luca stepped back and hefted the gun instinctively when Joe slowly raised a shaking hand but quickly realised that the man posed no threat. He seemed to be looking at something else in the room but Luca didn't know what. Joe smiled, and Luca frowned.

'What the fuck you grinning at, you dumb son-of-a-bitch?'

But Joe just kept smiling and the hand fell down to his side. Luca saw what little light there was in his old friend's eyes gutter and die, like someone softly blowing out a match.

'You stupid fuck,' he said to the corpse, 'You stupid, dumb, Polack fuck. Why didn't you just see sense, huh? Why couldn't you have just for once played ball? Why did you have to make me do this? Huh? Why?'

Luca realised then that he was crying.

23

BANNATYNE stood on the polished wooden floorboards at the door of the study and gazed at Joe Klein's body with sadness, sure that he was witnessing the end of an era. Joe was still propped up against the side of his desk, the thickened, dark blood staining the front of his shirt, his skin pale and waxy. A police photographer leaned over the corpse and snapped his camera, the sudden flash momentarily bleaching the skin even more. It was after midnight and the gangster had been dead for over three hours.

The other corpse was in the process of being loaded into a black body bag. Bannatyne took a final look at the young face as the zip was fastened, then watched as the two attendants hauled the bag up and manhandled it from the room. He had seen babies dead in cots, strangled by their mother or beaten by a drunken lover. He had watched the mangled bodies of children being removed from a car wrecked by a parent who had been driving too fast, or too drunk. He had stood over the bodies of young girls and boys who had been raped and murdered by some sicko. He had watched teenagers who had died in a pointless street brawl being dissected in a drab, clinical mortuary. He was, like most coppers, hardened to such sights, but still he felt sadness over the tragedy of a young life being snuffed out.

All around Bannatyne the controlled tumult of a murder investigation flowed and ebbed. Officers, clad like Bannatyne in white disposable coveralls, searched the room, looking through all the books on the shelves, peering into drawers, probing into cupboards. The photographs on the wall were studied, surfaces were dusted for fingerprints. A half-finished glass of milk sat on the desk and was marked with a number and photographed, as was the tumbler lying on the carpet beside Joe's hand, the remains of its whisky having long since soaked into the carpet. And then there was the knife, a big, heavy old weapon lying on the floor, the blood that had dripped from its blade long since dried on the hardwood. It too had been numbered and photographed for posterity.

Frank Donovan and Jimmy Knight stood behind Bannatyne. 'The boy's James Sinclair,' said Donovan, just inside the door. 'Known as Jazz.'

'One of Johnny Jones' boys,' said Knight.

'Back door's been forced open,' Donovan continued. 'We reckon he broke in earlier, waited for Joe to pop him before he knew it. Didn't work out that way, though.'

'Aye, looks like Joe got the drop on him, stuck him with the knife, but the boy got one off before he died.'

It was plausible, but Bannatyne remained unconvinced. He knew Joe Klein and he was unlikely to have been taken unawares – and equally as unlikely to step away from the boy until he knew he was dead. 'Who called it in?' He asked.

'Anonymous,' said Donovan. 'From a call box down the corner.'

'We'll not find anything, but get the call box dusted anyway.'

'Getting done, boss,' said Donovan.

Bannatyne pointed to the phone on Joe's desk. 'And get Joe's phone records, see who he called tonight, if anyone.'

Knight said, 'This is gonnae cause ructions, you know that, don't you, boss?'

Bannatyne looked at the big detective. 'Jimmy, "ructions" is an understatement. This is going to rip this bloody city apart if we don't stop it.'

* * *

Davie was in his flat with Audrey when he learned of Joe's death.

She had asked him earlier in the day if he fancied going to the opera as she had been given tickets by someone in the office. Naturally, Davie had never been to the opera before – the truth was, neither had Audrey – but he agreed without any hesitation because the chance to spend more time with her was too good to miss. It was a production of *La Bohème* at the Theatre Royal and although it was sumptuously staged, Davie couldn't help but be bored.

'What did you think?' Audrey asked as they came out into the night and Davie paused a moment, wondering if he should be honest.

'It was different,' he said, finally.

Audrey gave a small laugh. 'You were bored.'

'No,' said Davie, 'it was interesting. Some nice tunes. What's the guy's name again? Puccioni?'

'Puccini,' said Audrey, 'and admit it, you were bored.'

'Well, maybe just a wee bit. But it was still interesting. One thing, though – if that woman was dying of cancer or TB or whatever, how come she looked so bloody healthy?'

Audrey laughed again. 'That's the opera for you,' she said, for all the world as if she was a season ticket holder.

They walked arm in arm to Albion Street, still joking about the opera, and reached Audrey's car.

When they reached Sword Street, they kissed again. This time he initiated it because he had decided it was time to stop Audrey having to make the first move. When they broke apart, he asked her if she wanted to come up for a coffee. He did, of course, have ulterior motives because he knew Rab was out. The coffee was duly made and they were in the flat's living room with the TV on. A political talk show was on when the first kiss came. It was particularly passionate because this was the first time they had done this indoors. Her tongue darted between his teeth and they fell back onto the couch.

What followed was awkward, ungainly even, a tangle of uncoordinated elbows and knees as their hands explored each other. Buttons were unclenched, zips unhitched and clasps untethered as they struggled to reach bare flesh. Neither of them cared much how clumsy they were. Abe's head came up as their breathing rasped, but saw nothing much in their inelegant fumbling to engage his canine mind and he settled back down again, although he continued to watch them from under active brows.

When the phone rang Davie ignored it. After all, he had been dreaming of this from the first time he had seen Audrey in the pub. But it kept ringing and finally he sat up and reached out to the receiver on a low table beside the couch.

'Hello,' he said, his voice a little hoarse.

'Thank fuck you're there, son,' said Rab, and Davie could tell by the thin tone in his voice that something was wrong.

'What's up?' He asked.

'You'd better get over to Joe's right away...'

Rab fell silent then and Davie waited, feeling the blood congealing in his veins.

'What's happened, Rab?'

And then Rab sobbed and Davie felt his heart breaking. He didn't need to hear what Rab said next, his voice cracked with emotion. 'They've shot him, Davie. They've shot Joe. The bastards have killed him, Davie...'

Audrey straightened slowly when she saw Davie's expression stiffen and his face pale. She pulled her blouse over her breasts, suddenly feeling exposed. 'Davie?' she said.

Davie hung up the phone and stood up, his eyes brimming with tears. 'Can you drive me out to Joe's place?'

* * *

Rab was standing as close to Joe's house as he could while keeping his distance from the sprawl of reporters, cameras and rubber-neckers. Audrey had parked her car further up the road, closer to a side street that led to Barlinnie Prison, and the two of them had sprinted back to Joe's house. As Davie moved to his side, Rab turned a pair of angry eyes towards him.

'They shot him, Davie,' he said. 'They fuckin shot Joe.'

Davie touched his friend's arm gently. 'Have they got anyone?'

'They're no saying nothing. All I know is that Joe is in that fuckin house and he's dead.'

Audrey scanned the knot of reporters who were standing together beside a police van and spotted Barclay Forbes. She touched Davie's arm and said, 'I'll see what I can find out.'

Davie nodded his thanks, turning his attention to the house.

Barclay Forbes threw a cigarette away as Audrey approached and looked past her to Davie and Rab. 'You with them, hen?'

She nodded, her face tight, not in the mood for any kind of lecture. 'What's happened, Barc?'

'Joe the Tailor got himself killed, that's what. It's no real surprise.'

'Do they know who did it?'

The older reporter shrugged and shook a fresh cigarette out of a pack of Embassy Tipped. 'They're no saying much. I've spoken to a couple of my police sources but they know fuck all.' He lit up the cigarette and looked again at Davie. 'So you're with them? No very clever, hen.'

Audrey glanced back at Davie before answering. 'I don't want to get into that now.'

'Fair enough. But this is gonnae change everything, hen, you need to know that. And your boy there is gonnae be in the thick of it. The shit is gonnae hit the fan over this, mark my words, and you need to be careful none of it splashes you...'

As they spoke the reporters, photographers and TV cameramen stood around in what appeared to be a bored fashion as they waited for something to happen. When Bannatyne, Donovan and Knight appeared in the doorway of the house and began to walk down the gravel driveway, their interest perked up and they surged towards them. The experienced Forbes surfed the crest of the wave while Audrey was merely carried along by the tide. Cameras flashed and questions were shouted but Bannatyne ignored them all. He looked past the blue and white police tape across the drive entrance and Audrey followed his gaze towards Davie and Rab, who had now been joined by a small, dark-haired man with olive skin and a thick head of wiry hair. She saw Bannatyne frown as the three of them walked away. She tried to call out to Davie, but he didn't look back at her. She stood alone in the middle of the crowds, feeling she was neither part of the scribble of colleagues still calling out questions, nor Davie's smaller group that was now walking towards the city.

24

THE COFFEE ON the formica table top in front of Davie was untouched. It had long since gone cold, but he didn't care. The sturdy white china cup and saucer were simply props for him to play with while he continued to process the fact that Joe was dead. He could hear Luca and Rab talking but their voices were distant, like a radio playing in another room. He was only two feet away from either of them as they sat in Luca's café, the shades pulled down over the windows to hide them from prying eyes, but he felt a deep sense of disconnection. He stared at the brown liquid before him, turning the cup on its saucer slowly as he tried to come to terms with the loss of yet another loved one. Only that morning Joe had been alive. Only that morning Davie had stood at his side over Barney Cable's grave, Joe's words *'it's not how you die that matters, it's how you live'* echoing in his mind. Joe had been gunned down in his home like a dog, but he had lived like a lion. Davie knew that many people hated him – cops, lawyers, other crooks – but he had loved him. Like a father, he had loved him.

But now he was dead.

And someone had to pay.

And as Davie thought of this he felt the numbness being burned away by the heat of his anger and the voices of his friends began to seep through.

'We shouldn't've left him alone...' Rab's voice. Quiet. Subdued. Saying 'we' but blaming himself.

'Don't think like that, kid.' Luca's voice. Equally quiet, but firmer. In charge now.

'He'd still be alive...'

'No, there'd be two bodies in the morgue, that's all.'

'I could've stopped it...'

'No, you couldn't, kid. What happened tonight was gonna happen no matter what. Joe always knew he'd never die in bed. Guys like him, they don't go peaceful.'

Rab shook his head, not so much in denial, more as if he was trying to clear it. He was staring at his coffee cup. Like Davie's, it was untouched.

'Whoever did this woulda taken you out, too.' Luca was still speaking, softly, reassuringly. 'It was Joe's time, not yours.'

'We know who did this,' said Rab, raising his eyes to stare at Luca. His eyes were hard and bright and filled with rage.

'Not for certain we don't,' cautioned Luca.

'The fuck we don't! It's that bastard Johnny Jones that's behind this.'

'Rab, it could be any one of a dozen...'

'No, it couldn't and you know it, Luca. It was Jones. We all know it. He wanted Joe in on this drug thing.'

Luca looked surprised. 'He told you about that? Joe?'

Rab nodded. 'Aye. The wee bastard saw Joe as a threat to his business so he did him in, pure and simple.'

'Joe was wrong about that business. He shoulda got into it...'

'Maybe so, but that was no reason for Jones to have him done in. He's out of order there. He's got to pay for that.'

Luca sat back and stared at the hulking young man across the table, his mind working feverishly. He had to steer Rab away from Jones somehow, dissuade him from any revenge. Sometime in the future Jones would be surplus to requirements, but right now Luca needed him. Just a while longer and then he could let Rab loose. He looked towards Davie sitting on Rab's right. The boy hadn't said a word since they took him away from the roadway outside Joe's house. Rab's grief and his anger were evident, but this kid was a different matter. His blue eyes were cold and distant and Luca couldn't read him. Never could.

Rab saw Luca looking at his pal and said, 'Davie agrees wi me.'

'He hasn't said anything,' Luca protested.

'Doesn't need to. Me and Davie, we know each other, we think alike. He knows Jones is behind this.'

Luca looked at Davie again, trying to read something in his blank expression. 'That right, kid?'

Davie looked up slowly and Luca felt a cold breath on the back of his neck as he looked into those icy blue eyes. He had stared into the eyes of dangerous men in Sicily and New York and he knew a killer when he saw one. Joe had always said it took one to know one, and as the words came to him, suddenly Joe was there with them, sitting at Luca's side. The Sicilian knew that Joe was not really present, but still he heard his voice, saw him watching Davie sadly, and repeat the words that had been uttered months before:

'People kill for many reasons, my friend. Most do it because they have to, some do it because they enjoy it. But in order to kill you must have something inside you, a talent for violence, that little spark of evil, if you like. I have it, you have it, Rab most certainly has it, Davie's father had it. I think Davie has it, too, but he fights it. Some day that fight will reach its final round and Davie will either defy, or embrace, his true nature. And when that day comes, I would hate to be the man opposite him.'

And then Joe was gone and all that was left was the frosty gaze of the young man before him. And Luca knew with certainty that one day he and Davie would face each other down.

Luca swallowed hard. 'We have to be smart here, guys. Sure, we could go out there guns blazing and take Jones out, but that's a sucker play. What is it they say – revenge is a dish best served cold? Sure, we'll get the son-of-a-bitch and we'll get him good, but Joe, God rest his soul, had it all wrong. This thing that Jones brought to him, it's a goddamn goldmine. We throw in with him now, play it out then when the cash starts to roll in, we take over the whole operation and we put Johnny in the ground. We move now, the cops'll know it was us and sooner or later they come knockin at our door. We wait, we take everything.'

Rab began to nod before Luca had finished speaking but Davie still hadn't moved. He sat perfectly still, listening, no expression and no sign of his eyes thawing. Luca began to wonder if he had over-played his hand and that the young man suspected something. Rab was street smart and cunning, but his greed would always supersede his emotions. Davie was different and Luca watched him carefully, searching for some clue as to what was going on behind those blue eyes.

'Makes sense,' said Rab. 'As long as sometime I get to put one in Jones' head, that's okay with me. Might as well make some profit first. What you think, Davie?'

For what seemed like a long time Davie remained silent and unmoving. Then, gradually, his eyes moved, then his head, and he looked at his pal and shrugged.

'I mean, Joe's dead, right?' Rab said, convincing himself as much as Davie. 'Doing that fucker now won't bring him back. We follow Luca's lead the now, then we get Jones later, okay?'

Davie's gaze shifted back to Luca and the Sicilian felt that cold sigh at the back of his neck again. 'Whatever you say, Rab.'

Luca relaxed a little. He had bought some time, hopefully enough to get the business he had worked so long to set up swing into gear. But Davie McCall's eyes troubled him. Sooner or later, he knew the young man would come looking for him and somehow Luca had to ensure he was the last man standing.

* * *

Boyle knew there was something wrong the minute he heard Joe the Tailor was dead. He just knew. He hadn't seen Jazz all day and that just wasn't like the boy. Boyle was in Johnny Jones' living room watching the telly when the phone in the bedroom rang and he heard Johnny answer. Boyle knew it was Johnny's mystery man, but even so it was a bit late for a call. He got up and walked down the hall to the bedroom and saw Johnny standing by the bed, a smile breaking out on his face.

'Well, that's fuckin good news,' he was saying into the phone, then frowned. 'Naw, it was nothin to do with me.'

Johnny glanced at the doorway towards Boyle. Normally he would have waved him away but this time he just stood there, the frown deepening. *Jazz*, thought Boyle, *what the fuck have you done*?

Johnny said, 'I never sent him...'

Johnny said, 'Who?'

Johnny said, 'Fuck...'

More was said but Boyle had stopped listening. Something had happened to Jazz, something bad, he knew it. The stupid bugger had gone and done something crazy. The same instinct that told him the phone call was about his pal now told him the boy was dead and he felt something stinging at his eyes. Jazz was a dumb, stupid twat but he was his mate. He refused to let the tears come. Not in front of Johnny, who was now hanging up the phone and staring at it thoughtfully.

'What's happened?' Boyle asked, hoping the words would take the pressure off his throat.

'Joe Klein's deid,' said Johnny, then he looked at Boyle. 'Your boy Jazz shot him.'

Good on you, Jazz, thought Boyle, but said, 'Where's Jazz now?' He knew the answer before Johnny told him.

'Jazz's deid, too,' said Johnny.

Boyle swallowed, trying to dislodge the lump that had lodged in his throat. 'Who?'

'That boy McCall, my guy says...'

At Johnny's words Boyle felt something cold settle over him. McCall, he should've known. And maybe on some level he had known. A McCall had taken his father and now another one had taken his best mate. The debt was long overdue for payback. Boyle was done waiting.

25

DAVIE SAW FAT MORRIE before Fat Morrie saw him. Davie knew he would run into him, of course, as they were both late night walkers. And this was no casual meeting. Davie had planned it. After he had left Luca's Café, Davie went back to his flat and picked up Abe, who was desperate for his walk. Then he set off down Duke Street towards Parkhead, knowing full well he would bump into Morrie at some point. After he passed the bridge over Duke Street railway station, the topography of the buildings changed. The tall tenements were left behind and squat retail and trade outlets took their place. Their roofs were flat and had obviously at one time formed the ground level of tenements just like those behind Davie. He had no idea what had happened to these sandstone buildings. Joe would have known. But Joe was gone and his knowledge with him.

The air was heavy with the threat of an impending storm and when Davie looked up he saw the stars and moon were obscured by thick, dark clouds. He could feel it pressing on his forehead and behind his eyes.

Their paths converged near a pill box-style pub-cum-disco in the shadow of a railway bridge. It was closed now and the area was deserted apart from Davie and the dog swiftly closing on the slow-moving Morrie, who walked with his head down and his hands thrust deep into the pockets of his parka, which was zipped up to the neck even though the humid air was stifling. They were almost upon him before the lumbering young man looked up and realised who it was approaching him. Davie saw his expression change from mild surprise to slight suspicion and then, inevitably, to unshakeable fear.

'Davie,' said Morrie, his voice trembling just slightly. Morrie was scared. Davie didn't think much on it. A lot of people were scared of him.

'Need a word, Morrie,' said Davie, positioning himself directly in front of the fat youth.

Morrie's eyes were generally little more than slits amidst fat cheeks, but Davie's words caused them to widen considerably. 'What can I do for you, mate?' *Mate*. Trying to sound casual and friendly. It was the technique of the bullied and the terrorised everywhere, make yourself their friend, maybe they won't hit you. Not too hard anyway. Davie had lost count of the number of people who had spoken to him that way, even though he was never a bully. He never needed to be.

'You punted anything to any of Johnny Jones' lads recently?'

Morrie took a slight step back and he gave the night-darkened street a sharp glance before he lowered his head and his voice to say, 'You know I cannae talk about my customers, Davie. They buy my discretion, you know what I mean?'

Davie nodded and stepped closer to the fat guy, his own voice dropping. 'Morrie, I've no got the time or the notion to persuade you. I want to know if you've sold a gun to any of Jones' boys. And you're going to tell me without me having to do you any damage.'

Morrie swallowed hard and licked his lips as he calculated the odds. Davie knew the armourer was far from stupid and would be aware that he wasn't one to make idle threats. He was now sizing up his options – to tell Davie what he wanted to know, or to protect his customer. Davie also knew that Morrie wasn't the bravest of individuals and would cave without any violence having to be dished out. To his credit, Morrie made a token attempt at resistance.

'Come on, Davie, you know I cannae tell you,' he said in a voice that was beginning to rise. If Davie kept up the pressure pretty soon only Abe would be able to hear the boy.

Davie gave an exaggerated sigh. 'Sorry to hear that, mate.' He made a show of looking around him, then gripped Morrie by a fleshy upper arm and pushed him towards the railway arch. Morrie yelped and tried to pull free but Davie's grip was too strong.

'C'mon, Davie, gimme a break!'

'I told you,' Davie said in a matter-of-fact tone, 'I don't have the time to mess around here. Under the arch there will do me just nicely.'

Morrie's fat legs moved faster than they had ever moved as Davie propelled him towards the shadows under the bridge. The gun dealer looked down at Abe as if the dog could help him but he found no solace there. Finally he said, 'All right, all right...' Davie stopped but kept hold of Morrie's arm, his fingers biting deep into the flab. He waited as Morrie visibly struggled with his conscience, a series of tics working his face like there was something burrowing around under his flesh.

'Jazz bought a piece from me a coupla days ago,' he said. 'An automatic with a suppressor.'

Davie nodded. That explained why Sinclair hadn't been at the funeral. He was probably hiding out in Joe's home, preparing to ambush him.

'I didnae know what he was gonnae do with it, you've got to believe me,' Morrie pleaded. 'In my line of business it doesnae pay to ask questions like that.'

'What about Boyle?'

'He's had a piece for a while now, a revolver. He said he liked the feel of it. He got a sawn-off at the same time and another automatic. All the pieces were clean, never been used. No in Glasgow, anyway.'

Davie recalled seeing the pistol thrust into Boyle's belt a few nights before. 'You seen either Boyle or Sinclair tonight?'

Morrie shook his head. 'Jazz's vanished, I hear. Saw Boyle up by Tollcross when I came out, but he lives up near there.'

Davie looked towards the railway arch, considering heading to Tollcross and tackling Boyle right away. In the café he had been happy to feign his agreement with Luca and Rab, but he never had any intention of letting Boyle or Jones away with it. They had gone too far. He knew Luca was keen to steer them away from striking back in order to profit from Jones' business deal, but Davie had little interest in money and none at all in becoming a drug dealer. He decided that Boyle would keep for now. It was late and he was tired. When he took Boyle on he wanted to be daisy fresh.

'You finished wi me or what, Davie?' Morrie asked and Davie turned back towards him. He let go of his arm and stepped away without a word. Morrie rubbed the area where he had had gripped him so tightly and moved off. He stopped when Davie shouted after him, 'Don't say anything to anyone, Morrie.'

Morrie turned back, still rubbing his arm, nodded and beetled off in the direction of the railway bridge. Davie watched him go for a few moments then turned and moved back along Duke Street towards home.

* * *

When his phone rang, Rab's first thought was 'What the fuck now?' He had just arrived home after hatching plans with Luca and he was bone tired. A glance at the clock told him it was just after four in the morning. He decided to ignore it and after a few rings it stopped. All Rab wanted now was to get to bed, get some kip and see what the next day brought. There would be a lot to do because Joe's death would hit the city like a thunderclap. Positions would have to be strengthened, messages might need to be sent. He'd discussed it all with Luca and they knew what had to be done.

Then the phone rang again and Rab decided he had better answer it.

His heart sank when he heard Knight's voice saying, 'Knew you were in, ya bastard.'

'Come on, Knight, eh? It's no a good time.'

'I realise that, son, I really do, but this is urgent. I need something from you.'

'This arrangement of ours is gettin kinda one-sided here. When am I gonnae see something from you?'

Knight chuckled on the other end of the line. 'Right now, son. My boss is very concerned about you and your boy McCall.'

'How?'

'Joe's death. He meant a lot to you, specially young Davie. We need to know that you're not going to go off on some revenge mission.'

'We're not.'

'See, I believe you when you say it, but what about Davie? Loose cannon, he is.'

'Davie'll be fine.'

'Wish I could believe you, son.'

Rab sighed. 'What you wantin?'

'We need to put your boy away for a wee while.'

'I told you, I don't grass Davie.'

'Nothing big, just for a wee while, till the heat dies a bit, you know? Now, I know you can steer me in the right direction.'

'No way.'

'Wrong answer, son. You need to do this.'

'I don't need to do anything.'

'Yes, you do. Because if you don't I'll be forced to come up with something myself. And believe me, if you make me do that it'll be something serious, you know what I'm saying?'

Rab fell silent, his fingers gripping the receiver so tightly he feared he might snap it in two. He couldn't fire Davie in for something, he just couldn't. But if he didn't he knew this bastard cop would fit him up for something big. He didn't doubt for a minute that Knight was capable of it.

Rab sighed and said, 'So how does this all benefit me?'

Knight gave a small laugh again. 'Because it's not you I'm after, son.'

* * *

Davie saw the car parked at the closemouth as he turned into the street from Duke Street. He knew it for a police car even if it was unmarked. He ignored it as he stepped towards the close, stopping only when he heard the copper's voice coming through the open window.

'Where you been, Davie?'

Davie turned and peered through the window. It was the cop, Donovan, the one who had questioned him after Norrie Kennedy's murder. Christ, was that really just a couple of weeks ago? The detective was alone, which was unusual.

'Taking the dog for a walk,' He answered, truthfully.

Donovan gave Abe a quick glance then his gaze reverted back to Davie. 'Things are well fucked, Davie.'

Davie nodded. He'd get no argument from him on that score.

'We don't want them getting any more fucked, son.'

Davie remained silent. He was taciturn at the best of times, but he knew to say even less to a cop, even if they were alone. Not that his silence would matter if this guy wanted to do something – cops were always good at providing their own corroboration when the need arose. Donovan didn't strike him as being that kind of cop, though.

'Mister Bannatyne wanted me to give you a message,' Donovan went on. 'Leave things to us. We'll get Joe's killer, put him away.'

Davie raised his eyes to the thick clouds filling the sky, as if looking for the squadron of flying pigs he knew must have been passing overhead.

'Don't be taking matters into your own hands,' Donovan went on.

Davie nodded. 'Okay. That all?'

Donovan sighed. 'I'm trying to be your pal here, son. I've been asking around about you – you're no stupid. You've got a rep for being a hard bastard, well-deserved from what I hear, but there's respect out there for you. Your pal, McClymont? He's maybe got the ambition but he's nothing compared to you. Don't be a mug over this. You know something, you come to me with it, okay? We told you before, you're no the law on the streets – we are.'

'I don't grass.'

'Even if it meant bringing Joe's killer to justice?'

Davie hesitated. He thought about telling Donovan that Jazz had bought a gun, and that Boyle was also armed, but decided against it. Donovan saw the hesitation and said, 'You know something, don't you?'

Davie stared at him, then said, 'We finished?'

Donovan returned the young man's grave look and shrugged. Davie turned without another word and stepped into the close, where the ground floor lamp was dark. Light fell down from the next landing and filled the close with a faint glow, but the bottom of the stairs was in a pool of shadow. The detective watched Davie and the dog vanish into the darkness then reappear as they began to climb the stairs before he twisted the ignition key. Bannatyne had asked him to speak to the boy and he'd done it. There was something about Davie McCall that set him apart from the others. Of all of Joe's boys, he was the most enigmatic, the least predictable. Donovan didn't think talking to him would do the least bit of good, but it was worth a try.

The detective pulled away from the kerb and was steering the car towards Duke Street when he caught sight of Clem Boyle turning the corner ahead. Donovan stared at him through the window as he moved slowly past, but the boy was oblivious to him as he walked towards Davie's closemouth, his face set in a purposeful scowl.

26

WHEN DAVIE WALKED through the main door of the flat, he found Rab standing in the hallway. 'You've got a visitor, in the living room,' said Rab, jerking his head towards the door, then went into his own bedroom. Rab's face was troubled, his eyes unable to meet Davie's, which he put down to grief. He walked down the hall into the living room, Abe at his heels.

'Well popular tonight, so I am,' he muttered.

Audrey was sitting in the armchair facing the door. She stood up when Davie came in and swiftly crossed the room to step into his arms. He pulled her close, appreciating the sensation of her body against his and the apple blossom smell of her hair.

'Davie,' she said and then said no more.

'It's okay,' he said.

'No,' she said, unwrapping her arms from his body and stepping away to stare into his face. He wanted to kiss her but something told him that was not what she wanted. 'Tell me you're not going to do anything stupid.'

For a fleeting moment he wondered if she had been speaking to Donovan, then he replied, 'I'm not going to do anything stupid.'

'Now tell me like you mean it.'

He saw the concern etched in her green eyes and he brought his hands up to her cheeks, letting them linger for a moment. However, he couldn't bring himself to speak. To say anything further would be a lie and he cared too much to lie to her. He saw tears well up and she gently pulled his hands from her face, stepping back from him as she did so.

'I don't know if I can do this,' she said. The words hit Davie like a powerful blow to the chest but he waited for her to continue. 'Your life... your world... it's...' She tried to complete her sentence but couldn't find the words. Davie silently finished it for her. His life, his world, was not her world and she did not fit in. Her world was safe, it was normal, it was having drinks with friends and going to the pictures and the dancing and going home to a nice house in Bearsden. It was having a nice boyfriend who came to meet the parents and stayed for a nice Sunday dinner. It was getting married and having nice kids and settling down in a nice house close enough for the in-laws to come and babysit whenever they were needed. Her world was nice. Davie's was not. His world was the streets and back courts of the East End. Davie's world was hard and tough and violent. He didn't fit in her world and she would never fit in his. Deep down, he had known that from the start. Even so, as he stood there looking at her, wanting to reach out and hold her close, something harsh and bitter lodged in his throat and wouldn't move.

'Okay,' he said. Just one word. He wanted to say more. He found he had no more to say.

She shook her head, dislodging the tears and freeing them to trickle down her cheek. He wanted to brush them away but he stood perfectly still, his arms at his side, his own eyes burning. So this was what it was like to be dumped, he thought.

'I just wanted to see you... to tell you...' she said and stopped again. She stared at him for what seemed like an age then she shook her head again. 'I don't know if I can do this... but I'm going to try.'

It took a moment for her words to sink in, so convinced was he that she was ending it. He opened his mouth to speak but no words came. The pain he had been feeling – in his throat, his chest, his eyes – dissipated and was replaced by something new. He didn't know what it was but he liked it.

But still a dark little whisper in his head told him she was making a mistake and he should tell her to get as far away from him as possible.

But Davie ignored that voice and told himself that he would never let anything happen to her. Ever.

And he meant it.

She moved in close again, a hand resting lightly on his cheek, her face upturned, and he kissed her. It was a soft kiss, with no urgency, no overpowering passion, yet it was the most remarkable kiss Davie had ever experienced. It made him forget Joe, forget Boyle, forget the voice that still hissed that he would ruin her life.

'Stay,' he said, but she shook her head.

'Not tonight. I've got work in the morning.'

She smiled and kissed him once more, then stepped away and moved towards the door. She stopped to give Abe an affectionate rub on the head before she looked back at Davie and said, 'Ask me again on Friday night.'

And then with another smile, a beautiful smile, she was gone.

Davie looked at the door for a full minute, a grin growing on his face. Maybe, just maybe, he could give it all up. Maybe he could stick two fingers up to destiny and change everything just like Joe had said.

He didn't know how long he had been standing there when he heard the gunshot.

* * *

Boyle had taken up position in the darkness at the bottom of the stairs, his back against the wall, eyes on the steps leading up to McClymont's first floor flat. He didn't know how long he would have to wait but he didn't care. He would stand here as long as he had to. Sooner or later one of them would come down those stairs and he'd put one between the eyes. He didn't much care who it was – McCall or McClymont. He'd prefer McCall but if it was Big Rab, fine. Somebody was paying for Jazz tonight.

He pulled the revolver from under his sweatshirt and clicked open the cylinder for what must have been the 20th time since leaving Johnny's place in Castlemilk. He didn't know why he kept opening it to check the bullets. It wasn't as if any of the six slugs could have fallen out. But he jerked it open, glanced inside and snapped it shut again. Then he made sure the safety was off and lowered his arm, letting the gun dangle there at his side.

A door on the next floor opened and closed, then footsteps descended the stone steps. He tensed, pushing himself away from the wall, the gun already coming up as he watched through the metal railings between him and the stairs for his first glimpse of a target. McCall or McClymont. Didn't matter. Really didn't matter.

* * *

Watching in his wing mirror, Donovan had seen Boyle disappear into the close and knew he had trouble in mind. The detective jerked the wheel and pointed the nose of the car towards the kerb. Something told him he had no time for fancy parking so he merely ensured the vehicle was as far off the road as possible before jumping out, leaving the keys dangling in the ignition, his mind on Boyle and his grim expression. Donovan stood on the pavement for a moment, wondering if he should call for assistance. *No,* he decided, *it may be nothing.*

He began to walk swiftly towards the tenement opening.

* * *

Audrey was still smiling as she stepped down the stairs. When she had arrived she'd no idea what she was going to say. No, that's not right, she kind of did. She was going to tell Davie that it couldn't work out between them, but as soon as she saw him, as soon as she looked into those blue eyes, she knew those words wouldn't come. She stopped on the landing between the first floor and ground level, looking down at the well of darkness at the bottom of the final flight but not really seeing it. She was thinking about going back upstairs, to be with Davie, to take him to bed, to finish what they had started earlier. Then she recalled how late it was and that in – God, three hours time – she had to be up and out to work. Leave it, she decided. Friday night would come soon enough.

She stepped down the last flight of stairs.

She didn't see Boyle as he lurked in the deep shadow, didn't hear him step up behind her as she reached the ground floor landing, didn't know he was raising the gun at her back.

* * *

Boyle had frozen when he saw it was the girl, the one McCall was seeing. He hadn't expected that and he stepped back again, planning to let her go on her way. But then he realised how late it was and wondered what she had been doing up there with McCall at this time of night. She must have been up there shagging him, he realised, the two of them at it like bunnies while his pal was going cold somewhere. Boyle didn't like that idea, not one bit. He smiled to himself in the darkness, deciding that she would do just nicely. He'd put one in her, put the bitch down, and that would hurt McCall. Yeah, she would do nicely.

He moved silently behind her as she passed and raised the gun to shoulder level, the sight centred squarely on the back of her head, his finger tightening on the trigger. All it would take was to tighten that finger slightly, just a wee pull, and she'd be dead.

But as he peered down the barrel at the back of her head he found he couldn't pull the trigger.

He stood there, holding his breath, his arm steady and true but unable to fire the gun. This wasn't like that day with Barney Cable and his boy. This was different. That day it was as if he and Jazz had been watching the killings on the telly. The adrenalin had been flowing, Cable had let off a few rounds at them and Boyle couldn't be sure if it was his bullet or Johnny's that had brought him down. One thing he did know, it wasn't him who had shot Peter Morton, knew that for a fact because he hadn't even been aiming in his direction. Jazz was lying face down on the road by that time so it must've been a bullet from Johnny's gun that had taken Cable's minder down. Cable was different though. When Barney had tried to get over that fence, Boyle had no trouble in blasting away at him. But here in this quiet close, watching the girl move towards the street, he knew he couldn't pull the trigger. He couldn't do it. He hated this lassie, hated the fact that she probably still had Davie McCall's smell all over her, but even so he couldn't fire.

But when Donovan appeared at the closemouth and yelled at the girl to get down, Boyle's finger jerked and the gun went off.

* * *

Donovan had just pulled the girl out into the street when he heard the shot. The bullet went a little wide, but not wide enough. He felt it punch into his chest then a split second later felt the searing pain. He slumped against the tiled wall of the close and slid down, *fuck, fuck, fuck,* screaming through his mind. He saw the girl's pale face over him and he was aware of Boyle moving down the shadowy corridor towards them, the gun still pointing in their direction. He heard a voice in his head telling him that he really should be arresting the bastard but he knew that wasn't going to happen any time soon and he just lay there saying *fuck, fuck, fuck* over and over to himself. Then he felt her hands on his shoulder and he tried to push them away. He didn't know why.

'Somebody help,' he heard her yell. 'Somebody phone an ambulance!'

That sounds like a good idea, he said. At least, he thought he said it, but he really couldn't be sure. Boyle still hadn't moved, the red-haired bastard just stood there looming over the two of them. The pain was gone now and all Donovan felt was numb and cold. Numb and cold, were they the same thing? Maybe they were. *No,* he decided, *you can be numb without feeling cold.* So, that was it decided then, he felt both numb and cold at the same time. *Happy now? Delirious*, he said. Or maybe he didn't say anything at all. He felt as if he was falling, pitching into a dark hole without a parachute, but he knew that couldn't be the case because he could still feel the hard stone beneath him. But then even that sensation was beginning to fade and he was still falling, falling, falling.

He wondered, *is this it? Is this what it's like to die*?

And then he thought of Marie and he thought of Jessica and then, just like that, he thought of nothing else.

* * *

Audrey was kneeling beside Donovan, her hands on his shoulder, wondering what she should do when she heard him say 'Marie' and 'Jessica.' Then he visibly wilted and his head slumped to one side. She didn't know what to do so she just sat there gently touching his shoulder and hoped someone had called 999.

Boyle stood behind them, the gun dangling all but forgotten in his hand. He didn't know what to do now. He had shot a cop. He didn't know what to say. He had shot a cop. He hadn't meant to do it but that wouldn't matter to them. There would be hell to pay now. He had shot a cop.

He whirled as he heard footsteps pounding down the stairs behind him.

* * *

As soon as he heard the shot Davie burst out the front door, Abe squeezing past his feet. He heard Rab blundering from his bedroom, a series of curses flooding from his mouth. Davie took the stairs two at a time, but even so the dog was still ahead of him, a growl rising in his throat as he leaped downwards. Davie turned at the landing and saw the three figures at the closemouth. Boyle was already turning in his direction, the gun in his hand levelling, and Davie just had time to take in the fact that Audrey was kneeling beside someone before he realised that Abe was flying towards Boyle and Boyle was lowering his aim.

'Abe! No!' Davie yelled, jumping down the remaining steps. But it was too late. Boyle fired.

Either Abe was moving too fast or Boyle's aim was hurried because the bullet missed the dog and careened off the tiled wall to fly harmlessly into the darkness of the back close. Abe lunged at Boyle's arm but he dodged out of the way and crashed the handle of his gun down on the top of the dog's head. Abe yelped and slumped, shaking his head to clear it, but kept his feet. Boyle swore once and glared at Davie, before turning and fleeing, practically leaping over Audrey as she crouched at the opening. Davie stopped and looped his fingers round Abe's collar, twisting round to Rab who was now at the bottom of the steps.

'Hold on to Abe,' said Davie and Rab nodded, taking hold of the collar. Davie took off after Boyle, his eyes meeting Audrey's briefly as he passed, his mind registering that it was Donovan lying bleeding on the closemouth but knowing there was nothing he could do now but catch the bastard.

Whatever the reason for the bad blood between them, it ended tonight.

And as he dashed along the street towards Boyle's swiftly moving back, there was a brief flicker of light in the sky and then a few seconds later the first low rumble of thunder.

27

DAVIE HAD TO ADMIT that Boyle could move. By the time he had sprinted up the street and reached the junction with Duke Street, the boy had made off like a hare. He knew he would never catch him on foot – Boyle had too much of a head start – but Davie had no intention of letting him get away.

That was when he saw Donovan's car lying to his left, the nose pointed at the kerb, the keys still in the ignition. Davie could drive well enough to steer in the right direction without hitting anything but he'd never passed a test. That didn't stop him. Wrenching open the door, he slid into the driver's seat, turned the key and fired up the engine. He glanced at the gear stick, checking where reverse was, and manhandled it into position, hearing the gears crunching. He pushed the brake off and hit the gas, sending the car jolting backwards into the middle of the street. He jammed his foot on the brake before he slammed into a parked car and then threw it into first. He pulled the wheel to the left and moved forward, slower this time, until the nose was aimed towards Duke Street. He paused for a split second, wondering if this was a good idea, before he punched the gas again and the car lurched forward into the main road.

It was late and the road was relatively quiet, but even so Davie heard the screech of wheels and the strident complaint of a horn, both of which he ignored as he twisted the wheel to the right. He was already scanning the pavement as he sped along Duke Street, looking for Boyle. He didn't so much as glance at the speedometer, though he knew he was going too fast. He was driving a policeman's car without permission – actually, he'd stolen it – he was unlicensed, uninsured and he was going to batter shite out of someone. A speeding ticket was the least of his worries.

He spotted Boyle's back, still legging it like an Olympic athlete going for Gold, and pressed down on the accelerator to draw level. He shot a look at Boyle through the driver's window but he was too intent on making his escape to pay attention to what little traffic was on the road. Davie spotted a gap in the line of cars at the kerbside up ahead and gave the steering wheel a sharp jerk, bouncing onto the pavement and stopping a fraction of an inch from the window of a small hardware store. Boyle skidded to a halt and raised the gun with a shaking hand just as lightening pulsed through the sky.

Davie climbed out of the car and sneered. 'Big man with a gun, eh Boyle?'

'I'll fuckin do you, McCall. I mean it…' said Boyle, his voice shaking with exertion and fear.

Davie tried to appear calm but inside he felt his guts knotting and tightening. Boyle was too far away to rush him, but not so far away that he would miss if he fired. Thunder rumbled somewhere above them as Davie said, 'Put it down, Boyle. It's just you and me now.'

'I'll put you down, ya fucker.'

Davie's mind raced as he gauged the distance between them, knowing for sure he would not make it. His only hope was to make Boyle drop the gun.

'What is it between you and me, eh?' Davie asked.

Now it was Boyle's turn to sneer. 'Don't gimme that, you know what it is.'

'No, I don't,' insisted Davie, keeping his voice steady, looking for an opening.

Boyle seemed to sense some danger and took two steps back. 'Your dad,' he said and Davie felt his stomach tighten further. 'He did my dad in.'

'I'm no my dad,' said Davie quietly while thinking, *I might have known.*

'No, but you'll do.'

Lightening ripped through the dark sky again, followed shortly by the rumble of thunder. *It's getting closer,* Davie thought as he considered his next move. Somehow he had to get Boyle to put the gun down.

'Fair enough,' said Davie, understanding the need for revenge. At first his own need had been focussed simply on Johnny Jones, then on Jazz, but now here was Boyle, who had fired a gun at Audrey. For that alone Boyle had to go down. He nodded and said, 'But let's do it the old-fashioned way, eh? No with guns.'

Boyle smiled but there was a distinct lack of humour in it. 'A square-go?'

Davie nodded again and he saw Boyle considering the proposition. He knew what was going through Boyle's mind. He was tough, three years older and he had more experience than Davie. He had also regained his wind after his run along Duke Street. Add to that he'd already given Davie one kicking and he was confident he could give him another, no bother. Boyle nodded once and slowly stooped to lay the pistol on the ground. Then he rose into a crouch and waited for Davie to make a move.

Davie felt his mouth tighten. He heard a wind rushing in his ears that had nothing to do with the growing thunderstorm and his vision was gradually narrowing on one thing and one thing only – Clem Boyle. Everything else around him was already fading, as if a mist had suddenly begun to form, leaving only Boyle clear and sharp. The roar inside his head grew in intensity and there was an additional sound, like waves on shale, and Davie knew he was ready.

They stared at each other for a few moments, each waiting for the other to begin. There was a severe flash and almost simultaneously a sharp crack as the thunderstorm raged above the city, but as yet there was no rain. Duke Street was deserted and it was as if they were the only two left on the planet. They stood on the pavement of the city street as the electric air crackled and rumbled around them, each one watching, each one tense, each one ready to bring this to an end.

It was Boyle who moved first.

Davie knew it would be.

The red-haired youth's face creased into a snarl as he launched himself across the void between them with a throaty growl. Davie was ready and neatly side-stepped to the left while at the same time lashing out with his right leg to sweep Boyle's feet away from under him. Boyle's hands stretched out to buffer his fall against the hard concrete, but he still went down hard and Davie knew the impact would have sent a shock wave of pain through his arms and shoulders. Not enough pain, though. Not nearly enough. Davie took a pace backwards and lashed out with his left foot, smashing it into Boyle's ribs with such force that the boy's body lifted slightly from the pavement. Davie drew back his foot again and delivered another brutal kick to the chest. Boyle cried out and rolled away, Davie following, but Boyle was fit and he managed to snap to his feet. He resumed his crouch, but Davie could tell by the way he favoured his left side that some damage had been done to his ribs. *That makes us even*, he thought.

Boyle smiled through his pain and nodded at Davie, as if he knew what he was thinking, then darted forward. Davie knew he would be expecting him to dodge away again so this time he stood his ground, planting his feet firmly and, as Boyle came close enough, shot out his right arm and crunched the hard heel of his hand into Boyle's nose. He put everything he had into the blow, the power coming from his back and shoulders. Boyle's head snapped back and Davie moved in closer and delivered another blow, again to his nose. Boyle staggered back, both hands darting to his face as blood flew from his nostrils, but Davie followed him, jabbing at his left side with his clenched fist, once, twice, a third time before he skipped away once more. Boyle twisted his body away, lashing out as he moved with his right hand in a fierce backhanded sweep that caught Davie under the eye, the chunky ring on his third finger slicing a lump of flesh from his cheek. Blood oozed from the deep gash, but Davie ignored the pain and began to circle round Boyle, looking for another opening. Boyle moved too and Davie thought he was simply waiting for a chance to pile in again. He was wrong.

Suddenly, Boyle stooped and came up again with the revolver. Davie charged across the pavement, gripping the wrist of Boyle's gun hand with his left hand to keep the barrel pointed away while with his right he slammed a series of blows into his injured ribs. Boyle retaliated, his left fist snapping at Davie's side. Agony burned through his body from his still tender ribs but he ignored it, concentrating on delivering as much punishment as he could while trying to keep the gun away. They grappled in close quarters, their breathing harsh and laboured as they struggled against each other, sweat sliming their flesh. The storm around them was growing in intensity, the air pressure a palpable creature surging around them. The thunder crashed simultaneously with the lightning flashes now, but still there was no rain to relieve the intense heat.

Then, with a titanic heave, Boyle threw Davie away from him and swung the weapon round. Davie dodged to the side as a bullet sliced through the air and then he spun back, ready to lunge at Boyle again, but he had already slid over the bonnet of the car and was sprinting along Duke Street. Davie broke into pursuit, determined that Boyle would not get away.

Boyle kept looking back over his shoulder as he pounded along the empty road and Davie was ready to throw himself to the deck if he stopped and pointed that bloody gun again. They were both slower than normal, Davie because of the ache in his ribs, Boyle from the bruising he'd received earlier, but they still managed a steady pace. Their footsteps reverberated from the tenement walls and seemed to echo the length of the night-time street. The rain still had not hit, but Davie knew when it did it would come like a tidal wave – simply bursting from the sky.

Finally he saw Boyle slow, his energy almost sapped, and begin to turn. Davie summoned up one final burst of speed and careered into him just as he brought the revolver to bear. Boyle cursed as he was thrown off his feet, the gun flying from his hand and clattering onto the pavement a few feet away. Davie and Boyle rolled together, each one trying to break free, each one knowing that the winner of this struggle was the one who got to the weapon. Davie didn't like guns but he wanted to reach this one. If he didn't, he was a dead man for sure.

They scrambled on the concrete, muscles expanding, sinews stretching, flesh scraping to blood on the hard concrete. Davie tried to crawl over and past Boyle, who writhed like a sweat-soaked snake in a bid to shake him off. A sharp elbow crashed into Davie's nose and the coppery taste of blood stung at his tongue, but still he hung on. He brought his closed fist down hard into Boyle's kidney, driving it into the flesh. Boyle groaned but continued to drag himself along the ground, knees and feet pushing, one hand reaching for the gun, which lay just out of the range of his splayed fingers.

Davie gripped Boyle's upper arm with fingers slippery with moisture, tugging at it to keep it away from the gun handle. His right hand hammered at Boyle's side, still trying to exploit its weakness, but Boyle was strong. He managed another monumental heave and threw Davie off, then twisted onto his back and shot out one foot, catching Davie squarely on the chest. Davie's already protesting ribs caught fire and he tumbled backwards, giving Boyle the chance to launch himself at the gun, hand closing over the butt.

Davie was about to move in again when he realised that the barrel was aimed straight at him. He was in a bad position, on his back, and no way to escape this time.

Boyle smiled as he slowly got to his feet, the gun never wavering.

'Davie boy,' he rasped, and in that moment Davie saw Boyle change. It was subtle, like a shadow passing over his face, but it was something he had seen before. Davie knew then that whatever murderous creature had nestled in Danny McCall also looked at him from within Clem Boyle.

'Game over, son,' said Boyle and began to tighten his finger on the trigger.

The report of the gun was incredibly loud and Davie braced himself for the impact.

But none came.

For a fleeting moment he wondered if the noise had been a sharp crack of thunder. But then he saw Boyle fly back and slump against the wall behind him, the gun dropping from his fingers to rattle on the concrete. Boyle hung there for a beat, something dark and wet blooming at his chest. Davie turned and saw two uniformed cops in the middle of the street, their car between them and the pavement, the flashing coloured lights dancing in the night. One of them had his arm resting on the roof and in his hand was a police issue pistol.

Davie looked back to Boyle again, who was glaring at him, his features contorted with either agony or hatred. Then the expression bled from his face as he slid down the wall, coming to rest in a sitting position, his head slumped to his chin, his face blank, his eyes open but sightless.

It was then that it began to rain.

28

JIMMY KNIGHT CARRIED the two cups of coffee to the table and sat down opposite Rab McClymont. They were in the tea room of Kelvingrove Art Galleries and Museum at ten in the morning and they were both confident they would not be seen by anyone from their respective professions. Sunlight slanted in the big windows and it looked like a fresh, early summer morning. It had rained for two days solid and the oppressive heat that had built up on the day Joe had died had been washed away. After Clem Boyle was gunned down, Davie had been taken in for questioning but later released. Given that Boyle had shot a copper there was little chance of any charges being brought against him. Davie had, after all, merely tried to facilitate a citizen's arrest.

Rab sipped his coffee and said, 'So it was lucky for Davie they cops drove by.'

Knight nodded. 'We had the lads from the Support Unit out in force after Joe got done. The bosses thought there would be trouble.'

'They weren't wrong.'

'Aye, sometimes the suits at Pitt Street get it right. Those two had been in Parkhead when the call went out about Frank Donovan.'

Rab had read it in the morning papers. The two uniformed coppers from the Support Unit had been speeding along Duke Street in response to the alert issued about a detective being shot when they saw Davie and Boyle fighting on the pavement. They said they stopped the car and called out a warning but Rab suspected that they didn't say a word before they put one into Boyle. Not that Rab cared much.

'The uniforms did us all a favour taking Boyle out that way,' said Knight, echoing Rab's thoughts.

Rab nodded. 'Bastard needed killing, right enough. How's your man Donovan?'

Jimmy Knight smiled. 'He'll live.'

'We thought he was a gonner.'

'So did he. They say he was gone for a minute or so – was walking into the white light – but the paramedics did their job. He'll be back on the job in a few months. He'll be fine – he'll get a medal.'

'You sound as if you wish you'd been shot instead of him.'

Knight's smile broadened. 'Nothing like a medal on your record come promotion time. Which is why I needed to see you.'

'You want me to shoot you, like?'

'No...'

Knight didn't need to say anything further. He simply stared at Rab, knowing that the young man knew full well what he needed. When Rab still hesitated he said, 'Don't play silly buggers, son. We both know you're going to give me something.'

Rab sat back in the plastic chair, still putting off what he knew was inevitable. Knight paused before he said, 'David McCall.'

Rab immediately shook his head. 'I told you, I won't grass on Davie or Joe. No way.'

'Joe's dead, son.'

'Davie's no.'

'He's dangerous, Rab.'

'No,' Rab insisted.

'Aye,' Knight said firmly. 'He's no like you and the others. You know it and I know it. Look at the way he went after Clem Boyle the other night...'

'The boy tried to kill his burd.'

'So what you saying, Rab?' Knight went on, 'You saying that you don't think Davie boy wouldn't still do something about Joe's death? You know he believes Johnny Jones is behind it.'

'Jones was behind it. Jazz Sinclair was one of his.'

'Jazz Sinclair was a fuckwit. Johnny's a bastard but he's no a stupid bastard. There's no way he sent that fuckwit to take out Joe Klein.'

Rab nodded. He had discussed this with Luca and they had reached the same conclusion. If Johnny had wanted to get Joe he would have called on someone with more experience, maybe from down south. Jazz Sinclair had gone after Joe for reasons of his own and got lucky. In a way. But what Knight said next moved those particular goalposts.

'You heard of gunshot residue? We call it GSR?' When Rab shook his head, Knight continued. 'See, whenever you fire a gun it leaves traces, they call it "blow back." You cannae see it with the naked eye but it can be collected when you treat the skin with chemicals. Thing is, Sinclair didn't have any on his hand.'

'So maybe he wore gloves.'

Knight smiled. 'They'd still be there, you know? No, no matter what way you shake it, it still comes out the same. Someone else was there.'

Rab's brow creased into deep lines. 'Boyle, maybe?'

Knight shrugged. 'Maybe. The way we see it, Joe did for Jazz before he could get off a shot, this other bloke then did Joe, left the gun behind. When this comes out – and it will – you know Davie's going to start thinking about Johnny again and it's only a matter of time before he does something about it. He's got a lot of fury in him, that lad, I saw it the first time I clapped peepers on him. A lot of angst that needs to be worked through, know what I'm saying? Could get in the way of business.'

Rab gave Knight a long, hard look, something in the cop's voice telling him that he knew about the drug deals. He tried to find some clue in the man's eyes but it was like trying to read Braille wearing a boxing glove. That was the problem with this guy – his breadth of knowledge verged on the supernatural, something he shared with Joe, and he only gave away what he wanted to give away. Something else he had in common with the old man. Rab wondered suddenly if this was what it was like when you dealt with the Devil. That horned bastard would know everything, too.

Rab dropped his eyes to the table top and considered what the cop had said about Davie, recalling the conversation in Luca's café. Davie had been very quiet throughout but Rab had known something was working away at him. Joe's murder had affected him deeply, which was unsurprising, given the bond between them. Knight was right – with Boyle and Sinclair dead, there was a slim chance that Davie would let it lie, but if he found out someone else was there Rab knew he would do something about Jones, screwing up a sweet deal for them all in the process.

Knight said quietly, 'Doesn't need to bc anything major, just something that would take him off the streets for a year or so.' Rab immediately thought of Barney Cable's warehouse and something must have shown on his face because the detective's eyes narrowed and he said, 'What?'

* * *

Donovan had more wires coming out of him than an up-market stereo and he hated it. Every time he moved he was aware of the bloody things pulling at his flesh, not that he moved very much. Marie had been at his bedside when he came to the morning after he'd taken the bullet. His wife's face was the first thing he saw, her eyes red-rimmed and puffy, her nose running and her skin pale. She was still the most beautiful thing he had ever seen. She was sitting at his bedside, his hand in hers, crying softly into a soggy tissue, and he lay there looking at her for a few seconds before he whispered, 'Is this because you can't find the insurance policy?'

When she looked up he saw all the pain and anguish she must have been feeling being washed away by deep, cleansing relief and she threw herself forward to wrap her arms around his neck. He grunted and reminded her he'd been shot and she sat back again, filled with apologies, her hand fluttering over his wound, fearful to touch it but needing physical contact, so she settled again for holding his hand in both of hers.

She said, 'We thought we'd lost you.'

He managed a weak smile and said, 'Kinda thought that myself.'

He saw the tears forming again. 'You died, you know. They told me. There in that close, on the ground, you died. They brought you back.'

He squeezed her hands as best he could and cleared his throat. 'I don't remember anything about it.'

She gave him a slight, brave smile. 'So, no heavenly choir? No hordes of angels?'

'Not even a solitary harp.'

They sat there together for some time, holding hands, smiling at each other like teenagers as they listened to the rain pounding against the window of his hospital room.

That had been two days before and he could already feel his strength returning. The wound still ached but the morphine drip helped. He was sitting up in bed reading an Ed McBain novel when Audrey appeared in the open door of his room. He recognised her, of course, but couldn't recall her name.

A nervous smile plucked at the corners of her mouth as she said, 'I'm sorry, am I disturbing you?'

He struggled further upright and said, 'No, not at all, just reading.'

She stepped into the room and raised the brown paper bag she carried. 'I've brought grapes, I'm afraid.' She shrugged apologetically. 'Not very original.'

'Grapes are fine, Miss...?'

She caught the question in his voice and she moved closer, her free hand outstretched, 'Burke. Audrey.'

He smiled. 'Nice to meet you, Burke Audrey.' He took her hand, trying not to wince as his body protested at the movement. Her hand was cool, her fingers soft to the touch. He looked into her face and saw her staring at his bandages with subdued horror.

'I just wanted to thank you, for what you did,' she said.

He nodded. 'If I'd known I was going to end up getting shot, I might not have done it.'

She smiled at him. 'Somehow I don't think that's true.'

Donovan smiled back, wondering if it was true or not. He had acted on instinct that night, yanking her out of the close when he saw Boyle levelling the gun. His big mistake was not getting himself out of the way, too.

'They tell me you're Davie McCall's girlfriend.'

The words were out before he knew it. He didn't know this young woman yet there he was asking her a personal question. But boredom had set in very quickly. There was nothing on the telly and his book could wait. After two days in hospital he was ready to speak to anyone who was not a brisk nurse or a doctor.

She was nodding, her eyes lowering to look at the green hospital top sheet on the bed as if it was the most interesting thing in the room.

Donovan asked, 'You like him?' *Christ*, he thought, *it was like being back in high school.*

She nodded, her eyes still downcast, and he sensed she was wondering why she was telling him this.

'You like him a lot?'

She looked up then and he saw a reservoir of tears welling in her green eyes. She was strong, she was holding them back, but then the dam burst and two goblets trickled down her face. 'I've made such a mess of everything...'

He reached out and grasped her hand, hoping to Christ that Marie didn't walk in and see him playing patty-fingers with an attractive young woman. 'Take it easy, hen, you'll have me going in a minute.'

She smiled and wiped the tears away with her free hand. 'If I hadn't gone to see him that night, you wouldn't be lying here with a bullet hole in you.'

'You can't think like that. It happened, that's it. You're alive, I'm alive, let's just be happy for that.'

'Boyle isn't alive.'

Donovan felt his face harden. 'Well, don't expect me to shed any tears over him. I owe your boyfriend for what he did and someday I'll repay the debt. Davie McCall's a complex guy. I've said I owe him and I mean that, but there's an old saying that if you save someone's life you're responsible for them forever. Don't know how that works, to be honest, but just in case it's true let me say this – he's not for you.' He could tell from her expression that she had heard this before but he pressed on regardless. 'Your lives are different. You're a good looking lassie, you've got a good job – reporter, right?'

She nodded.

'Take my advice – stay away from him. He's bad news, and believe me, it pains me to say it cos I actually quite like the guy, and I don't like neds on principle.'

'Davie's different…'

'I'll give you that, he's not like the rest. But he's still a ned, and a particularly violent one at that. You and him, you're like oil and water. You can be together but you sure as hell don't mix. My advice? Stay away from him. He'll be the death of you.'

But when he looked into her eyes he saw her strong will shining through again and he knew he was wasting his breath.

* * *

Luca knew who Bannatyne was, even though he had never actually met the man. Joe had pointed him out at Barney's funeral, but even before then the Sicilian had marked the smartly-dressed grey-haired man as a cop. Now here he was, sitting in the same alcove where just a couple of nights before Luca had discussed the future with Rab while worrying about how Davie would react. That night ended in more violence, with Davie at its centre. Luca hadn't seen the young man since but he was never far from his mind. There was a chance Davie suspected his hand in Joe's death and that was a chance Luca was not willing to take. Joe had understood Davie, but to the Sicilian the workings of his mind were a mystery. Luca didn't like mysteries; they made him nervous. Luca did not like to be nervous.

Now here was this cop with the smart grey suit and the clear brown eyes sitting in his café, sipping his coffee and eating one of his wife's scones. Luca was anxious, which annoyed him. He had dealt with the police all his life and yet here he was feeling dread clutch at his belly like food poisoning.

'Mr Vizzini, right?' Said the cop. 'Detective Inspector Bannatyne, Baird Street CID.'

Luca forced a broad smile as he stood by the table, drying his hands on a paper towel. 'Pleased to meet you,' he said and held out his hand.

Bannatyne shook it, his grip firm and dry. Luca cursed himself for he knew his hand was still slightly damp from cleaning dishes in the kitchen. He hoped Bannatyne didn't think his palms were sweating.

'You were a friend of Joe Klein's,' said the cop, taking a sip of his coffee.

'*Si*, we were good friends. May he rest in peace,' said Luca. No need to lie, it was common knowledge that Joe was his partner in the café.

'Terrible thing.'

Luca nodded solemnly, waiting for the next question.

'Did you know that you were the last person he phoned before he died?'

Luca adopted a look of shock. 'No...'

Bannatyne nodded, slipping a chunk of buttered scone into his mouth. 'Lovely scone, by the way. Homemade?'

Luca nodded. 'My wife.'

'My compliments.'

Luca inclined his head slightly. '*Grazie*...'

Bannatyne sighed. 'Aye, phone records show that he phoned your home that night. Care to tell me what the conversation was about?'

Luca shrugged. 'The usual. Business, Mister Cable's funeral...'

'You were there, weren't you?'

'You know I was – you saw me with Joe.'

Bannatyne smiled. 'Yes, I did. I have to admit, I had to ask who you were. You've kept very much under our radar.'

Luca spread his hands. 'I am just a café owner, nothing more.'

Bannatyne tore another segment of scone off and threw it into his mouth. He regarded Luca with a slightly amused expression before he said, 'Of course you are. So that was why Joe phoned you that night? Just to talk about the day's events.'

'Joe often called me at night, just to talk. We were friends.'

Bannatyne nodded. 'Sure.'

'But I thought you found the guy who did it beside Joe. That's what it says in the paper.'

Bannatyne looked thoughtful at this. 'Yes, we did find the body of an individual.'

'So, case closed, right?'

The detective wrinkled his nose a little. 'Well... let's just say there are a few unanswered questions.'

'Like what?'

'Ah, Mister Vizzini, you wouldn't expect me to discuss an ongoing investigation, I'm sure. You know how it works.' Bannatyne raised his eyes to look directly into Luca's. The café owner saw a challenge in the brown irises and he knew then that this cop knew more about him than he let on. His guts fluttered again.

'So you think someone else did it, not this boy Sinclair?' Luca said, more to say something than anything else.

'Let me just say that the case remains open,' said Bannatyne.

'Then if he didn't do it, I hope you get the son-of-a-bitch who did.'

'So do I, so do I,' said Bannatyne, swallowing the final crumb of scone and washing it down with the rest of his coffee. He stood up, fishing in his pocket for some coins and Luca held out his hands in dismissal, saying, 'No, please, it is my pleasure.'

Bannatyne smiled. 'That's kind of you, Mister Vizzini, but I'd prefer to pay.' He dropped a 50 and three ten pence pieces on the table top. 'Wouldn't want people to think you're trying to bribe me.'

Luca smiled back at him and scooped up the coins. 'Heaven forbid, Detective Inspector.'

Bannatyne smiled and held out his hand again. 'Well, good to meet you.'

'*Si*,' said Luca, grasping the hand again. Despite his growing nervousness, this time his hand was as fresh as Bannatyne's. If their palms had been any drier they could've started a fire.

'I'm sure our paths will cross again,' said the cop.

Luca wondered whether that was a promise or a threat as he watched Bannatyne step outside into the sunlight.

* * *

Davie was in bed when they came for him. Abe was lying on the bedspread beside him and he must have heard a noise on the stairway because he raised his head and growled. There was a fierce rapping on the front door and Davie knew by its sound that it was The Law. They had a way of knocking a door. He glanced at the clock beside the bed and saw it was six-thirty. That clinched it – they liked to come early, catch you unawares. He heard Rab's bedroom door open and the big guy padding towards the front door. Davie leaped out of bed and got dressed. Abe was already standing at the closed door, his nose pressed to the gap at the bottom to sniff out what was happening in the hall. Davie jerked open the door to find two uniformed cops just about to burst in.

'David McCall?' One asked, and he nodded. The two officers reached out and gripped him by the arms, one stepping behind him, the cuffs already in his hands. Abe's growl deepened and he bared his teeth.

'Keep your dog back if you don't want it shot,' warned the other cop and Davie told Abe to *sit and stay*. The officers weren't armed, but it would be a simple task to call for support. Abe fell silent but his lips still quivered as he watched the two cops push his master out into the hallway. The dog tried to follow but one of them held him back with his foot and closed the door on him.

Rab was standing in the hallway, still in his pyjamas, and Davie saw that big cop Knight at his side with another two uniforms. 'Robert McClymont and David McCall, we are arresting you for a housebreaking at the premises of the SwiftMart Warehouse in Queenslie. You have the right to remain silent, but anything you do say will be taken down and may be used in evidence against you. Do you have anything to say?'

'Can I put some clothes on?' said Rab.

He and Rab appeared in the Sheriff Court the following morning and Joe's old lawyer managed to get them bailed. The depute procurator fiscal handling the case against them did not oppose the motion.

As they walked out of the court building on Ingram Street, Rab said, 'So where the fuck was Mouthy?'

* * *

Mouthy stared across the table at Rab, his face white with fear. 'Honest, Rab – I never said nothing!'

Rab grimaced. 'Don't fuck me about, son. You were lifted the day before us but you've no been charged wi nothing. You were seen.'

'Aye but they never even mentioned the warehouse job. They just took me in for questioning about Boyle and them, asking me what I knew. The warehouse wasnae even mentioned, honest!'

They were sitting at a corner table in Luca's and Bobby Newman, sitting beside Rab, leaned over and hissed, 'Come on, Mouthy – you expect us to believe that?'

'Raise my hand to God, Bobby, it's the honest truth, on my mammy's life, so it is. I would never tell the police nothing. I'm no a grass.'

'Well, somebody did,' said Rab, 'and it sure as fuck wasnae me or Davie. So who?'

Mouthy's brow furrowed as he thought about this. 'It wasnae me,' he said plaintively.

Rab glanced at Bobby, who shrugged, unsure whether to believe Mouthy or not. Rab sighed and said, 'You're lucky Davie doesn't want anything to happen to you, Mouthy son, cos if it was up to me you'd be face down right now with a bullet in your head.'

Mouthy's eyes widened and he said, 'Rab, I...'

Rab leaned in closer to the smaller youth and he snarled, 'Shut the fuck up now or I'll use that teaspoon there to take your fuckin eye out.'

Mouthy's jaws clamped tight.

'Now,' said Rab, 'here's what you're gonnae do. Go home, pack up your stuff and get the fuck out of Glasgow by tonight. We don't ever want to hear from you again, understand? We see you back here, we take your head off, understand?'

Mouthy nodded.

'Bobby, we'll go with him,' said Rab, 'just to make sure he understands we mean it.'

Bobby nodded and pushed himself to his feet. Mouthy hesitated for a few seconds then rose, too. From behind the counter Luca watched them leave. Rab paused in the doorway and glanced back at him. Luca gave him a single nod. Rab nodded back.

The following morning, a cleaner walking to work in a primary school found Mouthy's body face down on a stretch of wasteground, a single bullet hole in the back of his head. On a broken down wall nearby the words 'Mouthy Grant is a grass' were scrawled in white paint. A pair of thick woollen gloves lay beside the body. Tests later revealed they had been worn by the shooter.

The murder was never solved.

* * *

The evidence against David McCall for the warehouse robbery was bog standard, but strong enough to win a conviction. The security guard was able to identify Davie, but only Davie, as one of the trio of robbers. He took off his mask once, he said, and had given him a good look. He was corroborated by his supervisor, who also said he could identify Davie. A fingerprint was also found on the barrow they had used. It was at that point that Davie knew he was being fitted up, albeit for something he did actually do, because he had never taken his gloves off throughout his time in the warehouse. Transferring a print from one place to another was easy enough if you knew what you were doing. And Knight would know what he was doing. Amazingly, neither of the men was able to identify Rab. Perhaps they were more afraid of him than they were an 18-year-old youth, Davie's reputation being reserved only for those in his immediate circle.

His defence counsel tried valiantly to switch the blame to Mouthy Grant, who had been in his grave for three months by the time the case came to court. However, there was nothing to connect the dead youth to the crime, even though the lawyer implied he had incriminated his client only to avoid prosecution himself. The prosecution had not mentioned him at all in their narrative. Davie regretted Mouthy's death and he knew Rab was behind it. Rab, of course, had denied all knowledge.

With the security guards unwilling to identify him, the case against Rab was dismissed while Davie was given four years. He listened to the sentence without emotion, his eyes finding Knight in the gallery. Why the Black Knight was fitting him up and not Rab was something he would think about in the coming months. The one thing he was certain of was that Rab would never turn against him. Not Rab. They were mates. They were brothers.

As they led them both from the box, Davie murmured to his mate, 'Look after Abe for me.'

Rab nodded. As he was led from the dock, he glanced at the public gallery and saw Knight grinning at him. Rab couldn't help but feel he really had made a deal with the Devil.

* * *

Davie was led from the rear of the court into a van to be taken to Barlinnie Prison, where he would spend the next couple of years at least. At the end of the lane he saw a group of people, some of them press photographers trying to snatch a picture, his street fight with Boyle having made him something of a celebrity. He had refused to speak to any reporters, even Barclay Forbes, but they never gave up. He had offered Audrey an exclusive but she had declined, saying she didn't want to use their relationship to further her career. He loved her all the more for that, but he worried about their future. He had told her not to come to court and was unsure if he wanted her to visit him in Barlinnie. He had almost got her killed and while part of him wanted her badly, a more sensible part told him to distance himself from now on.

He paused at the rear of the van and glanced down the alleyway to the mob at the end, scanning the faces, hoping he might see her, but she wasn't there. He felt disappointed and relieved at the same time. Then, just as two burly prison officers helped him up the steps into the secure compartment, he saw a face. It was a flash, a glimpse, and at first he thought he had been mistaken. Even so, he felt an electric shock run through him. As the doors closed he darted another look towards the crowd but the face was gone.

When he sat down on the hard bench inside beside three other lads being sent up for some crime or another, he felt the beating of his heart in his temples and his mouth was dry. He ran his handcuffed hands through his hair, his fingers trembling against his scalp, all thoughts of Audrey banished by what he had seen.

He replayed the brief snatch of the face in his mind, telling himself he was wrong, that it was too fast to be certain, that it could not be him. But as the van lurched into motion, he knew in his heart that it was true. Davie was certain. He knew it was him.

Danny McCall was back.

Epilogue

DECEMBER 1980

Johnny Jones had never felt safer. Okay, he had lost Clem Boyle and Jazz, but on the upside Joe Klein was dead, Rab McClymont was keeping his head down and McCall was only three months into a four year stretch for housebreaking. The agreement with the wee Italian was holding strong and pretty soon they'd be making money hand over fist. All the other faces invited from the west coast had stumped up their investment money and the first consignment of heroin was due from Turkey the following week. They were all playing nice, but that wouldn't last. When the rift came, and it would come, Johnny would make sure he was well away, living off his rapidly growing nest egg. For the moment, everything in Johnny's garden was decidedly rosy.

He didn't know how Luca had taken McCall out the picture. Of course, Johnny would have preferred a more permanent solution for both him and Rab, but the wee Tally didn't seem to want that. McClymont would be useful to them, he had said. McCall was in the jail and no threat for now.

But he'll get out in a couple of years or so, Johnny had said.

Rab will keep him in line, Luca had said.

Aye, you thought the Tailor could be kept in line.

Luca had glared at him. *Rab and Davie are not Joe Klein and never will be.*

Not if they've got bullets in their head, Johnny thought, but he kept it to himself. There had been too much killing, too much attention, too much heat. Let things cool down, let things lie and see what happens. Everything comes to he who waits.

Johnny was driving back to Castlemilk from Duke Street as he thought this all over. He sat in a line of traffic at the bottom of the High Street, where the road curved round the old Tolbooth tower. This was the site of the old town jail, his dad had once told him, and the tall clock tower was the only part of the building left. The radio was on and a track by The Who was playing, *Behind Blue Eyes*. The song made him think of both Joe Klein and David McCall, blue-eyed boys both. *Well, fuck 'em*, he thought.

He heard the motorcycle before he saw it. He glanced in his wing mirror and saw the leather-clad biker weave through the stationary traffic behind him, his head and face completely encased in a black helmet and visor. Jones had never been on a motorbike, never been attracted to them, but watching this guy skipping up the line, he could see the benefits. The bike came to a rest beside his window and Johnny studied the powerful machine. Yeah, might be something in two wheels, right enough. Nippy wee thing, get him across the city in no time. *Don't fancy the leathers, though, the way he was hunched over there looked like a big, black cr–*

The bullet shattered the driver's side window and plunged into Johnny's right eye, spraying a clump of blood and brains from the back of his head. There was very little noise and no one paid attention to the sound of breaking glass. Johnny's body slumped in the seatbelt and the biker slipped the silenced automatic back under his leather jacket before roaring off through Glasgow Cross. He was well away down the Saltmarket before the angry horns began to blare.

On Clyde Street, with the river on one side and the walls of the city's High Court on the other, the rider pulled the bike into the side and walked swiftly away, still wearing the dark helmet. One or two people looked at him as he passed, but he ignored them. He crossed Stockwell Street at the Victoria Bridge, then made his way to the walkway along the edge of the river. He by-passed the suspended footbridge that led to the south bank and headed for the shadows below Glasgow Bridge. There, where no one could see, he peeled off the leathers to reveal a light windbreaker and dark jeans. He thrust the garments into the helmet and dropped them over the side into the dark waters of the Clyde. He knew they would be found eventually, but by that time he would be long gone and was confident they would yield no real clues. The gun he threw separately, as far out into the water as he could. As he did so, he wondered just how many shooters rested in the river's silty depths. Enough to arm a small country, he was sure. Even if they did find it, he was certain it wouldn't lead them to him. No one knew he was in Glasgow, in fact he could arrange to have a handful of people swear that he was with them in London when Jones was shot. With one final, careful glance around him to ensure that no one had seen his face, he moved back into the daylight and began to walk to Central Station to catch the next train south.

The man had accepted the contract with Joe on the day he had died. The Tailor had been a good customer and the man had fulfilled the obligation free of charge, as a sign of respect.

Joe Klein had killed his last man.

Enjoyed Blood City?

Here's a sneak peak of *Crow Bait*, Book II
in the Davie McCall Saga...

The boy was running across a field, the long grass around him sighing softly as a warm breeze whispered through its stalks. He was running, yet he moved slowly, like a film being played back at half-speed.

The boy was happy. It was a good day, the best day ever, and his young heart sang with its joy. They had taken him out of the city, away from the black buildings, away from the stench of the traffic, away from the constant roar of engines. A day in the country, where the sun didn't need to burn through varying levels of grime to warm the land. His first day in the country and he revelled in the feel of soft grass caressing his legs as he ran.

He could see them waiting for him at the far end of the field, mother and father, the car his father had borrowed from his boss parked under trees behind them. They smiled at him as he came nearer and his father put his arm around his mother's waist. It was a tender moment and the boy was sorry the day had to end.

But the air cooled as the gap between them narrowed and the field darkened as if a cloud had passed over the sun. The boy looked up, but the sun was still there, burning brightly in an unbroken blue sky. And yet, the day had shadowed and the grass had lost its colour. The green and sun-bleached yellow was gone, replaced by blacks and greys.

The boy stopped and looked to his parents for an explanation, but they were no longer there. In their place was a dark patch, a deep red crying out amid the now muted surroundings, and the boy knew what had caused it.

'Dad, don't...' he heard himself say.

'Dad, please don't...' he said as he backed away, fearful of what he might see in that pool of crimson. His mother, he now knew, was gone, never to return. But he also knew his father was there, somewhere in the red-stained darkness, waiting, watching.

So he backed away and he began to turn, all the joy replaced by a deep-seated dread, and he turned, for all he wanted to do now was get away from that corner of the field and the sticky redness of the grass, so he turned to run, he turned to flee, he turned to hide.

But when he turned he found his father looming over him, the poker raised above his head, the love he had once seen in the man's eyes gone now and in its place something else, something the boy did not fully understand, but something he knew would haunt him for the rest of his life. Something deadly, something inhuman.

And then his father brought the poker swinging down...

* * *

Davie McCall woke with a start and for a moment he was unsure of his surroundings. Then, slowly, the grey outline of his cell, what he had come to call his *peter*, began to take shape and the night-time sounds of the prison filtered through his dream-fogged brain: Old Sammy snoring softly in his bed; the hollow echo of a screw walking the gallery; the coughs and occasional cries of other inmates as they struggled with their own terrors.

He had not had the dream for years and he knew why it had returned. It was something Sammy had said earlier that day, something about Davie's father that had brought the memory back. The field was real and he had run through it on just such a warm summer day, when his mum and dad took him to the Campsie Hills to the north of Glasgow when he was eight. They had been happy then. They had been a family then. It ended seven years later.

Danny McCall vanished when Davie was fifteen.

But the son knew the father was still out there, somewhere.

He had seen him, just once, little more than a fleeting glimpse, a blink and he was gone. It had been ten years before outside a Glasgow courthouse, just as Davie was being led away to begin a four-year sentence for robbing a warehouse. He could not be sure for it was just a flash, but the more he replayed it in his mind, the clearer the face became, as if someone had tweaked the focus. It became a face he knew as well as his own, for the son was the image of the father. It bore a smile on the lips yet there was a coldness in the blue eyes.

And then, just as Davie was pulled away, a wave. He had not registered it at the time but as the months passed and he replayed the scene in his mind, he became sure of it. A wave that said *I'm back*.

Some other books published by **LUATH** PRESS

Death of a Chief

Douglas Watt

ISBN 978-1-906817-31-2 PBK £6.99

The year is 1686. Sir Lachlan MacLean, chief of a proud but poverty-striken Highland clan, has met with a macabre death in his Edinburgh lodgings. With a history of bad debts, family quarrels, and some very shady associates, Sir Lachlan had many enemies. But while motives are not hard to find, evidence is another thing entirely. It falls to lawyer John MacKenzie and his scribe Davie Scougall to investigate the mystery surrounding the death of the chief, but among the endless possibilities, can Reason prevail in a time of witchcraft, superstition and religious turmoil?

This thrilling tale of suspense plays out against a wonderfully realised backdrop of pre-Enlightenment Scotland, a country on the brink of financial ruin, ruled from London, a country divided politically by religion and geography. The first in the series featuring investigative advocate John MacKenzie, *Death of a Chief* comes from a time long before police detectives existed.

Move over Rebus. There's a new – or should that be old – detective in town.
I-ON EDINBURGH

the author vividly brings to life late 17th century Edinburgh.
JOURNAL OF THE LAW SOCIETY OF SCOTLAND

Testament of a Witch

Douglas Watt

ISBN 978-1-908373-21-2 PBK £7.99

I confess that I am a witch. I have sold myself body and soul unto Satan. My mother took me to the Blinkbonny Woods where we met other witches. I put a hand on the crown of my head and the other on the sole of my foot. I gave everything between unto him.

Scotland, late seventeenth century. A young woman is accused of witchcraft. Tortured with pins and sleep deprivation, she is using all of her strength to resist confessing...

In the wake of the Scottish Parliament's Witchcraft Act, the Scottish witch-hunt began. Probably more than a thousand men and women were executed for witchcraft before the frenzy died down.

When Edinburgh-based Advocate John MacKenzie and his assistant Davie Scougall investigate the suspicious death of a woman denounced as a witch, they find themselves in a village overwhelmed by superstition, resentment and puritanical religion. In a time of spiritual, political and social upheaval, will reason allow MacKenzie to reveal the true evil lurking in the town, before the witch-hunt claims yet another victim?

Stealing God

James Green

ISBN 978-1-906817-47-3 PBK £6.99

Jimmy Costello, last seen at the epicentre of a murder investigation and a gangland turf war, is now a student priest in Rome. Driven to atone for his past sins, Jimmy is trying to leave the hardbitten cop behind him, but the Church has a use for the old Jimmy.

When a visiting Archbishop dies in mysterious circumstances, Jimmy is hand-picked to look into the case. With local copper Inspector Ricci, Jimmy follows the trail from the streets of the Holy City via Glasgow and back to Rome, where they stumble on dark forces that threaten everything Jimmy hopes for. But who is really behind their investigation – and are they supposed to uncover the truth, or is their mission altogether more sinister?

An explosive sequel to *Bad Catholics*, the first in the Jimmy Costello series.

Yesterday's Sins

James Green

ISBN 978-1906817-39-8 PBK £9.99

Deliver us from evil...

Why would anyone put a bomb in the car of a retired USAF Major who writes cookery books in a small Danish town? Charlie Bronski has a past and it looks like it's catching up with him.

Charlie recognises the bomb attempt as professional and he should know because it used to be his line of work. When Charlie asks for help from the people who provided him with his new life and identity they ask him for a favour. It shouldn't be too hard, just to kill a middle-aged widower who's doing a placement as a Catholic priest. Name of Costello, Jimmy Costello.

A race against time begins. Can he get Costello before somebody gets him?

The third in the compelling Jimmy Costello series.

An intelligent and well-written thriller.
THE HERALD

Eye for an Eye

Frank Muir

ISBN 978-1-905222-56-8 PBK £9.99

One psychopath. One killer. The Stabber.

Six victims. Six wife abusers. Each stabbed to death through their left eye.

The cobbled lanes and back streets of St Andrews provide the setting for these brutal killings. But six unsolved murders and mounting censure from the media force Detective Inspector Andy Gilchrist off the case. Driven by his fear of failure, desperate to redeem his career and reputation, Gilchrist vows to catch The Stabber alone.

What is the significance of the left eye? How does an old photograph of an injured cat link the past to the present? And what exactly is our little group? Digging deeper into the world of a psychopath, Gilchrist fears he is up against the worst kind of murderer – a serial killer on the verge of mental collapse.

Everything I look for in a crime novel.
LOUISE WELSH

Rebus did it for Edinburgh. Laidlaw did it for Glasgow. Gilchrist might just be the bloke to put St Andrews on the crime fiction map.
DAILY RECORD

Hand for a Hand

Frank Muir

ISBN 978-1906817-51-0 PBK £6.99

A bright new recruit to the swelling army of Scots crime writers.
QUINTIN JARDINE

An amputated hand is found in a bunker, its lifeless fingers clutching a note addressed to DCI Andy Gilchrist. The note bears only one word: Murder.

When other body parts with messages attached are discovered, Gilchrist finds himself living every policeman's worst nightmare – with a sadistic killer out for revenge.

Forced to confront the ghosts of his past, Gilchrist must solve the cryptic clues and find the murderer before the next victim, whose life means more to Gilchrist that his own, is served up piece by slaughtered piece.

Hand for a Hand is the second in Frank Muir's DI Gilchrist series.

The Glasgow Dragon

Des Dillon

ISBN 978 1 842820 56 8 PBK £9.99

What do I want? Let me see now. I want to destroy you spiritually, emotionally and mentally before I destroy you physically.

When Christie Devlin goes into business with a triad to take control of the Glasgow drug market, little does he know that his downfall and the destruction of his family is being plotted. As Devlin struggles with his own demons the real fight is just beginning.

There are some things you should never forgive yourself for.

Nothing is as simple as good and evil. Des Dillon is a master storyteller and this is a world he knows well.

Des Dillon writes like a man possessed. The words come tumbling out of him. ...His prose... teems with unceasing energy.

THE SCOTSMAN

Me and Ma Gal

[B format edition]

Des Dillon

ISBN 978 1 842820 54 4 PBK £5.99

If you never had to get married an that I really think that me an Gal'd be pals for ever. That's not to say that we never fought. Man we had some great fights so we did.

A story of boyhood friendship and irrepressible vitality told with the speed of trains and the understanding of the awkwardness, significance and fragility of that time. This is a day in the life of two boys as told by one of them, 'Derruck Danyul Riley'.

Dillon's book is arguably one of the most frenetic and kinetic, living and breathing of all Scottish novels... The whole novel crackles with this verbal energy.

THE LIST 100 Best Scottish Books of All Time, 2005

My Epileptic Lurcher

Des Dillon

ISBN: 978-1-906307-22-6 HBK £12.99

The incredible story of Bailey, the dog who walked on the ceiling; and Manny, the guy who got kicked out of Alcoholics Anonymous for swearing.

Manny is newly married, with a puppy, a flat by the sea, and the BBC on the verge of greenlighting one of his projects. Everything sounds perfect. But Manny has always been an anger management casualty, and the idyllic village life is turning out to be more *League of Gentlemen* than *The Good Life*. As his marriage suffers under the strain of his constant rages, a strange connection begins to emerge between Manny's temper and the health of his beloved Lurcher.

It's one of the most effortlessly charming books I've read in a long time.

SCOTTISH REVIEW OF BOOKS

Six Black Candles

Des Dillon

ISBN 978-1906307-49-3 PBK £8.99

'Where's Stacie Gracie's head?' ... sharing space with the sweetcorn and two-for-one lemon meringue pies... in the freezer.

Caroline's husband abandons her (bad move) for Stacie Gracie, his assistant at the meat counter, and incurs more wrath than he anticipated. Caroline, her five sisters, mother and granny, all with a penchant for witchery, invoke the lethal spell of the Six Black Candles. A natural reaction to the break up of a marriage?

Set in present day Irish Catholic Coatbridge, *Six Black Candles* is bound together by the ropes of traditional storytelling and the strength of female familial relationships. Bubbling under the cauldron of superstition, witchcraft and religion is the heat of revenge; and the love and venom of sisterhood.

The writing is always truthful, immediate and powerful.

SCOTLAND ON SUNDAY

Animal Lover

Raymond Friel

ISBN 978 1 908373 72 4 PBK £9.99

A tale of love, loss and trying too hard.

Tonight. Tonight is all that matters. Everything else, all this, neon lights and the smell of disinfectant and dead chickens, don't let it get to you, Danny. Baked beans, not a problem. On the shelf they go. Super Danny. By day, a quiet supermarket shelf stacker, but by night...

Well. It didn't quite work out the way I'd planned. My first attempt at animal liberation was a disaster. It was all going so well until... Well, I guess you'll find out. But after that night, everything started to spiral out of control. Everyone at work was out to get me for something or other. The woman I loved was becoming more extreme by the day. My ratio of animals saved versus animals killed was changing rapidly. And not in the direction I wanted it to.

Super Danny? Not quite. Not even close. It's treble or nothing time, and next week, the circus is coming to town.

The Girl on the Ferryboat

Angus Peter Campbell

ISBN 978 1 908373 77 9 HBK £12.99

'Sorry,' I said to her, trying to stand to one side, and she smiled and said, 'O, don't worry – I'll get by.'

They say it is the things in life that you don't do that you regret. For Alasdair and Helen, a chance encounter on the ferry from Oban to Mull leads to a lifetime of wondering what might have been.

This vividly evoked novel is a mirage of memories; a tale of love, loss and regret woven around that single, momentous meeting on a ferryboat one summer.

I have no doubts that Angus Peter Campbell is one of the few really significant living poets in Scotland, writing in any language.
SORLEY MACLEAN

Angus Peter Campbell has a very considerable gift indeed.
NORMAN MACCAIG

Extraordinary imaginative writing.
THE INDEPENDENT

Luath Press Limited

committed to publishing well written books worth reading

LUATH PRESS takes its name from Robert Burns, whose little collie Luath (*Gael.*, swift or nimble) tripped up Jean Armour at a wedding and gave him the chance to speak to the woman who was to be his wife and the abiding love of his life. Burns called one of 'The Twa Dogs' Luath after Cuchullin's hunting dog in Ossian's *Fingal*. Luath Press was established in 1981 in the heart of Burns country, and now resides a few steps up the road from Burns' first lodgings on Edinburgh's Royal Mile.

Luath offers you distinctive writing with a hint of unexpected pleasures.

Most bookshops in the UK, the US, Canada, Australia, New Zealand and parts of Europe either carry our books in stock or can order them for you. To order direct from us, please send a £sterling cheque, postal order, international money order or your credit card details (number, address of cardholder and expiry date) to us at the address below. Please add post and packing as follows: UK – £1.00 per delivery address; overseas surface mail – £2.50 per delivery address; overseas airmail – £3.50 for the first book to each delivery address, plus £1.00 for each additional book by airmail to the same address. If your order is a gift, we will happily enclose your card or message at no extra charge.

ILLUSTRATION: IAN KELLAS

Luath Press Limited
543/2 Castlehill
The Royal Mile
Edinburgh EH1 2ND
Scotland

Telephone: 0131 225 4326 (24 hours)
Fax: 0131 225 4324
email: sales@luath.co.uk
Website: www.luath.co.uk